THE SEVENTH BLACK BOOK OF HORROR

Selected by Charles Black

Mortbury Press

Published by Mortbury Press

First Edition
2010

This anthology copyright © Mortbury Press

All stories copyright © of their respective authors

Cover art copyright © Paul Mudie

ISBN 978-0-9556061-6-8

This book is a work of fiction. Names, characters, businesses, organisations, places and events are either the product of the author's imagination or are used fictitiously. Any resemblance to actual persons, living or dead, events or locales is entirely coincidental.

All rights reserved. No part of this publication may be reproduced, stored in a retrieval system, or transmitted, in any form, or by any means (electronic, mechanical, photocopying, recording or otherwise) without the prior permission of the author and publisher.

This book is sold subject to the condition that it shall not, by way of trade or otherwise, be lent, re-sold, hired out, or otherwise circulated without the publisher's prior consent in any form of binding or cover other than that in which it is published and without a similar condition including this condition being imposed on the subsequent purchaser.

Mortbury Press
Shiloh
Nantglas
Llandrindod Wells
Powys
LD1 6PD

mortburypress@yahoo.com
http://mortburypress.webs.com/
http://twitter.com/mortburypress

Contents

THE PIER	Thana Niveau	5
MINOS OR RHADAMANTHUS	Reggie Oliver	15
MORNING'S ECHO	Joel Lane	29
IT BEGINS AT HOME	John Llewellyn Probert	33
FLITCHING'S REVENGE	Gary Power	45
REST IN PIECES	David Williamson	65
WALK TO THE SEA	Rog Pile	75
ROMERO'S CHILDREN	David A. Riley	85
THE GREEN BATH	Paul Finch	99
TELLING	Steve Rasnic Tem	125
SWELL HEAD	Stephen Volk	134
WALKING THE DYKE	Alex Langley	151
THE CREAKING	Anna Taborska	158
BERNARD BOUGHT THE FARM	James Stanger	168
TED'S COLLECTION	Claude Lalumière	183
NEW TEACHER	Craig Herbertson	197
THE IN-BETWEENERS	Tony Richards	204

Dedicated to David A. Sutton

*****

Acknowledgements

The Pier © by Thana Niveau 2010
Minos or Rhadamanthus © by Reggie Oliver 2010
Morning's Echo © by Joel Lane 2010
It Begins at Home © by John Llewellyn Probert 2010
Flitching's Revenge © by Gary Power 2010
Rest in Pieces © by David Williamson 2010
Walk to the Sea © by Rog Pile 2010
Romero's Children © by David A. Riley 2010
The Green Bath © by Paul Finch 2010
Telling © by Steve Rasnic Tem 2010
Swell Head © by Stephen Volk 2010
Walking the Dyke © by Alex Langley 2010
The Creaking © by Anna Taborska 2010
Bernard Bought the Farm © by James Stanger 2010
Ted's Collection © by Claude Lalumière 2010
New Teacher © by Craig Herbertson 2010
The In-Betweeners © by Tony Richards 2010

Cover artwork © by Paul Mudie 2010

*****

Also in this series:
Six more volumes of unadulterated *HORROR!*

THE PIER

Thana Niveau

The sea was flat and grey, mirroring the leaden sky, yet offering no reflection of the Victorian pier that marched into the water on spindly legs. The charred remains of the central pagoda gave little hint of the pier's former grandeur. Jagged bits of timber lay scattered across the pier-head where frock-coated gentlemen and wasp-waisted ladies once strolled. Alan glanced at the information-sign showing a sepia photograph of the pier in its heyday. It was hard to believe that this was the same place.

Across the channel he could see the mountains of South Wales and to the south, Cornwall. A ferry was said to have once run tourists across to Cardiff, but the docking platform collapsed in a storm and had never been repaired.

A derelict hotel crouched on the rock face beside the pier. Alan could just make out enough faded letters on its façade to supply the rest of the name: The Majestic Hotel. It was one of those ostentatious Gothic palaces that would have been decorated with plundered Egyptian artefacts and overseen by an army of servants. Now it was just a hulking ruin held together by scaffolding and protected by razor wire.

"The ticket office is shut," said Claudia, panting as though she'd exerted herself in going to look, "and there's nothing in the gift shop."

"I didn't want postcards," Alan said with a trace of annoyance. "I wanted to go out on the pier."

She gave him a flat look. "I mean there's *nothing* in the gift shop. It's empty. Deserted. Like this eyesore." She gestured dismissively.

"It's not deserted. Look, there are fishermen on the promenade."

"Well, I don't like it. It doesn't look safe."

He rolled his eyes. "It looks perfectly safe. There'd be keep

The Pier

out signs if it wasn't."

"But the fire—"

"It's not on fire *now*, is it? Come on, I want to see."

Without waiting for her he walked out onto the pier. The boards were warped but they looked sturdy enough. Not bad at all considering the damage salt and the sea could do. Below him the water was silky smooth but peering down through the slats threatened to make him dizzy.

"It must have been nice once," Claudia said.

"I think it's nice now."

"It's depressing. Like that rotting hotel over there. Probably crawling with rats and God knows what else."

Alan bit his tongue. There was no point in starting the tired old 'eye of the beholder' argument. She'd never been able to appreciate the strange beauty of graveyards or abandoned buildings. Junky antique shops made her nervous and she couldn't stand the smell of old books.

He'd spent the past few days suffering in silence. His shrill in-laws had kept him constantly on edge with their paranoid *Daily Mail* rants about immigrants and foreigners. A week was more than anyone should be expected to endure his wife's family and he'd congratulated himself on making it through without killing one or all of them.

"How could they let it fall into disrepair like this?" Claudia continued. She had clearly inherited her parents' need to find someone to blame.

He sighed. "I'm sure *they* didn't do it on purpose."

"Are you going to patronise me all day? Because if so—"

"I'm not patronising you," he said carefully, trying hard to mean it. "You're just so ... unadventurous." It was the kindest word he could manage.

"But it's old and ugly. Why can't we look at country houses and museums like normal people? Why do we always have to go slumming in places that ought to be condemned?"

"'Always'? Hey, we go to plenty of places you like. And they're always heaving with tourists and families with

The Pier

screaming babies. Isn't it nice to get off the beaten path once in a while? See something with real character?"

"I just don't like this place, Alan. It gives me the creeps."

He was about to tell her she didn't have to stay when he noticed the plaques. All along the promenade were little brass memorials, set into the wood of the decking and the railing.

OUR DEAREST ISABELLA, TAKEN TOO SOON
GRANDPA GEORGE, GONE FISHING
TOO MUCH OF WATER HAST THOU, POOR OPHELIA

"Look at these," he said.

But Claudia had already spotted them and was eyeing them with disapproval.

MY BELOVED JOHN, LOST AT SEA, HOME AT LAST
ANNA, YOU GOT THERE FIRST
HOW DOES IT FEEL NOW, DARLING?

Claudia grimaced. "Is this for real?"

"They're just commemorative plaques."

She advanced several uncertain steps, shaking her head in response to what she read. "There's something not right about them. I mean, look at this: 'You reap what you sow'. What the hell kind of memorial is that?"

Alan chuckled at the one he'd just found. "'If you can read this, you're next'."

"Ugh! That's in such bad taste."

"Not as bad as this one: 'Go on, push her in'."

"Alan, that's not funny."

"Don't blame me. I didn't write it."

"No, but you obviously don't see anything wrong with it."

"As a matter of fact, I don't. It makes a refreshing change from that clichéd 'in the arms of the angels' crap."

"Well, I think it's horrible."

"You think everything is horrible," he muttered. No matter where they went it seemed she was determined to have a lousy time. And to make sure he did too.

DO IT, YOU KNOW YOU WANT TO

The plaques were certainly unusual. Did the town just have a

The Pier

weird sense of humour? He read as he walked, fascinated by the universally morbid tone.

"Alan?" Claudia had stopped a few paces behind him.

"What is it now?"

"Haven't you noticed something?"

"Noticed what?"

"They're all memorials."

"Yeah, so?"

She stared at him as though waiting for him to catch on. He shrugged, oblivious to whatever it was she'd spotted that he hadn't.

"No birthdays or wedding anniversaries. No 'World's Best Mum'. No 'Happy Retirement'. They're all about death."

They'd only come about a quarter of the way down the pier but Alan estimated he'd seen at least a hundred plaques so far. And she was right. Some were more cryptic than others, but they all shared a single theme.

FOR BILLY, WHO LOVED THIS PIER. NOW YOU'LL NEVER LEAVE

"Yeah, I suppose that is a bit strange."

Claudia wrapped her arms around herself, though it wasn't remotely chilly. "I don't like this at all."

"So you keep saying."

"I mean it. It gives me a bad feeling and I don't want to stay here. We're leaving now."

Alan squared up to her like a gunslinger. "No sweetie, *you're* leaving; I'm staying here."

Her eyes flashed as her mouth worked at forming a retort. "Fine," she said at last through clenched teeth. "I'm going back to the hotel. I'm going to order room service and a bottle of their most overpriced wine. I'm sure you won't mind. *Sweetie*." She smiled icily and then stalked away, her pointy-toed heels clacking on the boards.

"Fine," Alan growled to himself. At least now he could enjoy the pier on his own. As Claudia's retreating figure dwindled and finally disappeared from sight, he felt all the

The Pier

unpleasantness of the past week vanish with her. All that was left was peace. Waves whispered beneath him, a low ambient hiss like voices on a radio station just out of range.

YOU LOST HER

He glanced up nervously, half expecting the voices from within the plaques to manifest themselves behind him. He wasn't surprised they had spooked Claudia, but now even he was finding them unsettling.

A fisherman stood halfway down the promenade, peering over the railing. He'd anchored a hefty fishing rod against the planking and its line disappeared into the water at a sharp angle. He looked up as Alan drew near, his weathered cap shading an equally weathered face.

"Nice day for it," Alan said with a friendly nod towards the fishing gear.

The man simply stared in response, the unwelcoming expression of a local confronted by an odious tourist.

Alan had hoped to engage him, to ask about the plaques, but his companion's unfriendliness intimidated him. He smiled nervously and cleared his throat before finding his voice again.

"Hey, listen, I'm sorry if I'm disturbing you. I couldn't help but notice the rather odd character of the memorials out here."

Again he was met with cold silence. After a week of his in-laws' strident opinions he wasn't sure how to handle the silent treatment.

For several seconds he felt sure the man would just continue to stare. But at last he broke eye contact and looked Alan up and down before parting his lips with an unpleasant smack. "Odd," the man echoed.

Alan wasn't sure if it was a question or an agreement. He added hopefully, "I wondered if maybe there was some local story behind them?"

The man nodded thoughtfully and a humourless smile made his lips curl slightly. Then he turned his attention back to his fishing line with a grunt. Clearly the interview was over.

Alan's face burned at the wordless rebuke. He backed away

The Pier

and then continued along the pier.

WE WANTED WHAT WAS INSIDE

IT WAS OURS

The plaques seemed to be getting weirder and weirder the further he went. He felt like he should have reached the end of the pier by now, but when he looked up he saw he was only little more than halfway along. The pier-head and its charred centre was still some distance yet.

Beneath him the water sloshed gently against the legs of the pier, soothing, hypnotic. He could imagine drifting asleep to the sound. A yawn overtook him and he shook himself. The argument with Claudia must have exhausted the little strength her family hadn't sapped from him. His spurned wife had had the right idea, though: a good meal and some wine was just what he needed too. He'd make it up to her after she'd had a chance to cool off. No doubt the week had been taxing for her as well.

ALAN AND CLAUDIA

His breath caught in his throat and he stood gaping at the little plaque. It was several minutes before he got hold of himself. It was an astonishing coincidence, but just that – coincidence. Their names weren't exactly unique. Still, he felt unable to move on.

He dug his phone out of his back pocket and set it to camera mode. Framing the inscription in the phone's window he pressed the button and saved the image. Then he sent it to Claudia. *You won't believe this*, he texted.

Then he saw the adjacent plaque. SHE DESERVES IT. And beside that: IT WON'T HURT.

A chill raced along his spine and he almost dropped the phone. He was too unnerved to photograph the inscriptions, but he wanted confirmation of what he was seeing. He spied another fisherman near the end of the pier and Alan made his way there, determined to find out what was going on.

"Excuse me," he said brazenly, "but what can you tell me about these plaques?"

The Pier

This man was even older than the first and looked so frail Alan marvelled that he'd managed to carry all his gear this far out along the pier. He blinked so long at the intrusion Alan wondered if the man was deaf or blind. But then his eyes fixed on Alan and he shrugged. "What's there to tell?" he said at last. "They remember."

This struck Alan as deliberately unhelpful. "'They remember'? Remember what?"

But he simply nodded as though Alan had answered his own question. Were the old timers just senile?

Spurred by a sense of inexplicable urgency Alan pressed on. "I really want to know about these plaques. I've never seen anything like them before. It's almost like they're alive. Reading my mind. Like someone's talking to me through them." He laughed. "I know that sounds crazy."

Something like fear shone for a moment in the old man's eyes. Then he looked away, out towards the sea. "No one reads those things," he said hoarsely.

"What do you mean? My wife and I were just reading them."

"Your wife?"

"She didn't stay. They upset her so she left."

Alan took the pensive silence for approval of Claudia's decision. But enough was enough. He was losing his patience. Angrily, he seized the man's coat. "Tell me what this is about!"

The man continued to stare out across the waves, his expression unreadable. Finally, he leaned in close and whispered, "Those messages aren't for you."

"What are you talking about? Who are they for?"

The man shook his head fiercely. "If you're seeing strange things in those plaques I'd advise you to turn around and go back the way you came."

"But I—"

"Go!" With that he tore free of Alan's grip and turned his back, keeping his eyes fixed on the water.

The Pier

Alan backed away, staring in bewilderment. It was some local sport, that's all, a game they played on outsiders. The pier clearly wouldn't last another hundred years. Probably not even another ten. Why not decorate it with cryptic messages to confound tourists until it fell to pieces?

"Crazy old geezer," he muttered, turning away. The ruined pagoda beckoned and he made for it in earnest, determined to get there without reading any more of the plaques.

Soon it was only a few yards away but his eyelids felt heavy again and he suppressed another yawn. Baffled by his sudden weariness he scrubbed at his face, producing starbursts behind his eyes. His cheeks felt like sandpaper. Had he forgotten to shave that morning? When he opened his eyes again tombstones slithered in his vision, rising and falling softly in the mud. Each time he blinked it took real effort to open his eyes.

A sharp pain in his hand brought him back to himself and he stared at the splinter embedded in his palm. He was standing on the bottom rung of the railing, his left hand bracing against the top plank. The ashen expanse before him was the sea, his graveyard only waves. Startled, he pulled the splinter out and backed away, bewildered and disoriented. Behind him, the old man was still looking out over the water, his back to Alan. Of the first man there was no sign at all. If Alan had fallen in, no one would have seen.

His back prickled with sweat and he dug out his phone. Claudia hadn't responded to his text so she probably had her phone turned off. When a polite computer voice confirmed that, he rang off. What was there to tell her anyway? That he'd fallen asleep on his feet and nearly done a header off the pier? He sure as hell couldn't tell her the plaques were talking to him.

The time display on the phone surprised him and he double-checked it against his watch. Although the sky had darkened considerably, that couldn't possibly be right. When had he sent that text with the photo? He scrolled through the menu and

The Pier

blinked uncomprehendingly at it. He'd been on the pier for nearly six hours.

YOU BELONG HERE

Alan forced himself towards the middle of the promenade, trying to get as far away from the railing as he could. He was nearly at the end of the pier and he felt a wild sense of victory, as though he'd been swimming against the current to reach a goal. When he finally arrived at the blackened pier-head he was exhausted. His legs ached as though he'd walked miles.

It might have been a bonfire that had gone out. Crooked trestles encircled the remains, bound at intervals by torn yellow tape. The low sun turned the debris into a mass of writhing shadows and for a moment Alan was convinced that the burnt and broken timber was trying to reassemble itself. That would explain the faint clacking sound he heard. But there was no breeze. The strips of tape hung limp as flags. The sea was dead calm.

He peered into the rubble and a flash of pale grey caught his eye. Something *was* moving in there. Birds picking at crumbs, perhaps? But while he remembered seagulls wheeling in the sky that morning, he hadn't seen or heard any since stepping out onto the pier.

He moved closer, squinting into the darkness. There was the smell of charred wood and the sea, along with something else, something rotten. He could just discern a few small pale shards, jutting like brambles from the ruins. It couldn't possibly be the bed of oysters it resembled, the shells broken open to relinquish the scattering of pearls at his feet. Even as his fingers closed around the tiny misshapen object, Alan knew it wasn't a pearl. He dropped the tooth and staggered back with a cry. His eyes soon found the lumps and hollows of a skull, then another.

The clacking was growing louder. Alan stared hard into the shadows, straining to see in the growing darkness. He fumbled for his phone again and used its display as a torch, bathing the ruins in a sickly greenish glow. Shadows leapt as he passed the

The Pier

light over the debris. Staring faces rose to meet the glow, their mouths stretched far too wide, their eyes glinting with a light of their own. The phone clattered to his feet, as he understood at last what he was seeing. The pagoda had never been made of timber at all.

His gaze fell on a series of memorials at the base of the ruins.

I WASN'T READY
CAN YOU FEEL ME?
I'M STILL HERE

The words spun in his head and he stumbled away from the plaques. He felt dizzy, spinning out of control and unable to find solid ground. Wind rushed in his ears and coalesced into a chorus of voices both menacing and alluring. Determined to resist the pull of the ruins, he turned away only to see the pier stretching on impossibly long, far away from the shore. And it was no longer deserted. Hundreds of people lined the pier, gazing coldly at him.

Behind him the bones crackled like flames while the silent masses watched him. Even if he had the strength to run, he'd never get past them all or survive the distance to the shore. The dizziness passed with the realisation and he sank to his knees on the planks. Shadows bloomed around him like a spreading stain, engulfing him. He didn't want to see what form they were taking behind him.

As he closed his eyes and waited to join the others, he knew the voices had lied. It *did* hurt. He only hoped it wouldn't be forever.

MINOS OR RHADAMANTHUS

Reggie Oliver

The sun was sinking behind the cricket pavilion, extending its long shadows over the grass of what had once been called the 'Great Field'. Caverner remembered how when he had first arrived as a homesick boy of seven in the summer of the year 1901 it had indeed seemed like a Great Field. Now after fifteen years the place looked to him very little and forlorn, transfigured though it was by the light of a perfect August evening. Caverner wondered why there were no small boys there, playing on the pitch or practising in the nets which adjoined the pavilion, until he remembered. Of course, it was August; it must be the summer holidays.

Caverner was beginning to ask himself why he had come. His time at St Cyprian's had not been a notably happy one, though it had been shot through with fragments of idyllic joy. There had been moments of ecstasy which had come upon him quite without warning and fled in the same way. Later, when he called them to mind, he had never been able to put those occasions into a succinct metaphysical category. Neither 'Oneness with God', nor 'Communion with Nature', nor even 'Youthful Exuberance' had ever satisfied as explanations or definitions of these experiences.

He remembered how at the end of his last summer term at St Cyprian's, he had been allowed to roam pretty much as he wished. He had gained his scholarship to Eton and during the end of term examinations he became what was called 'a leavite', a piece of pedantic facetiousness used to denote someone who was still at the school but free of its academic shackles. He spent this time riding his bicycle along the Kent coast, stopping where he wanted to, spending his pocket money on whatever he chose to eat or drink, lying in the long grass by the roadside or on the short springy turf of cliff tops. He knew even while he experienced it that this strange

Minos or Rhadamanthus

unburdened interlude was to be savoured, bitten through to its core.

One cloudless afternoon he had come in his wanderings to a church not far from the sea and parked his bicycle in the porch. The church itself with its knapped flint walls and its plain Early English windows was not very exciting; equally, the interior had been pleasant enough but had offered little of interest. There were no ancient tombs or brasses for him to rub; the glass was intensely Victorian and would not do. Caverner, at thirteen, was beginning to suffer from a slight case of Antiquarian Snobbery. As he came out of the church, he suddenly remembered that he had not yet had the lunchtime sandwiches with which he had been provided, so he decided to eat them in the churchyard which was on a slope with a view through trees of the sea. There it was, deeply blue below the paler blue of the sky.

He sat down facing it, resting his back against a tombstone that tilted gently away from it and stretched out his legs on the long, nodding summer grass that glittered in the heat. The sandwiches had contained some kind of meat paste and were not very palatable, but the apple which he had been given by way of dessert seemed to taste of the summer that surrounded him. When he had finished he remained sitting. A deep calm entered him, not soporific at all, but wide-awake, like a glass of clear cold water. He had the feeling that he could see to the end of the world. It occurred to him that it would be more accurate to say that he could see to the end of time. That was the quality of the experience, a very particular quality like no other: it was absolutely of the moment and the place, yet, as he put it to himself, 'ancient'. That word 'ancient' had always seemed to him one of the loveliest in the English language. The sea before him, the warm lichened stone at his back, the bright sun above him, the dead beneath him under the grass all contributed to the flavour of the instant. It was a thing as unique as himself; not in time, nor out of time, but somehow for all time. For a few seconds he seemed to have in his grasp

Minos or Rhadamanthus

the meaning of Eternity. It was no longer the shapeless cloudy entity that it had been in sermons and hymns and drowsy Bible readings before bedtime. Above all, there was, for once, no fear in it, no fear at all.

A breeze stirred and with it the sensation began to drift away. He tried to retain it even while he knew it was as useless as trying to hold smoke in his hands. He got up and bicycled down into Sandgate where he bought an ice cream and wandered along the pier. The feeling had gone, never to be recovered in exactly the same form, but he knew he had been changed by it. When he arrived back at St Cyprian's later that afternoon, he was expecting, rather absurdly, that people would see the change in him, that he would appear transfigured. A part of him, though, knew that this was laughable.

At evening prayers in the chapel some of the exalted state of the afternoon came back to him. It was rather unexpected because he had come to loathe the unctuous tones with which the headmaster, the Rev. C.W. Margetson conducted the rite. Sitting almost opposite Margetson, he watched the man closely as he knelt at his desk praying, as he always did, extempore. The hands like polished yellowed ivory were knotted together; the balding cranium sprinkled with sparse black hairs nodded in tune with his holy ejaculations. Caverner who had once been impressed and frightened by these pieties now knew more of the man inside, or thought he did.

That evening Caverner saw him without the usual feelings of revulsion. He saw a hypocrite, but he also saw what a hypocrite was: a man in torment. Pity and compassion was not what he felt; perhaps, he thought later, such things are beyond a thirteen-year-old, but he did have a fleeting intuitive understanding. Caverner had been momentarily touched by the suffering behind the cant. The thin, bony, mean looking man opposite him was somehow appropriate to the occasion, part of the necessary furniture of evening prayers in St Cyprian's chapel, even of the world and universe beyond it.

Minos or Rhadamanthus

Then Margetson had announced the hymn: 'The Day Thou Gavest, Lord, is Ended', and Caverner allowed the drowsy sentimentalism of the tune and words to wash over him and carry him away. His cheeks burned from his day in the sun and the wind from the sea. All was well, even Margetson.

As far as he could remember, Caverner had never actually hated Margetson; his feelings towards him were always more complex. He had begun his life at St Cyprian's by fearing him and his punishments. Margetson possessed two canes of differing thickness and suppleness which he called Minos and Rhadamanthus after the judges in Hades, the Classical Land of the Dead; then there was the wooden paddle with which he would punish his youngest charges, and this he called Cerberus after its guard dog. None of the boys knew why Margetson had given names to his instruments of torture, nor did they understand the significance of those names, beyond the fact that they had to do with final judgement and retribution. No one would have dared to ask the Head, as he was called; but the very fact that these instruments had names invested their exercise with an additional and sinister terror.

Caverner never again knew such fear as he had known between the ages of seven and eleven at St Cyprian's; not even in the trenches in the seconds before the whistles blew and he and his men had climbed over the parapet to begin the treacherous walk through No Man's Land. Then the fear had been acute, but purely physical. The terror he had known at St Cyprian's was also moral and spiritual. When he was summoned to 'see the Head' he felt acutely the anticipation of physical agony, but more acutely still what he came to know as 'conviction of sin'. The Head used the word sin a great deal and made his victims feel that the pains he inflicted were but a pale foretaste of the eternal agonies meted out to sinners in the life to come. Some boys pretended to shrug this side of the matter off, but Caverner could not. His parents were somewhat remote, god-fearing people whom he knew would be grieved to know that he was a miserable sinner and that, thanks to

Minos or Rhadamanthus

Margetson, he had already sampled the torments of the damned.

Margetson had a curious way of dealing with his victims. In the first instance they would be summoned to 'see him after lunch', and that usually rather disgusting meal would be further blighted by his reading, before Grace, of a list of those who were to see him. In this post-lunch interview he would tell the boy at some length quite why and how he had offended so grievously; then he would ask the boy in question to come to see him 'after tea', at about six o'clock, for what he invariably called 'a licking', or, if he was feeling particularly judgmental, 'a good licking'. To the day of his death Caverner could never hear the word 'licking' without a physical feeling of nausea rising in his throat. Its metaphorical resonances had sickened him from the very first.

So, after tea, the thing itself would happen. In the spring and Michaelmas Terms sentence was carried out in the Head's study in the main school building, but in summer Margetson chose to use the cricket pavilion on the Great Field as his place of punishment. The ostensible reason for this was convenience: the hour after tea was the time he spent coaching the First Eleven in the nets next to the Pavilion.

During his early years at St Cyprian's, Caverner had simply been in awe of the Head, and, at times, desperately afraid. Then one summer term, shortly after his eleventh birthday, he had been found guilty of a particularly heinous misdemeanour. Caverner could not quite remember what it was: was it talking after lights out, or laughing during one of the Head's sermons? No, he had forgotten the crime, but not its consequence. After lunch he had been told to meet the Head in the pavilion after tea at six.

The pavilion itself was an innocent looking building of white-painted weather boards with steps leading up to a veranda, fretwork on the eaves and balustrade giving it a touch of the picturesque. Inside, it was slightly stuffy after a long day in the sun, smelling of creosote and linseed oil. There were

Minos or Rhadamanthus

team photographs on the wall, pads and bats scattered about on the wooden benches. Caverner had waited a good five minutes for Margetson to arrive, terror and shame increasing with every derisive tick of the pavilion clock.

When Margetson came he was carrying his two canes, Minos and Rhadamanthus. He told Caverner to 'prepare' himself, a ghastly euphemism which meant that Caverner was to take down his shorts and underpants, then bend over one of the benches. As Caverner did as he was told Margetson asked him whether he preferred the punishment to be inflicted by Minos or Rhadamanthus. Caverner by this time was trembling so much that he could not speak, but something about the tone of Margetson's question – "Minos, or Rhadamanthus?" – had astonished him. There had been a higher pitch to his voice, and a tremor which Caverner could not mistake for anything other than pure excitement.

It was just as the dreadful business was coming to an end that quite by chance Caverner noticed something. His head had been bowed and turned away from his torturer, but the force of one of Margetson's blows had shifted him slightly so that he saw what he had never seen before: the Head in action. He saw the look on the man's face, the disarray of his clothes, the gross physical evidence of sensual excitement.

Caverner had been an innocent boy, brought up in innocence, but there are times when innocence knows and can see farther than experience. Caverner not only saw, but somehow knew, and Margetson, for his part, knew that he had been discovered. He immediately stopped the beating and told Caverner to "get dressed at once." Caverner did so and left the Pavilion before Margetson. He walked down the steps in a state of numbness, almost a trance as he reflected on what he had seen. He had been horrified, but also, somehow, liberated. Conviction of Sin would not torment him again. He began to understand that evil may not have a motive, but it must have a cause.

It would not be true to say that Margetson never punished

Minos or Rhadamanthus

Caverner again, but Minos and Rhadamanthus were rarely used on him. He preferred to give Caverner 'lines' instead. This meant copying out a hundred or more hexameters of Virgil, a task which Caverner, a dreamy but studious boy, found almost congenial.

Caverner kept his experience in the Pavilion to himself, but he gave it a great deal of thought and, as he did so, certain aspects of Margetson's curious character began to make sense. Long afterwards Caverner realised that it was this speculation which kept him from simply hating the Head.

In the first place there was Margetson's wife, invariably and rather strangely called 'Mrs Head'. Mrs Head was a lumpy, doughy woman, with deep-set, suspicious eyes, curiously dull and featureless of countenance. She acted as Head Matron in the school, frequently forcing castor oil, liquorice powder and hot poultices on her charges with the same dedicated ferocity with which Margetson applied Minos and Rhadamanthus. From what little casual conversation she let fall, Caverner gathered that she was the daughter of a Bishop and something of a snob. Childless, she lavished what few maternal instincts she possessed on the occasional sprig of nobility that came as a pupil to St Cyprian's. Those, like Caverner, whose parents were neither rich nor aristocratic, she treated as barely tolerable nuisances.

Caverner, like most children of his age, regarded almost all adults as more or less physically repulsive, but he recognised gradations of hideousness, and Mrs Head he thought of as belonging to the lowest circles of Hades. What little he understood of carnal relations convinced him of the impossibility of their existing between the Head and his wife. This, he later realised, could have been the prejudice and aesthetic snobbery of youth, but he certainly could detect nothing tender in their relationship.

Margetson would sometimes mention the scholastic achievements of his youth in a tone which suggested a grievance that he had not risen higher in the world. He had

Minos or Rhadamanthus

taken a good degree at Oxford, and had once played cricket for his university. He had taken holy orders; he had married the daughter of a Bishop. Caverner studied the appropriate reference books and discovered that the bishop had died shortly after his daughter's marriage. Perhaps, thereby, hopes of preferment had been dashed. Caverner tried to imagine the brilliant, hopeful young curate Margetson might once have been, but failed. Something had happened to him. Had it been an event; or was it simply the heavy foot of time that had trodden him into the mud?

Once or twice Caverner thought he had caught glimpses of the old Margetson, the fine classical scholar. There were times during a lesson when Margetson would quote Horace or rhapsodise over the gobbets of Virgil they were construing; then with a sigh he would return to the dreary business of drilling his charges for the scholarship examinations, or for Common Entrance. At this stage of his education Caverner did not quite understand how a piece of Latin could be regarded as a thing of beauty, which was mainly Margetson's fault because most of the time learning was taken simply to be a means to a marketable end. Scholarships on the honours board of St Cyprian's attracted parents: another pupil, another fee.

For a Christian cleric, Margetson was curiously obsessed by pagan mythology. The legends even entered his sermons which were long, rambling and might, for all Caverner knew or cared, have been brilliantly erudite. In these discourses Jesus remained the blonde-bearded, white-gowned Aryan Scoutmaster of the Sunday school poster; even the bloody warriors and thundering prophets of the Old Testament were pale and sickly figures. But when, in an odd aside, Margetson turned to the classical legends, it was as if he had turned a light on in a strange but very real world. Caverner remembered Actaeon, torn to pieces by his own hounds, Agave holding the severed head of her own son believing it to be that of a Mountain Lion; here were Odysseus and Aeneas venturing underground and visiting the land of the dead. The boys of St

Minos or Rhadamanthus

Cyprian's became oddly familiar with the geography and personnel of Tartarus.

To Margetson the Greek and Roman Hells were more interesting than the Christian one whose torments, even in Dante, were seldom entirely bespoke. Margetson revelled in the particularity of pain. So Caverner and his fellows heard about Ixion on his wheel, Sisyphus and Tantalus, or Tityos whose liver perpetually regenerated itself in order to be pecked to bloody fragments again and again by vultures.

Caverner did not question the validity of this world of punishments, even after his encounter in the cricket pavilion. He only questioned Margetson's justification of his own activities: that pains were to be inflicted in this life in order to warn the offender against those of the life to come. Caverner, who could summon up no great affection for the Scoutmaster Jesus with which he was presented, saw himself as doomed in any case. One punishment more or less in this life would make no difference in the life to come.

Once, towards the end of his time at St Cyprian's Caverner had found himself on what was called 'the private side', that part of the school buildings which was reserved for the Margetsons' domestic use. He had been sent to the Head with a message by one of the masters. Not finding Margetson in his study he ventured further into this secret domain than he had ever been before. It was not particularly exciting. Margetson's home territory was not exactly Spartan – certainly not by comparison with the conditions in which his charges existed – but they were drab. Ornament was discarded in favour of severe and unostentatious conformity. What pictures there were consisted mainly of monochrome steel engravings of church buildings, or portraits of ecclesiastical dignitaries. Then Caverner saw, in a corridor, a picture that he actually liked. He could not help stopping before it. This picture was different from the others. It was admittedly not in colour, but it was the sepia print of a recent painting.

In front of a vague, rocky landscape were seven tall,

Minos or Rhadamanthus

beautiful young women, one of them bare breasted, draped in flowing, classical robes. They carried rounded metallic water pots which some of them were emptying into a cauldron in the centre of the picture. The general atmosphere was one of slow, dreamlike tranquillity. The only slightly troubling element in this scene was that the cauldron had an opening in its bulbous side in the shape of a grotesque head, like a flattened mask of tragedy, from whose wide, angry mouth the water poured away into a dark hole. The activity of these beauties appeared to be futile.

"Do you know who they are?"

Caverner started violently and his back brushed against something. It was a rusty black suit belonging to Margetson who had crept up silently behind him. Caverner, blushing and terrified, turned round to face the Head, who seemed however to be in a genial mood and appeared almost amused by Caverner's obvious discomfiture. Caverner rapidly explained his presence there and presented the note to Margetson who put it in his pocket without even a glance at the contents. His steel-blue eyes, slightly magnified by heavy round spectacles, fixed themselves on Caverner.

"Do you know what is being represented?"

Margetson was not a handsome man, but he had an impressive presence. He was tall, loose-limbed and spare, with a beak of a nose, a long neck and an unusually prominent Adam's apple. His skin was the colour and texture of polished ivory. Caverner had always felt that there was something not quite real about the man.

"Well, boy?"

Caverner shook his head.

"Then I shall tell you, in order that you may be better informed." Margetson often talked in this ironic, stylised way. It contributed to the air of remoteness and unreality.

"These are the daughters of King Danaus of Egypt," he said pointing to the seven beauties. "They were commanded by their father Danaus to murder their husbands on their wedding

Minos or Rhadamanthus

night. All but one did so. The murderous daughters were subsequently killed, and in Hell they are condemned by the inexorable judges of that place perpetually to pour water into a leaking vessel which will never be filled. This is the scene which that excellent modern artist Mr John William Waterhouse has chosen to depict."

Caverner stared at the picture again. What had seemed like serenity was now shown to be a profound melancholy sadness. For Caverner it overwhelmed all the dreamlike beauty he had once found in it. If Margetson had not been there he might have wept; instead he fought back the tears. His grief was tinged with indignant anger: whatever these lovely creatures had done they did not deserve this.

"You appear to be moved, boy. What is the matter? Do you think that the dread crime of killing one's spouse should *not* be punished with the utmost severity?"

Caverner shook his head.

"Run along then."

Caverner recalled the moment with vividness, standing there by the Pavilion some ten years later, but the grief had somehow gone out of it. So much, so many terrible things had intervened. Again he began to wonder what had brought him back to St Cyprian's when he could have been spending his leave in London.

He was not quite sure how long he had been there. It seemed an age to him, yet it could not have been. The shadow of the Pavilion had barely lengthened; the even, golden light was not yet ensanguined by the sun's fall towards the horizon. The only change to the scene was that it was not now entirely deserted. A small black figure was moving towards him across the Great Field.

At the opposite edge of the field from the pavilion was a line of trees masking a knapped flint wall. Behind this lay the scout huts, the carpentry shed and the school buildings to which access could be obtained through a gap in the wall. From this gap had come the black figure that resembled a strange, ragged

Minos or Rhadamanthus

flapping bird. As it approached, Caverner could see that this crow of a man was in fact a schoolmaster in a black suit with a black gown over it. Then he began to make out the white dog-collar below the long pale neck, the familiar, slightly bounding stride, the glint of spectacles. It was Margetson.

Caverner retreated to the steps of the Pavilion, then stood his ground. He was, after all, an officer in uniform; there were three wound stripes on his sleeve. Nevertheless he waited as if waiting for a battle. Margetson only noticed him when he was halfway across the square of the cricket pitch. He hesitated, a puzzled frown on his face. After a while he came on again. When he was about six feet away from Caverner he stopped once more and peered at him through his spectacles.

"Caverner, isn't it?"

"That's right, Margetson."

Margetson was taken aback by the naked use of his surname. There was a pause before he was able to say: "Ah. On leave, are you?"

"On leave. Yes. A leavite, you might say."

"Hmm. Not a deserter, then?" Caverner did not dignify his remark with a reply. "My little jest," added Margetson, almost apologetically, "Just my little jest. One of our brave boys, then, eh? Splendid. Splendid." Having delivered himself of this conventional piece of patriotic piety he seemed at a loss again. His rusty black suit looked to Caverner, rustier and shinier than ever. Could it possibly be the same one after nearly ten years? In a lower, less confident voice, Margetson said: "What do you want, Caverner?"

"I think I wanted to see you."

"Was that wise?"

"It may have been necessary."

"Oh, you foolish boy. You foolish boy. Did you think I would be impressed? Did you think I might fall on my knees and worship the conquering hero? I am sorry to disappoint you. To me you are a grubby, ignorant little boy, I am afraid, and will ever remain so. That is the penalty of being a

Minos or Rhadamanthus

schoolmaster. We are invincible realists. We know that all boys are grubby, ignorant little reprobates and thus they remain. It is not the uniform that makes the man. Many are called, but few are chosen. Original sin, you see, is so very unoriginal."

Caverner watched Margetson unmoved. He looked up at the sky which appeared, strangely, to be getting lighter. Finally, he said: "I read about you in the *Times*. The Coroner brought in an open verdict."

For a moment Margetson appeared startled, then he came back at Caverner. There was now a touch of real venom in his voice.

"Well I saw something about you. Mametz Wood, wasn't it? July 1916?"

"It is August now. The term is over. The holidays have begun."

"I did not take my own life. It was taken from me."

Caverner looked at Margetson for a long time. "I think I despised you once," he said, then he smiled.

"How dare you, sir!" Margetson was silent for a time. He appeared to be struggling to articulate something. Finally he said: "It was not suicide, whatever the Coroner may have thought; whatever other people said. It was not."

"Who hanged you then?"

"I did not mean to…"

The image was conveyed to Caverner, as vividly as when he had first been given the details. When he had read the bald announcement of Margetson's death in the newspaper, he had immediately written to a friend in England and asked for further information. Though guns and death surrounded him, he burned to know. The friend, a fellow sufferer under Margetson, had been happy to oblige.

One morning, early, towards the chilly end of a Michaelmas term, when it was barely light, the boys of St Cyprian's had trouped into the gymnasium where, according to the school's inflexible routine, they were to line up before going into

Minos or Rhadamanthus

chapel. Something was dimly swinging from one of the ropes that hung from the rafters of the gym's great beamed roof. The process of realisation that this was the Head, the Reverend C.W. Margetson, and that he had hanged himself, came to the boys surprisingly slowly but was all the more terrible for that. The Head was in his usual rusty black, with his dog-collar, even his master's gown. His long neck had been stretched still further by the rope; the face was almost black but recognisable and his spectacles clung to his nose. Stranger yet was the fact that his trousers had come loose and were gathered in exhausted corrugated bags around his ankles. The effect for an instant might almost have been comic. Witnesses declared that the vision burned itself indelibly into their minds: it remained with them day and night. It remained with Caverner too, even amid the stench of death in Flanders, even though he had received the news at second hand.

"You cannot hurt me now," said Caverner.

Margetson clawed at the air around him, a gesture of such impotent rage that Caverner almost laughed.

Caverner said: "Very soon you will meet Minos or Rhadamanthus. Perhaps even Cerberus too." That was what he had come to say. It was not to see the terror in Margetson's eyes, so he turned away from him before he could.

Margetson turned too and began to hurry from the field towards a belt of dark firs in the distance. A host of shadows followed after him. Caverner remained standing in the ancient light by the Pavilion but he no longer felt alone. The Great Field was 'Great' once more, greater even than the War in which his body had perished.

MORNING'S ECHO

Joel Lane

It was the strangest kind of dating I ever experienced. But at the time, I was quite young. I hadn't been in the police force long, and I'd only just moved to Birmingham from the Black Country. In a way, it was how I got to know the city. Years later, when I was getting serious with Elaine, I told her a little about that. I said Carla had still been in love with her ex. Which was true, but it wasn't the whole story.

One evening, a girl of eighteen or so turned up at the Digbeth station in some distress. She wanted us to help her find her boyfriend. When we asked where he might be, she said: "He's in the ground." Denny was the head of a local teen gang, the Falcons, that had some minor criminal involvement – a couple of my colleagues knew him. He'd recently been threatened by an older and more dangerous gang, the Jackals, about whom we knew a lot more. Now he'd disappeared.

We spoke to the leader of the Jackals, a vicious little scrote who was probably capable of murder if someone else cleaned up after him. He claimed not to know who the missing boy was. We had no evidence. Carla wasn't able to say where the body might be, though we went round a few parks and waste grounds with dogs. We suspected Denny had done a runner and Carla was covering for him. But we didn't have the heart to accuse her of wasting police time. She was a thin, dark-eyed girl with spiky hair and a fragile loneliness that encased her like a shell.

A fortnight after we'd stopped looking for the missing boy, I had the first dream. I was with Carla in a ruined factory somewhere, open to the sky. There was a new moon. I dug with a spade through weeds and loose soil, took out a few shattered bricks, found a package wrapped in newspaper. In the moonlight, I began to unwrap it. Carla's fingernails gripped my arm. I woke up shivering, though it was only October.

Morning's Echo

That night was the beginning of something for me. I knew that it would be stupid to tell my colleagues about the dream – but at the same time, that I had to do something. Carla's passive face glimmered at the edge of my vision. The next day, I phoned her. She knew the place from my description: it was in Tyseley, just off the Grand Union Canal.

We went there after midnight. I was living alone, so there was no need for an excuse. Just as I'd dreamt, I dug up a buried newspaper package. This time, I unwrapped it. Thinking of 'pass the parcel' games in junior school. It contained the hand of a young man – drained white, but not in the least decayed. Carla took it from me, wrapped it again, and kissed me on the mouth. Then she walked away, leaving me to replace the soil and fragments of brick in the ground.

About a month later, I had a second dream. Another place I didn't know. Trees on the edge of a flooded running track, behind a decaying wall of red stone blocks. The same pale sliver of moon. Carla watched me dig in the marshy soil and uncover another small package. I felt her breath on my face.

Once again, I called her and she knew where it was. Near the university, behind some tenement houses where students lived. Because the running track was in a valley, the rising water table had made it a swamp. There was a strong odour of decay and unclean growth. But once again, what I found was perfectly preserved: the pale, narrow foot of a boy. Carla's kiss left me as frustrated as if I had woken up, though I was still in a moonlit landscape that seemed unreal. I wondered if it belonged to her memory.

The next time was a railway bridge in Digbeth: another foot. Then where a narrow river came above ground: a buried arm. It was always an abandoned place, and there was always a new moon. I was so keen to dream that I wasn't sleeping well, and Carla was in my mind all the time. But she wouldn't see me except when I'd dreamed about finding more of Denny. I asked her if she was keeping the pieces together. She said: "They're not just pieces. He's coming back."

Morning's Echo

Carla had a baby son she said was Denny's. I heard him crying a few times when I phoned her, and I saw them together one time when our paths crossed in the Bull Ring market. It was strange to see her so bound up with normality. The only thing that kept my obsession with her in check was how desperately busy we were that year. There was a rising level of street crime, some of it linked to the Jackals. Their leader was killed in a fight, but an even nastier piece of work replaced him. Things seemed to be on the edge of a chaos no police work could unravel.

Every month, another bitter dream. Another date with Carla in a place that she knew and I didn't. Another newspaper-wrapped part of her boyfriend. Another brief kiss that brought me no closer to her. I thought of something I'd read in college: the hermeneutic circle of learning, how you reached the whole through the parts and the parts through the whole. The hands, feet, arms, calves, thighs, and then a torso with the penis cleanly severed. Almost a year of madness.

Finally, it was October again. She led me through the Vyse Street cemetery to a half-circle of stone ridges that was strangely like a Greek theatre. I could hear water running underground. There was a disused air-raid shelter here, I knew. Long rats crept through the grass between headstones. At the heart of the structure, I saw a ruined vault. This time I didn't need to dig: the package could be reached through a break in the stone. No creature had interfered with it. I peeled away the layers of newsprint from the unblemished face. His eyes were still in place, seeing.

This time I walked away. Not wanting to see how Carla looked at her lover's head. Then I felt her hand on my arm. I turned. She embraced me, pressed her open mouth against mine. We stood together for a few seconds. Then she said: "There's still one part missing."

"I don't think that's going to turn up," I answered.

Carla shrugged. "It's always the way."

A cloud slipped over the moon like a scarf over a damaged

face. "What's going to happen now?" I asked.

She paused, uncertain. "Denny and I will go away together. He's back now. The balance is restored. But we can't stay here." She looked back to where Denny's head was waiting in its cradle of local news. Then she turned back to me. "You'll meet him again," she said. "And he'll be fair to you. Because you helped."

At the time, I thought she was talking about the police's dealings with the Falcons. It wasn't until years later that I realised she might have meant something quite different. She was, after all, mad. But I think about what she said more and more these days. Sometimes it's all the comfort I have.

IT BEGINS AT HOME

John Llewellyn Probert

"That child isn't crying enough."

Derek Martin, head of MartImages, took a fountain pen from the left inside pocket of his immaculately tailored suit jacket. The pinstripe which ran through the worsted blue wool was almost the same shade of pink as the blood vessels etched across the whites of the starving child's eyes. He uncapped the pen and, holding the dark green marbled barrel delicately, drew two large circles around the distressed African orphan's orbits. "The belly's not swollen enough either," he said, indicating the same on the picture with an arrow.

Paul Reynolds, who had taken the picture, looked at Martin with a mixture of shock and disappointment.

"I'm sorry?"

Martin put his pen away as his voice assumed the tones of an elderly headmaster addressing an errant ten-year-old.

"We have been asked to supply images to accompany the 'Disaster in Tanzania' appeal. The charities need something that will shock people into coughing up some of their hard-earned cash. That," he said, indicating Paul's photograph of the desperately hungry little girl he had found on the streets of Dar Es Salaam, "will just have them shrugging their shoulders and giving their loose change to the fucking donkey sanctuary instead. We'll lose the charities' business and someone else with a bit more creativity will be in there like a shot making the money we should be, and all because the photograph we gave them wasn't sufficiently emotive. So like I said, that child isn't crying enough. Add some more tears. And lose the snot – we know potential donators come mainly from a social class that find any kind of body fluid other than tears and blood a turn off."

It took a while for his boss's words to sink in.

"You want me to alter the photo?" Paul said eventually.

It Begins at Home

Martin shook his head.

"No son, I just want you to improve it a little."

Paul pointed at the folder crammed with the pictures he had painstakingly printed out last night after his new boss had explained that he 'couldn't stand looking at the things on a fucking computer monitor'.

"Mr Martin, those were the best pictures I could take."

Martin balanced the file in one hand before letting it slide into the dustbin.

"Well your best needs to get better," was his reply.

Paul frowned. He had spent the best part of two weeks taking images of starving locals.

"I took over five hundred photographs, Mr Martin – these are the positively the most heartbreaking I have."

Martin leaned over so that his eyes were only inches from Paul's own, and when he addressed him it was in the tones of the kind of bully Paul thought he had left behind years ago in school.

"Reynolds, I can see I'm going to have to spell things out in words of one syllable for you," he said. "If you can't find subjects that are more heartbreaking, more sympathy inducing, and most of all more middle-class-money-relieving than that then you need to create them yourself, understand?"

It was obvious from Paul's expression that he didn't.

"Okay," said Martin with an exasperated sigh. "You know Greg Phillips, right?" Paul nodded.

"He's gone freelance now – sells stuff to the majors."

"That's right. Well he started out in this business. Managed to do some very nice work for me." Martin scribbled on a pad, tore the sheet off, and thrust it at Paul. "Here's his website address and his phone number. Have at look at what he was able to come up with because it's what I need you to do. Then give him a ring. He can give you more advice than I can, or than I would want to."

*

It Begins at Home

"What do you mean 'the pictures weren't any good'?"

Paul's wife Anna dropped a plate of beans on toast in front of him and went to attend to their screaming baby son. Little Michael had just managed to spill something liquid and chocolaty all over the front of his face and bib and was now doing his best to smear it all over the table as well.

"Derek didn't like them," he said, in between forking chunks of burnt toast into his mouth. "He said they might need to be done again."

"Well I hope that doesn't mean you're going to have to go away again," she said, mopping up the mess and jamming a red rubber dummy into the baby's gaping maw. "It was hard enough the last time. I can't look after him by myself, you know."

"I know, my darling," said Paul, doing his best to defuse the imminent exasperated outburst he could see coming. "But you know how much I need this job."

"How much *we* need it more like," said Anna, wiping sticky fingers on a jam-streaked tea towel and glancing round their tiny flat. "Mr Chalmers was here asking about the rent again today. I promised him you'd have it by tonight so he's calling back tomorrow. You were supposed to come back with a nice fat cheque for all that work. Now what the hell am I supposed to do?"

"Stall him again, I guess," said Paul, finishing off his food and knowing better than to ask for dessert.

"That's what you always say. Well what I want to know is how, exactly? Honestly, one day you'll come home and find me and Michael in the street. And then what will we do?" She leaned over him and was about to start on another tirade when the telephone rang. "And we've had a red bill for that as well," she said, picking up the receiver. She rolled her eyes and handed it to Paul.

"Who is it?" he asked.

"Guess," she hissed, before grabbing the now gurgling baby from his resting place and dragging him off to enjoy the pleasures of bath time.

"Hello?" Paul said cautiously into the receiver.

"Mr Reynolds, it's Forest Grove here."

Paul cringed as he recognised the voice of Edina Relton, general manager of the care home at which his elderly father was now resident. "I'm sure you know what I'm ringing about."

Paul knew only too well, but it was only now, when faced with yet another financial demand on his non-existent resources, that he could feel his resolve starting to break.

"As I said to you last time," said Paul. "I will get the money to you just as soon as I am humanly able."

"That was three months ago, Mr Reynolds. Three months! Do you have any idea how much it costs to take care of a man in his early eighties suffering from senile dementia for three months?"

Paul knew exactly as a matter of fact, but only because he had the care home's latest bill under the clock on the mantelpiece.

"I do know, Mrs Relton, and I—"

"It's Ms Relton, if you had cared to read the documentation I sent you in sufficient detail, something which you obviously haven't done as otherwise you would be contacting me to discuss your father's immediate placement elsewhere."

Paul coughed in shock.

"I beg your pardon?"

The voice on the other end of the line spoke with the calm, measured delivery of someone who had done this sort of thing many times before.

"Because of non-payment of fees your father is scheduled to be discharged from our care at the end of the week. Which means tomorrow. Now, in case you are wondering, we are not the kind of institution who would do something so cruel as to leave him standing at the side of the road. Instead, one of our special ambulance cars will be bringing him over to the address we have for you where he will be left standing outside

It Begins at Home

your front door for however long a period it may take before he wanders off on his own unless you are there to meet him. And we both know he has a tendency to wander, don't we?"

Paul made a half-hearted attempt at a reply but it was clear that Ms Relton was having none of it. As he put the receiver down he heard someone start to cry. It took a minute for him to realise he couldn't tell if it was his child or his wife.

Or him.

*

"So Derek Martin gave you my phone number did he?" said Greg Phillips through a haze of cigarette smoke. "Naughty Derek. I'll have to have a word with him about that." He moved a stack of large format books from a sofa that looked like a relic from the 1970s, but then so did Greg. "Have a seat, then," said the photographer, going over to the drinks cabinet in the corner. "Want one?" he asked as he poured what looked to Paul like a lethal amount of vodka into a straight glass. Lethal for ten o'clock in the morning, anyway. Greg propped himself on a chair that had seen better days and lighter bodies than Greg's, put his cowboy boot encased feet up on a coffee table that judging from the numerous stains was more coffee than table, and took a deep swig. "So why did Derek suggest you see me?" he said eventually after obviously relishing the effect of his early morning alcohol fix.

"He thought you might be able to give me some advice on my charity pictures," said Paul, reaching for the portfolio case he had propped beside him. "He says they're not quite what he's looking for."

Greg's face drained of the ruddiness that had only just been imparted to his cheeks by the booze.

"No," he said, his demeanour suddenly less boisterous. "They wouldn't be."

"I've got some here," said Paul, sifting through the images to find one of what he thought was his best. "Perhaps if you

It Begins at Home

could give me some advice on what I need to do to improve them I'd be very grateful."

Greg reached over and laid a hand on his arm.

"I don't need to see your pictures, son," he said. "I can tell you what you need to do without looking at them, fine though I'm sure they are. The question is," he said, lighting a cigarette and giving Paul a cool stare, "are you sure you want to know exactly what Derek was getting at?"

Paul shrugged.

"I suppose so," he said.

The older man snorted.

"There's no suppose about it, my friend," he said, taking another gulp from the glass. "It's a funny old world we live in, one that can turn on us in a second if we don't know how to turn it to our advantage. Take my mother." Paul didn't want to and would have interrupted but he had the feeling that once Greg went off on a tangent he was probably pretty difficult to stop. "She ran the local hunt for fifteen years. Lovely woman, my mother, looked after me and my brother wonderfully, plays the organ in church on Sunday all for free as well. Couldn't give a flying fuck about foxes though. Did that make her a bad person? Shit no. What it made her was someone who recognised these animals for the pests they were and didn't see a problem in making a little money on the side by engineering their necessary despatch into something a little more entertaining, more appealing to those willing to pay for the privilege." He took another puff, another swig, and stared out of the window at the city skyline. "God knows there's little enough else to do in the countryside these days, especially now all the local girls have moved to the city to make internet porn. Do you see where I'm going with this?"

Paul had absolutely no idea.

"I don't really see what it's got to do with charity photographs," he said.

Greg sighed, took a huge bunch of keys from the bottom drawer of the desk, and went upstairs. A few moments later,

It Begins at Home

after a fair bit of rattling and cursing, he returned with a bulging manila folder. He took a picture from it at random and handed it to Paul. It depicted a teenage African girl in tears, a livid bruise marking the right side of her face. The slogan beneath read 'Stop the Atrocity Now!' followed by details of a third world charity and how to donate.

"What you are looking at is someone who has been made to cry, who has been made to appear damaged in such a way as to evoke sympathy in the average middle class Briton who will then dig deep and give to the charity who employed the company who gave them that picture. Who in turn will then employ that company again. I took that picture, but I did more than take it. I created it."

Paul looked up at the figure looming over him.

"You mean you composed the shot?" he said.

"I mean I created it. I paid a girl a couple of streets from here who needed the money to come into the studio for a morning's work and eventually got that picture. It took a bit of work mind you."

Paul was still having trouble understanding.

"Are you saying this picture wasn't taken in Africa?"

Greg snorted again.

"Does that advert say that it was? Put a picture with some words and add a charity and people make all kinds of assumptions. It's not a case of lying to the public, that would be wrong. It's just a case of not telling them the entire truth. And you have to admit the end result does the business."

Paul nodded.

"She's certainly a good actress."

Greg paused.

"Oh she's not acting," he said. "Cost me a bit more but Derek loved the picture and that was what counted at the time." Before Paul had a chance to say anything Greg was handing him another image. "Now look at this."

The next picture showed five men buried up to their necks in the middle of a dirt road in what looked like an African township. All showed signs of injury and in two cases the men's faces had been battered beyond recognition. Close by Paul could see three heavy rocks the size and shape of bowling balls, clumps of hair and blood still adherent to one of them.

"You can't tell me you shot this down the road!" said Paul, looking appalled.

Greg shook his head and drained his glass.

"Oh no – I actually had to go to Tanzania for that one," he said. "In fact that was one of my first. I spent two weeks in that shitty fucking country and got nothing. They were meant to be in the middle of a fucking war and no one ever did anything when there was a photographer around. So I paid some of the local militia to round up a few of the villagers and put them in a pit. Looks great, doesn't it?"

Paul refused to believe what he was hearing.

"You're saying you paid people to do that to innocent men?"

"Good God, no," said Greg. "We got their wives to roll those rocks at them. It was a game you see – the last one left alive would get to go free. It's amazing how competitive these people can be when the life of their only source of income is at stake. Plus of course the photographs of all those distressed womenfolk afterwards were to die for as well. Here, have a look. Of course I kept a few back to use in other campaigns. There's no way you'd find me going out there again."

Paul put the latest set of images on the table without looking at them.

"But what if anyone were to find out?" he said.

Greg held up his hands.

"No one who knows about this is telling anyone, either because they've been payed enough, or threatened enough. And I can't imagine you're going to tell anyone, son. You must be in a pretty shit place financially or Derek would never have sent you to me for this little chat. Very canny bloke is Derek. Only employs people who are desperate. And talented, of course. And you must be bloody desperate for a gig if he trusted you to come to me. I'll bet you owe more money than

It Begins at Home

you could hope to pay back in a month of Sundays and you need to start earning some serious cash, seriously quickly. Am I right?"

Paul thought of the rent, and the bills, and Anna, and his Dad.

"You're not wrong," was all he could think of to say.

"Good boy. So not a word of this to anyone." He brought his face close. "Because as well as the fact that Derek, and I, and the rest of our little group would deny everything, and as well as the fact that you wouldn't be able to prove a thing, we also happen to be on friendly terms with certain individuals who can pay you a little visit and render you incapable of writing your own name in crayon, let alone taking another photograph ever again. Understand?"

Paul felt sick as he did his best to nod his acquiescence.

"Good." Greg stood up, finished his drink and went to fix another. "When you think about it, it's just the same as what my mum did with the foxes. The people in those pictures are disposable. Their lives are going nowhere. At least this way they're making a bit of money for someone, if not themselves. And if you can make a bit of a game of it as well then it doesn't get totally boring for you."

*

Paul barely had time to think as he made his way from Greg's flat to Derek's offices. He needed the money so badly – more for his family than for him. But was his family's own need sufficient to justify the suffering of others? He shook his head. Of course it wasn't. And yet…

He was all his family had. And if he refused the assignment, Derek would just find someone else, wouldn't he? Any suffering that might be necessary to produce the 'right' kind of pictures would take place anyway, it just wouldn't be his family that benefited from the money it would bring in.

As he dragged himself up the stairs and knocked on the

frosted window of MartImages he still had no idea what he was going to say to Derek, although the idea of having to go back to one of those godforsaken third world countries had almost made his mind up for him.

*

"I don't need you for the Third World stuff anymore."

Paul had scarcely taken a seat in front of Derek's desk before the news was delivered. Any relief he felt was quickly obliterated by the desperation that now overtook him as he realised that the choice of whether to take the job or not had never been his to make anyway.

"So it was a waste of time me seeing Greg?" he said, realising that he was far more disappointed at losing the gig now than he really ought to be.

"Not at all," said Derek. "Greg rang me before you got here. Said you were just the sort of man we could trust. And that kind of thing's very important in our business, I can tell you." He threw a copy of the local paper towards Paul. "Appalling, isn't it?"

Paul glanced at the headline. 'Shocking Evidence of Abuse in Care Homes' he read.

"Glad my mother isn't in one of those places," Derek continued. "Mind you, if she was, she might benefit from the help of this organisation."

Now Paul was looking at a shiny white sheet of paper, blank except for the banner at the top that advertised a charity-run organisation dedicated to improving the conditions in some of the worst residential homes for the elderly.

"They want some pictures from us," said Derek, leaning over as if to ensure Paul could hear him. "The right sort of pictures. I'm sure you know what I mean. You've got two weeks. Payment will be on delivery." He scribbled a sum of money on the pad in front of him, tore off the sheet and handed it to Paul. "Happy with that?"

It Begins at Home

It was more money than Paul had earned in the last six months. He staggered back down the stairs and barely noticed the bus journey home.

Where his family was waiting for him.

*

"Mikey's got diarrhoea," Anna barked, as he came into the kitchen. So that was what the smell was, Paul realised. He looked away as she stuffed brown-streaked cloth nappies into the washing machine and pressed the start button. The machine rattled once and then refused to do anything.

"Fucking thing!" said his wife, stabbing at the button. Her actions did little other than to cause the machine to rock from side to side. "That's another bloody thing that needs to be mended," she said, looking up at her husband. "So now I'm going to have to hand-wash the lot. And let me guess, you still haven't been able to come up with any work?"

"Maybe," Paul mumbled, shuffling into the lounge, and away from his wife's accusing expression. At least the baby would be in his cot at this time of day so he could have the room to himself.

But the lounge wasn't empty.

There was someone sitting on the threadbare sofa, someone who barely registered Paul's presence, partly because of the gardening programme that was on the television, but mainly because his brain was too old and too encrusted with the scars of Alzheimer's disease to allow him to remember much at all.

"Oh no," Paul muttered under his breath as he sat next to his father, laid a hand on his thigh and tried to attract his attention.

"Hello Dad," he said.

"They dropped him off here an hour ago," said Anna from the kitchen. "I told them to take him back but they wouldn't. *Did* you say you'd managed to get a job after all?"

With almost infinite slowness, Arthur Reynolds turned to look at his son. The dull gleam in his grey eyes bore no trace

It Begins at Home

of recognition, neither did he say anything to suggest that he knew who Paul was. But that was not what made his son draw breath in alarm.

It was the purple bruise spread over the old man's left temple.

"Almost as soon as he got here he fell over," came the voice from the kitchen again. "He's really unsteady on his feet. And he can't stay here. Did you hear me, Paul? He. Can't. Stay. Here."

"Okay," Paul called back, not knowing what else to say. He sat for a moment in silence as the old man turned his attention back to the young lady on the screen talking about the best way to fertilise petunias. The temporary calm was broken by yet another cry from the next room.

"I asked you if you'd managed to find a job, then?"

Paul looked around the room. There was the picture he had been meaning to hang for the last few weeks, the hammer and nails all ready for him to dredge up the enthusiasm to actually do it. Next to it, on a chair in the corner, sat his camera. Then he turned his gaze back to his father. His bruised father. Who could almost look as if he had been abused. Paul's face was grim, but he tried to make his voice sound as optimistic as possible as he called out to his wife.

"Yes, darling, yes I have. Really good money too."

He looked at his father and reached for his camera.

Then he picked up the hammer.

FLITCHING'S REVENGE

Gary Power

When Stefan Makarovskyi came to, he found himself inside a dilapidated barn, sitting in a sturdy wooden chair. His hands were nailed to the armrests and his ankles shackled with barbed wire to the ornate legs. He'd have let out a scream of horror if it hadn't been for the sweaty sock that had been tightly rolled-up and wedged into his mouth. Curiously, despite his barbaric imprisonment he couldn't feel a thing. He bawled through the stale sock and thrashed his corpulent body from side to side, but trying to escape *was* an excruciatingly painful and futile exercise.

Finally, through sheer exhaustion, he just sat there, soaked in sweat and straining to regain his breath. His eyes were bloodshot and his pallor such a sickly shade of grey that it seemed he might expire at any moment.

From the shadows on the far side of the barn, five men stepped forward. Stefan recognised them immediately and his eyes widened.

Furthest to his right was Lucan Cowell, the local doctor. The small village of Flitching was quintessentially English and didn't take kindly to foreigners moving in. But Doctor Cowell, a man of Polish descent (real surname Kowaliski) had lived there for almost fifty years; his knowledge of the village and all its indiscretions had earned him almost reverential respect.

"Trying to escape is pointless," he said with his gaze fixed steadfastly on the eyes of the unwieldy Ukrainian. He pushed his glasses further up his long nose and scrunched his gaunt face into a sadistic smile. "Struggling is not recommended. I have injected a considerable dose of anaesthetic into your hands; pain will follow soon though, I assure you."

The short, stocky man next to him shook his head in frustration.

"It is fairly obvious why you are here," said Kevin Spall,

Flitching's Revenge

Flitching's resident policeman. His manner was precise and professionally abrupt. He flipped open a notepad and read from meticulously written notes. "Tracy Wyatt's body was found in Flitching Forest, December of last year. She'd been strangled with her own tights and subjected to a particularly brutal assault: facial contusions, ruptured eyeballs, fractured skull all indicative of a frenzied and sustained attack. Nasty. Very, very, nasty."

An elderly man with a mop of grey hair and such appalling kyphosis that his gaze was fixed permanently towards the floor, coughed loudly. He lifted a handkerchief to his mouth and made a noise that suggested he was retching up the entire contents of his stomach. This was Max Tremble, the local solicitor. He was standing furthest to Stefan's left.

The athletic but somewhat uncoordinated man next to Max Tremble stepped forwards and kicked Stefan's shins several times. It was a vicious assault, but the big man didn't even flinch, he just glared angrily back. James Fortescue, local MP and close friend of the murdered girl's father, turned to the others in a 'hold me back someone' sort of way, but when nobody moved he retreated awkwardly with an embarrassed but smug grin on his face. "You know you did it," he said. "We know you did it … and … and…" Stefan's intimidating stare made him stutter so much that he could barely speak.

"And if it was left to our pathetically, politically correct legal system," continued PC Spall in a much less flustered manner, "you'd either get off with a feeble reprimand or a spell of community service."

Conrad Wyatt, Tracy Wyatt's father, stepped from between Fortescue and Spall and pressed his hands together in thoughtful repose.

"So we have decided to sort out the whole sordid incident ourselves."

There was a muffled sound as Stefan uttered something that would have still been unintelligible even if he didn't have a rancid sock stuffed in his mouth.

Flitching's Revenge

Conrad Wyatt was a chillingly calm man. It was impossible to know what was going on inside his head. "You murdered my daughter. I have grieved and come to terms with that now. I don't merely want revenge though; I want your suffering to be slow and painful. Doctor Cowell has injected you with a cocktail of drugs. We've called it 'Flitching's Revenge'," he said with a bitter smile on his face. "It's quite an exotic concoction really; something to take your mind and body on a rollercoaster ride of misery and torment. There is nothing we can do to bring my little girl back, but this will go some way to redressing the balance of a shocked and wounded community." Conrad moved closer to Stefan and stared into his eyes. He sniffed deeply at the sweat rising from the man's odious body and whispered into his ear:

"You're going to suffer more than you could ever fucking imagine."

The big man could take no more. His fury was impassioned and his strength immense. There was a resonant 'pop' as he pulled one of his hands free leaving a lump of grisly flesh on the rusty head of the nail.

Max Tremble retched again. Stefan pulled the sock from his mouth and hurled it in Fortescue's direction. Much to his utter disgust, the sweaty, blood-drenched missile struck him squarely in the face.

"Evidence!" shouted the Ukrainian as he waved a clenched and bloody fist. It actually sounded like 'heavy dance' but those present knew what he meant and didn't really want to ask such an insanely angry man to, 'repeat himself , only a little clearer.'

PC Spall stepped forward with his notepad like a dodgy extra from *The Bill*.

"Evidence you want… Right then: footprints close to the body come from your boots; eyewitness of you being in the vicinity at the time of the murder…" Then, in frustration, he threw down his pad and pointed his freshly sharpened HB pencil at the accused. "Look matey – everyone knows how you used to watch her walk past your caravan on her way to school; the way you leered and undressed her with your eyes. You're just an … an … unwanted vagrant living like the bloody gypsy that you are and getting up to god knows what kind of filth. We all know what you're like and we don't want you in our village."

Stefan called him a "Fargin icehole." Spall couldn't understand what he said and looked to Conrad who politely whispered, "Fucking arsehole."

"I'd make the most of your last moment if I were you," advised the doctor looking at his watch. "I'd say my cocktail will take effect any second now."

For a few moments the five men stood in silence. Daylight was fading and a radiant mist had rippled into the barn from the fields. The men stood like ghosts before him, and it was then, swathed in ghostly light, that the captive man summoned the strength and help of his ancestors.

Stefan sat back and observed the doctor through slit eyes. His vision was becoming blurred and voices quite muffled. Speaking English did not come particularly easy to him, but understanding it was not so difficult.

"By midnight tonight you will be dead," announced Cowell chillingly.

"In Flitching, nobody can hear you scream," whimpered Fortescue and then he laughed and snorted at the same time.

Conrad cut a contemptuous glance at the insufferable MP and then turned his attention back to Stefan. "We will see to it that your death is put down to natural causes. I think that between us we can tie up all the loose ends."

"You'll have a low key cremation. We'll mix your ashes with a bit of pig feed and let the little buggers dine on you," added Max Tremble without once making eye contact. "Finalising the legalities of your death certificate will be quite easy for me to do."

Stefan flew into a violent rage. He glared furiously at the five men standing before him and hurled a volley of abuse in

Flitching's Revenge

their direction, looking at them each in turn and focusing his vehemence with frightening intensity. The doctor listened intently. When he'd finished the big man appeared to have a seizure. His eyes rolled upwards and then he slumped back lifelessly into the chair.

Fortescue in particular, seemed disappointed. "I thought he was going to last a bit longer than that." He looked over to the doctor. "Agonising death, you said." His voice was shrill and whiney. He was like a spoilt child who'd just been given a disappointing Christmas present.

Cowell went over to Stefan's body and examined him. There was a suffocating stench in the air from where Stefan had obviously fouled himself.

"He's dead," he said. "Quicker than I expected, but the end result's the same I suppose. Justice has been done; that's what we all wanted."

"So what did he say?" asked Tracy Wyatt's father.

The doctor peered over his glasses with a distant look in his eyes.

"Well, it was quite interesting really; he cursed us."

"Cursed us?" said Conrad, and he laughed mockingly.

"Yes," said the doctor. "He said that for each year from this date, on this same day of April, each of us will die a cruel and painful death and be made to suffer the same injustice that has been forced upon him."

Stefan's words were not taken seriously; they were nothing more than the ramblings of a desperate man. His charred remains were found in the burnt out barn a few days later by passing hikers who'd curiously been misdirected on their way from Flitching. The local paper reported suicide. The story went that Stefan had been depressed and couldn't live with the guilt of murdering that poor, innocent girl. Pills, alcohol and a petrol can were found near to the body. Loose ends, as predicted, were neatly tied. Paperwork was done and the whole sordid affair brought to a quick and satisfying conclusion.

Flitching's Revenge

Or so everyone thought.

One year on and the five men found themselves feeling curiously anxious as the fateful day approached. It was nonsense, of course, but nevertheless, they decided to spend the evening together in the Five Bells.

They were all enjoying a pint of locally brewed ale. James Fortescue had been honoured with the task of naming it. Proudly and not without a small amount of self-gratification and irony he named it Flitching's Revenge. Legal man Max Tremble was just about to take his first sip when his attention was drawn to a resonant creaking sound coming from just above his head. A five-hundred-year-old beam on which was ironically daubed 'Mind your Head', fell from the ceiling, collided with his cranium and sent him sprawling into the hungry flames of the Inglenook fireplace. He suffered an agonising death; trapped by the beam with his upper torso and head slow roasting in the burning embers. They eventually managed to drag his charred body free. The stench of crisp, burned flesh and screams of pain would stay with them as long as they lived – which possibly wasn't going to be that much longer. As the ambulance took Tremble's blackened corpse away they looked to each other in contemplative silence and shared one common thought; the curse had begun with a vengeance.

The next twelve months passed all too quickly and there was much conversation about Stefan's foreboding prediction. Conrad Wyatt survived a massive heart attack. Maybe he was made of strong stuff, or perhaps fate had preserved his life so that he might suffer according to Stefan's fatal declaration – at the predicted date.

A week before the second anniversary of Stefan's death Police Constable Spall went missing. He was found two weeks later in the basement of a derelict house just a few miles outside of Flitching. Close to his body was an empty Jack Daniel's bottle. He'd fallen through rotten floorboards onto a

Flitching's Revenge

concrete floor. Both his legs were broken, his shinbones poking through gaping flesh wounds. There were signs that he'd tried to crawl from the cellar; his fingers were no more than bloody stumps and there was a trail of blood across the floor. Most disturbing was the lack of flesh on his flayed and naked body. It seemed the rats had fed well for a few days, and it was more than likely that he'd been alive while the scavenging rodents feasted on him. He would have seen it all – until they had eaten his eyes, that is. His face was fixed with an expression of unimaginable horror. Death, when it came, must have been a welcome release. The coroner's estimated time of death was a chilling reminder of the accuracy of Stefan's curse.

Fortescue, Wyatt and Cowell met soon after the policeman's death to discuss how best to deal with a certain matter of destiny.

"It's happening, isn't it?" said Fortescue who was by now in a state of sheer panic. "That bloody gypsy really has cursed us, hasn't he? So which of us will it be next year?" he whined.

"That's not the only problem," said Conrad. "Kevin had been drinking too much and saying things around the village."

Fortescue looked agitated. "So what's that idiot policeman been rattling on about?" he asked. "I mean I blame him for all this mess really. If he'd pulled his finger out and got rid of that bloody foreign gypsy in the first place…"

Conrad raised a hushing hand to Fortescue and then continued:

"He'd been spending a lot of time in the Five Bells, rambling on about Stefan laying a curse on the village. We don't want people becoming inquisitive; we've got enough Miss Marples and Inspector Morses in this corrupt little village of ours."

"Did he name names?" asked Lucan Cowell.

"No … but only because he was so drunk. I tried to talk to him but the poor man was clearly cracking under the strain."

Fortescue was pacing up and down and wringing his hands

together frantically.

"Look, let's just forget about that inept excuse for a policeman and start considering what we're going to do now. This is the twenty-first century for God's sake; some bloody foreigner spouts off and people start dying. It's not rational ... sticks and stones and all that bollocks."

"Words will never hurt me?" mused Cowell. "Stefan's words were a lot more than that. The man came from a long line of Ukrainian gypsies. You have to understand the nature of a curse."

"You sound like you believe in the bloody stuff!" scoffed the MP.

"Don't you?" replied the doctor.

There was a telling silence.

"I've done a bit of research." The doctor was choosing his words carefully. "Where such 'supernatural' matters are concerned there is always a price to pay if the issuer of a curse does so purely out of anger." Conrad wanted to hear more. Fortescue seemed more interested in an incoming text on his Blackberry. Cowell continued: "Misuse of such dark matters apparently has the habit of backfiring on the practitioner. Stefan was a man about to die. His words were filled with passion and fury and drew on the spirits of his ancestors. He truly believed he was suffering an injustice – that is why he cursed us."

Fortescue mocked the doctor's words. "Hah! So that makes him an innocent party. Maybe we should go public." He laughed. "Go in front of a camera at the next anniversary for twenty-four hours and see if anything happens then. A sort of reality show. Who dies wins."

It seemed the infuriating MP was fast losing the plot.

"I fear one of us would definitely die," replied the doctor.

Fortescue's mind was working overtime though.

"What if one of us topped ourselves? That would break the cycle," and he grinned smugly as though he'd just worked out the answer to the problem.

Flitching's Revenge

"Hardly a result in our favour," observed Conrad. "Unless of course, you are contemplating suicide?"

"What about Stefan's family?" said Fortescue. He was struggling desperately for a solution. "Let's track them down and say if one of us dies we'll kill the bloody lot of them. That'll make them lift the damned curse."

"I think you're clutching at straws," said the doctor.

"At least I'm clutching at something, you Polish bloody idiot."

Cowell had been insulted enough.

"Perhaps you have nothing to worry about," he said as he walked out. "Maybe you will be the one to survive next time – then again, maybe you won't."

Days, weeks and months sped by and all too soon the third anniversary was upon them – and it seemed that Stefan's curse was becoming a little impatient.

James Fortescue decided to spend the fateful day in London in the company of a journalist friend who would document his every move and have a very good story if anything happened. He grew a beard, cut his hair and changed his name to Paul Metcalfe. In his arrogance he decided that the curse would be fooled by a change of identity.

He'd just passed through an arched exit way from Victoria station when a woman standing on the other side of a bus lane suddenly started screaming at him. It was a curiously surreal moment until he saw that the small child holding onto her hand was looking above where he was standing. Instinctively he too looked up and saw, to his horror, several hundredweight of metal scaffolding falling in his direction. If he'd had the reactions of a gazelle then he might have got out of the way in time.

Unfortunately he didn't.

Lucan Cowell had taken a sabbatical year from his practice and dedicated the time to pursuing a solution to the predicament. He decided his best option was to trace Stefan's family and see what they had to say. After several weeks he

Flitching's Revenge

traced them to a small town a few miles inland from the coastal city of Odessa. He posed as a western journalist looking to clear the name of the maligned man and as such was greeted warmly. It was at about the same time as Fortescue was being crushed by falling metal that the doctor developed an agonising pain in his right arm. A pain that quickly spread to his body. Five minutes later, he was lying on the ground clutching at his chest and gasping for breath. His suffering soon ended and Stefan's brother-in-law turned to his wife and said, "Our visitor has had a heart attack. He is dead."

On that same day Conrad Wyatt took his wife, Samantha, and son to the Greek island of Lesvos. They found a quiet retreat, Kharamida, a tiny village on the east coast, and rented a cottage there for the week. Conrad found himself in surprisingly upbeat mood when the third anniversary finally arrived. The weather was perfect. Not a cloud in the sky and just a gentle cooling breeze to take the edge off the midday heat as they lunched beneath the shade of a tree. It made him laugh when he saw his teenage son, Joshua, throw his arms about his head in a frenzy as he attempted to fend off the unwanted attention of a particularly persistent wasp.

"Bloody thing's back," cried his son and then he leapt around flapping his arms in a way that suggested uncoordinated madness. Conrad laughed again and then looked to his wife who was sipping a gin and tonic and staring dreamily into the distance. Intuitively she turned her head and smiled back. There were tears in his eyes. The death of their daughter was still a heavy burden, even more so in such idyllic surroundings.

"Have you seen the size of those damned things?" said his son as he sat down. "They're mutants."

One of them was crawling across the table. It had a swollen, red-striped body and was dragging a sting that looked big enough to kill a horse. The vile insect scrabbled across the cloth, feeling its way with constantly quivering antennae, then it took off and buzzed around their heads for a few seconds

Flitching's Revenge

before spiralling into the air and disappearing from sight.

"Gone," said Conrad as he ruffled his son's hair.

His wife passed him a glass of rosé wine and then stood behind him lightly massaging his shoulders.

"You alright, darling? You seem a little pensive."

"Yeah, fine," he lied. For some reason the killing of Stefan had done little to relieve his sense of anger and injustice and he could hardly confess his concerns regarding the curse. He took the glass and smiled reassuringly back, "Just what I needed – thanks." The wine was perfectly chilled. He sniffed deeply at the cherry aroma and cast a knowing grin. "Hmm, the San Giacomo. What are we celebrating?"

"Nothing really ... just being here." She smiled. "Perfect place, perfect moments."

He took a large gulp and immediately lifted a hand to his throat. He'd swallowed something. At first he thought a small olive had fallen into the glass from the tree, but then he felt it move. He felt a scratching sensation on the inside of his throat. A terrifying thought occurred to him. One of the damned wasps had made a kamikaze dive into his drink just as he'd put it to his lips. Now the bloated insect was lodged in his throat and starting to panic. Soon it would plunge its sting into him. Conrad knew his time had come; the curse was about to take its fourth victim. With tears in his eyes he called to his family.

"Sam, Josh ... I ... I love you," he said. Curiously he wasn't frightened. He consoled himself with the thought that soon he'd be reunited with his daughter. He just hoped that a gargantuan wasp sting in his throat wouldn't be as agonising as he was expecting it to be.

Josh suddenly looked frightened. He could see the panic in his father's eyes. "You okay, Dad?" he asked.

Conrad felt a sudden stabbing inside his throat, like a needle piercing his flesh. Venom flooded into his bloodstream and inflamed the tissue in his windpipe. Within seconds he found himself unable to draw breath. He gagged for air and fell from his chair, clutching at his throat as he tried to speak. Josh panicked. "Mum!" he screamed. "There's something wrong with Dad."

His wife immediately came to his aid. "Call an ambulance!" she cried, as she loosened her husband's collar.

Conrad watched the world fade away. Everything was distant; sounds were resonant and images detached. He could see his son stabbing furiously at a mobile phone and his wife crying desperately as she tried to comfort him. Then, just as Fortescue was being crushed and Cowell was having a heart attack, a terrible darkness descended upon him.

The fact that James Fortescue escaped the falling scaffolding without even a scratch was nothing short of a miracle. He emerged from the wreckage unscathed and knew straight away that he would be living to see another year. In his bizarre and unconventional mind he thought that it was a bit like winning something on a game show.

He was immortal.

He was a God.

Having decided that the threat of imminent death was no longer there he ditched the journalist, who he decided was quite boring and quite frankly a bit of a tosser, and celebrated his good fortune in Swallows, a rather seedy lap-dancing club just off Dean Street in Soho. A pair of impressively large, augmented breasts were being jiggled just a few inches from his eyes and it suddenly occurred to him that maybe he'd got it wrong and perhaps his fate might be to die from suffocation by implant. There were certainly worse ways to go. His body was filled with a concoction of drugs and alcohol that would keep him in a state of euphoria for at least enough time to see out midnight. He was laughing quite hysterically and throwing enough money at the dancer to keep her in his company well into the next day.

When the deadline was well and truly passed he celebrated with a bottle of Louis Roederer Cristal champagne and a bevy of lap dancing beauties, all in a private room. "I'm alive!" he announced to his glamorous entourage much to their

Flitching's Revenge

bemusement, and then he sent one of them out to get another bottle of champagne.

As for Lucan Cowell, nobody was more amazed than Stefan's brother when the old man opened his eyes and asked, "Any chance of a cup of tea?" It seemed that his fatal coronary was in fact a nasty bout of indigestion; the grim reaper obviously had other business to tend to that day.

The next twelve months slipped by and the fourth anniversary of Stefan's curse arrived all too quickly for the last two anxious men.

Lucan Cowell contacted Fortescue and asked that they meet in the now derelict ruin that had been the barn in which Stefan died. He had spoken of a breakthrough concerning the curse.

There was a curious silence between the two men at first. The day of reckoning for one of them had come. Now the odds of survival were even.

"So what have you got to say, Doc?" demanded the slimy MP.

Fortescue's manner was quite contemptuous, but then he'd always been like that. He'd obviously been drinking, and it was more than likely that he'd snorted something through his upper class nose as well.

"I spoke with Stefan's family," replied Lucan Cowell calmly. He sat at on a rickety old chair and rubbed the bridge of his nose so that his glasses lifted to his brow. "I learnt some interesting facts."

Fortescue was annoyingly fidgety; he moved around the room constantly and avoided any eye contact. "So tell me. I don't want to hang around here longer than I have to. To be honest I want to be the one that sees the day out. Nothing personal; I'm just being honest."

That was when he saw the small pistol jutting from beneath the doctor's belt.

"Hah…" he said, "So that's why you wanted me here. To shoot me and have another year's grace."

"I would have thought that was more your territory,

Fortescue," replied the doctor as he pulled out the gun and aimed it shakily in his direction. "You're a desperate man. This is just protection, that's all. Just listen to what I have to say and maybe we can both survive this ordeal."

Fortescue seemed unfazed by the gun and made an impatient hand gesture for him to continue.

Cowell sighed loudly at the man's arrogance.

"A curse such as Stefan's can only be issued by a man who believes himself to be innocent – to do so otherwise would guarantee a fate worse than death. His damning words have been spectacularly successful; it is my belief that he did not murder Tracy Wyatt."

"Speculation," sneered Fortescue. The doctor raised a hand of silence and continued.

"All that got me thinking. Let me enlighten you a little more. What I am about to tell you is a breach of confidentiality, I'm afraid, but under the circumstances quite necessary."

Fortescue cast a suspicious glance in his direction.

"I had been treating your wife for depression. You apparently had serious money problems. At first she thought you were gambling until it became obvious that you were seeing someone else. In itself no revelation; half of this corrupt little village are either alcoholic, having affairs or are sexually deviant."

Fortescue remained silent.

"During the past year," continued the doctor, "I decided to play a little game of 'who had reason to see Tracy Wyatt dead?' I spoke to her brother and he showed me her personal diary." Cowell produced a pink book from inside his jacket and waved it accusingly before Fortescue's face. "Reading between the lines, teenage code and such, it is obvious that she was seeing an older man on a regular basis. She was besotted by him and obviously had a physical relationship with him. But he tired of her. She was distraught and tried to blackmail him into staying. The dates coincide with those of her disappearance and murder."

Flitching's Revenge

There was a pensive moment as the two men studied each other.

"And your conclusion?" mused Fortescue.

"You murdered her," stated the doctor. "With hindsight it's obvious really. Poor Stefan was your perfect scapegoat; an opportunity to cleanse the village of another foreigner and the ideal cover for your devious plan. Nobody in this bigoted village was sorry to see him gone. It was quite a clever plan really."

The smug look on Fortescue's face confirmed his guilt.

"Very clever," he said and gave the doctor a slow handclap. "Quite the village Poirot aren't we? So how does this resolve our little dilemma?"

"A confession of guilt and the death of one of Stefan's victims on the chosen day might lift the curse. That was what I gleaned from my visit. It's a long shot but what other options are there?"

Fortescue's brain was working overtime.

"I'm surprised the police missed such a gem of evidence as the diary. In fact I remember Tracy telling me that she didn't keep a diary, the little minx. Still that's teenagers for you. I can tell you one thing though; she was a little rocket in the sack."

Fortescue edged forwards as he spoke and held out his hand. "Can I have a quick look before you shoot me…? If you do I'll give you the confession that you obviously so desperately want."

Foolishly the doctor passed the diary to him. Fortescue acted without hesitation; he swiped the gun and the book with surprising agility. Suddenly the tables were turned.

"Guilty as charged," he said. "It was time to move on; on to new pastures and all that. The little bitch had fallen in love with me, bless her; she was going to ruin me… I couldn't stand for that. Pity really … she was a fit little filly." With one hand he flicked through the diary and glanced at the pages; they were all blank. He roared with laughter at that.

"I had to be sure of my accusation," said the doctor. "It was

Flitching's Revenge

the only way I could ensure a confession from you."

Fortescue chuckled again. "What a clever, foreign quack you are." He lifted the gun and aimed it at Cowell's head.

"Well you've got your confession and now you're going to commit suicide. The villagers won't miss someone who knows so much about their various indiscretions. The curse gets its sacrifice and best of all, I become a free man. Sort of ironic isn't it?"

Cowell looked to the floor and waited for the shot.

"Stupid old man," said Fortescue contemptuously, and then he pulled the trigger. There was a deafening explosion and a flash of light. Cowell looked up to see Fortescue fall backwards and slump onto the floor. He was covered in blood. His face was a mess of loose flesh and gristle. The doctor chuckled to himself and then in Fortescue's dying moments he whispered in his ear.

"There, it's done. That was the final ingredient my rude and arrogant friend; a heartfelt apology for Stefan's murder and the sacrifice of a life." There was a grotesque look of surprise on what was left of Fortescue's face. "A little bizarre I'll admit," continued the doctor, "but I'm afraid I'm not in a position to be sceptical." Lucan Cowell removed the flesh coloured surgical gloves he was wearing and poked them into his breast pocket. "I don't expect the village will mourn the loss of a spineless MP. You weren't a popular man at all. One of Stefan's relatives modified the gun to backfire by the way. We spent a few vodka nights chatting about you being chief suspect and how best to get rid of you; our little plan worked better than I expected."

With Fortescue gone Stefan's curse entered its final year. Lucan Cowell could only hope that his efforts had redressed matters and saved him from being the fifth victim. His life in Flitching returned to normal although the fateful day in April weighed heavily on his mind. When the fifth anniversary arrived, he passed the hours as normally as possible. He ran a clinic, worked late and then with an hour until midnight,

Flitching's Revenge

poured himself a large whisky and sat in his favourite chair – and waited.

The minutes slipped uneasily from his old grandfather clock.

A light wind ruffled the curtains; Lucan closed the window and in doing so couldn't help noticing the rather ominous clouds gathering in the sky. He thought he saw someone standing at the edge of the woods. It looked like a young girl. Her face looked pale and her eyes black as the night. She whispered something to him and it sounded like the wind hissing in his ears. Her flesh was bruised. She stared through hungry, angry eyes and Lucan's heart skipped a beat.

Tracy Wyatt had returned from the grave.

In the blink of an eye she was gone.

Lucan returned to his favourite chair and poured another double shot of whisky. Reluctantly he glanced at the clock; it was half past eleven.

Thunder rumbled in the distance and a blustery wind rattled the old window frames. Lucan tried in vain to distract himself; he read a book, he watched TV but concentrating proved to be an impossible task. With just ten minutes to go he shuffled uneasily in his chair and took a swig of whisky from the bottle.

A splintering crack of thunder rattled the old house to its foundations and Lucan found himself clutching at the arms of his chair as though for grim life.

Lightning flashed and for a split second the silhouette of the great oak that stood in his garden played across his windows. It groaned like a beast as it strained to stand up to the might of what had now become a gale-force wind. The constant barrage of wind and rain was weakening its roots. It occurred to him that the elements were conspiring to bring down the old tree and crush his house with him in it.

Now there were only five minutes to go. Surely nothing could happen in five minutes. He rattled his fingers impatiently on the arm of the chair and watched the minute hand with increasing trepidation. Beads of sweat burst onto his forehead and his heart began to pound furiously as the second hand

Flitching's Revenge

swept past four minutes. Lightning struck ground outside his house and Lucan lurched to the window. It had struck at the base of the old oak tree. The roots were smouldering and the tree was leaning precariously in his direction. Lucan found himself frozen to the spot. The sound of the storm was deafening. It was as though he was at the centre of a tornado. Checking the time he saw there was just a minute to go. He stared in earnest at the clock, willing the minute hand to reach midnight. Then he would celebrate more than he had ever done before. Just seconds to go and he would glory in life. The great oak tree was still upright – just. It was teetering above the cottage and threatening to squash both him and the building like a bug. The old roots were straining, but he knew that they were strong. They would last.

Lucan stood perfectly still with his eyes fixed steadfastly on the clock face.

Stefan's curse was not going to make it an easy ride though; with just thirty seconds to go, the second hand stopped moving.

"No…" gasped the doctor, "That's not possible."

Suddenly there was silence. The tranquil atmosphere that prevailed was quite unnatural.

Lucan stepped outside his front door. The trees were like statues and the air perfectly still. Crows perched like spectres in the branches, watching, waiting. The only sound he could hear was the frantic pounding of his heart. It was as though the world had stopped in its tracks.

Standing at the base of the old oak tree there loomed a figure. Stefan Makarovskyi had returned from beyond the grave. The huge man began to laugh and as he did so the oak tree leaned a little more. Lucan saw that he was not alone; four other men were standing at the fringes of the forest: Max Tremble, his body crushed and burned almost beyond recognition; James Fortescue with flesh and gristle hanging from what had been his face; PC Spall, his body half eaten by rats, and finally Conrad Wyatt with bloated wasps pouring

Flitching's Revenge

from his mouth.

The men that he had known so well were now things of evil returned to haunt him. Lucan looked to Stefan and begged for him to spare his life. "I solved the mystery," he pleaded. "I cleared your name and lifted the curse. I brought the guilty man to confess his crimes and made him pay the price. You must let me live," he demanded. He dropped to his knees and sobbed helplessly. The strain was too much for him to take anymore.

Stefan's eyes burned furiously in the darkness.

"But it was you that took my life, Doctor Cowell. It was you who injected my veins with that fatal cocktail," he boomed, "and for that you should pay with your life."

Lucan pleaded with him once more. "And it was I who cleared your name and returned respectability to you and your family."

Stefan reached to the sky and spoke in his native tongue and as he did so the storm returned with a vengeance. With the wind howling in his ears like the woeful cries of the dead Lucan knew that the next few moments would decide his fate.

For thirty seconds at least he held his breath. For thirty seconds he closed his eyes and waited. The old oak tree creaked and groaned but the doctor remained where he stood. If his destiny was to die now then so be it. In its own way it would be a relief. For five years there had hardly been a day when he hadn't wondered if that year would be his last. Prescription drugs and alcohol had been his saviour. But his body had become frail and his mind weak.

In his head he counted the seconds; when he got to forty he knew that the final moments of Stefan's curse had passed.

He had survived.

With a heavy sigh he opened his eyes. Neither Stefan nor the spectres of Max, James, Conrad and Kevin were there. He was alone once more. The curse was lifted.

When he returned to the house it was as though a great weight had been taken from him. The feeling of euphoria was immense. The fifty-seven-year-old vintage malt whisky standing in his drinks cabinet that he'd kept especially for this occasion was beckoning to be opened. He settled in his favourite chair and chuckled gently, and through the sound of his mirth he heard several loud cracks. The roots of the great oak were snapping like twigs under the strain.

Just five minutes after midnight the turbulent storm felled the huge tree and sent its mighty trunk crashing through the roof of Lucan's cottage.

The doctor had managed to survive the wrath of Stefan's curse.

Nature it seemed was a little less forgiving.

REST IN PIECES

David Williamson

The idea came to him as he was applying the final touches of rouge to the cheeks of the corpse lying on the table before him.

The woman would have been in her early twenties and Harry Jones was doing his best to make her look presentable prior to the relatives viewing their late departed, before her one way journey to the cemetery the next morning.

The notion was so stunningly simple, that Harry wondered why he had never thought of it before. He was in the ideal situation. It was absolutely brilliant!

"Is she ready yet, Harry? The parents are waiting outside."

The assistant undertaker almost literally jumped with surprise. He'd been so engrossed with his own thoughts, that he hadn't heard old Jackson open the door and creep in behind him.

"Er ... sorry Mr Jackson ... yes, just finished with her." Harry replaced the lid on the tub of make-up and quickly gathered up the other cosmetics scattered about the stainless-steel trolley and shoved them all into a small box.

"Pull yourself together, man. We've got a busy day ahead of us!" added Jackson, before he swept majestically out of the mortuary viewing room to the waiting mourners, a well-practised empathetic smile springing to his thin lips.

Harry fixed the black crepe sheet and carefully adjusted the dead girl's long blonde hair so that she appeared more asleep than deceased, then left the room via another door so that the girl would be the only occupant when the parents came in for their final farewell.

His earlier thoughts drifted to the back of his mind as the day's business demanded more of his attention. They had three funerals that day, so little or no time for private daydreams.

However, as he walked into his house and hung his coat on the rack behind the door, his earlier idea came leaping very much to the fore.

"You're late. Again! That's the second time this week and it's only Tuesday!" screamed his wife, Valerie, from her armchair in the lounge. "You're dinner's ruined and it's in the bin..." On and on she prattled until he could take it no more and stormed out into the back garden for the first of his three allotted cigarettes of the day.

His hands had that familiar unpleasant twitch to them and he knew that if he remained within tongue-lashing distance of his wife, they would do far more than just twitch.

Valerie refused to try and understand him. She refused to acknowledge that a man in his line of business – dealing with death and misery each day – well, they needed a drink or two on the way home from work – just to unwind a little.

"And how many sobbing relatives have you had to console today? How many maimed bodies have you had to try and make half-way decent before they could be viewed?" he'd asked one evening, as he'd prodded without enthusiasm at the cold grilled trout which stared back at him from an equally cold plate.

Valerie was unable to show the slightest iota of sympathy towards him. "It's your job! You chose it, you can bloody well get on with it!" she spat, before snatching the still full plate and tipping its contents into the bin.

There was no point in him arguing with her. He hadn't chosen the job – God forbid, it would have been the very last thing he'd have wanted to do to earn a living. But after two years on the dole after being made redundant as chief clerk from an engineering company, two years of Job Club and all the form filling, applications and general humiliation of being unemployed, he had gladly taken the first real, full-time job offered to him.

Times were bloody hard and needs must and all that crap, and at least it would help pay off the rest of the mortgage.

But of course Valerie couldn't care less. She'd been spoilt

Rest in Pieces

when he was earning decent money. All she was concerned with was whether she had enough chocolates and other luxuries to maintain her eighteen stone bulk in the manner to which it had been accustomed.

It had started to drizzle, so Harry moved into his favourite refuge – his beloved greenhouse. A harbour of sanity in the sea of life's daily storm that was his wife. Of course, matters had got a lot worse ever since Valerie had found out about his little 'indiscretion' with Maggie Robertson, who lived just along the lane from their little bungalow. Valerie certainly wasn't the forgiving type and as the weeks had passed, her animosity and loathing towards him had grown and grown, so that life was now nothing more than a one-sided slanging match every time they were in each other's company.

He idly picked up his spray bottle and began to squirt the tomato plants, doing his best to imagine that the tiny blackfly covering the leaves were miniature Valeries. If only he could get rid of her as easily.

His earlier idea came flooding back, and as he squirted the little black insects, the thought grew and more ideas came and slotted neatly into place until he had the bare bones of a plan in his mind. It would take a lot of preparation. Every conceivable danger would have to be carefully thought through, but it was possible. It was very possible.

"Harry Jones, boy from the valleys – you're a bloody genius!" he whispered as he stretched up to close the greenhouse louvres against the chilled night air.

The next day, Harry was at work earlier than usual. He was always the first to arrive, but this morning he needed extra time to go through the Day Planner and check on the week's list of burials and cremations. Luckily, the schedule was a pretty full one. Everything should run smoothly so long as there were no unexpected delays. Twenty minutes later, he had it sorted out in his own mind. It was all in the planning, and Harry enjoyed planning stuff.

Rest in Pieces

It would happen tomorrow, Thursday, with phase two taking place on the Friday.

"Tidy!" he said aloud, to an empty chapel of rest.

The remainder of that day passed in a blur of further planning and fine honing. As an extra bonus, old Jackson was leaving early on Friday for one of his Rotarian meetings, and Harry took that as a sign from the Gods that all was well and they were on his side.

At six o'clock, he strolled across to his battered old Toyota, and, after checking that all his purchases of that day were still in the rear foot well, he drove off to his nightly confrontation with Valerie.

Everything had gone far better than he could have ever imagined.

Valerie had started her usual tirade as soon as he'd opened the front door. Harry let her have her say for about five minutes, he watched as she grew redder and redder, a strange little smile playing across his face.

Then, just as she was bent over the waste bin engrossed in scraping his cold bacon and eggs into it, he did what he'd been longing to do for years.

The heavy, cast-iron milk pan landed on the back of her skull with a sickening squelchy thud, sending a crimson spray of blood squirting onto the tiled work surface and across the cushion flooring below.

Oddly, she didn't collapse like a sack of turnips as he'd imagined, but stood there, staring dumbly at Harry, her mouth working but no sound escaping.

Then she just sort of crumpled slowly onto the floor, knocking over her much beloved waste bin, and lay like a beached whale next to the washing machine.

Harry left her where she was and went out to the car to collect his shopping. There were only two bags, and as he closed the front door behind him, he could hear a faint moaning coming from the kitchen.

Rest in Pieces

Valerie was the cause. She was trying to sit up, staring at the thick blood covering her hands through, misty, pain-filled eyes. And, as was her wont, she was moaning, only this time, with good cause.

Harry tut-tutted loudly and promptly gave her another whack with the cast-iron milk pan, then another for good measure. Now she was dead!

He strolled into the lounge and drew the curtains. It would be light for a while yet, but he didn't want any prying eyes at this stage of the game. He moved the coffee table and the settee to the far end of the room and then spread his newly purchased rubberised groundsheet across the patterned Axminster. Perfect. Ideal for the job!

Then, he unrolled the shiny new and very expensive set of butcher's knives and marvelled as they twinkled like a line of deadly steel soldiers.

The actual manhandling of Valerie's gross body into the bathroom, involved the use of a wheelbarrow, together with much sweat and even more swearing. Her mighty bulk was only barely contained within the confines of the barrow, and it took Harry several attempts to lift her in without it tipping over, which would cause him to start the whole arduous process over again.

When he eventually wheeled her bath-wards, with Valerie's hefty legs spread akimbo and dangling either side of the wheelbarrow in a bizarre and sickening parody of a sexual pose, he couldn't help but glance at her lolling, battered head as it glared accusingly at him, sometimes moving from side to side with the motion as though disapproving of him, even in death.

Harry was very pleased that she'd nagged him into buying a bungalow, rather than a house. The only useful idea she'd had in all their time together, as it turned out. Humping her carcass upstairs would have been impossible.

There was one of those old fashioned clothes drying racks suspended from the ceiling above the bath, which Harry had managed to strengthen the night before, but even with the new four-inch screws, the pulley and the joist it attached to, both groaned their protests as he hauled his dead wife's body by her puffy ankles so that she was suspended a foot or so above the plughole of the enamelled bath.

Harry was by now shattered and had to sit on the laundry basket to regain his composure. He watched in fascination as Valerie's corpse swung gently to and fro, and the blood dripping from her head made almost perfect circles on the white enamel. Very artistic!

Revived, he raised the boning knife and with one swift slice, he severed her throat down to the spine. The gaping wound now poured rather than dripped her bodily fluids into the bath, and Harry had to run the taps to thin the sticky gore into a more manageable consistency.

He left her hanging like that for the next two hours while he mopped up the kitchen and then had a nice supper of sausages and beans on toast. He even smoked four cigarettes, throwing all caution to the wind.

He was no expert, but Harry thought she carved beautifully – just like a piece of the finest fillet steak – her fatty meat almost falling off the bone with the help of the new knives.

He wasn't too sure about what effect the meat cleaver was having on the Axminster beneath the groundsheet, but he wielded it with great deliberation, and no small amount of skill.

In just over two hours, Valerie had been chopped and carved into more manageable segments and parcelled up into either bin liners or covered with clingfilm or both, and she was spread across the large rubber sheet.

It had still been surprisingly messy, even though he'd taken all that effort to drain her of blood first. But then he thought, converting any eighteen stone person into handy joint-sized pieces was bound to be a tad mucky. After all, his usual customers had blood that had started to clot and harden in lifeless arteries – nowhere near as messy.

Rest in Pieces

The worst part by far was finding something to put the organs and general viscera into. Something that wouldn't leak and would be easy to carry and dispose of. What better than Valerie's much-used and much-loved kitchen waste bin? Ironic too.

The whole process, from the initial bash on the head to the final mopping up operation had taken almost four hours. All he had to do then, was wait until it was late enough for passers-by not to be passing by, and then load the car with his 'passenger'.

He'd always been grateful that they lived in such a quiet little lane overlooking the River Thames, but never so much as he was now. There'd be no nosy neighbours or twitching net curtains around here.

There had been that one heart-stopping moment when a man walking his dog had called out: "Fine evening for a stroll!" and his bloody spaniel had come sniffing around the boot of the car, but a swift kick up the backside had soon sent the thing yelping into the night to be comforted by its stupid owner.

Harry drove the last three hundred yards to work with his car lights off and glided silently into the staff car park. He let himself in by the side door, and as quietly as possible, he slid open the double doors to what they referred to as 'the unloading bay' – the place where bodies were brought by private ambulance ready for the undertaker's attention.

He backed his car into the unloading bay and slid the big doors shut once more. So far, so good, now for the real business of the night.

Harry had selected his victims with the greatest of care. He had taken into account their size and weight, and had also allowed for anyone wishing to see their dear departed for one last time. To that end, he'd selected anyone too disfigured to be on display and a few very elderly men and women who, from Jackson's meticulously kept records, he had gleaned that there were no close relations likely to arrive out of the blue.

Rest in Pieces

The only anomaly was a man of forty-two who had died from a massive stroke the week before. But Harry had dealt with the man's widow and he knew from experience, that she was one woman who wouldn't be grieving for very long. Far too good looking for that, and there was something in her eyes...

It took him almost as long to unscrew all the coffin lids, place Valerie's bits and pieces in with the occupants, and then re-fit the lids as it had to chop her up in the first place, but he was mightily relieved when it was all over. Shame he'd run out of bin liners by the time he remembered her head, but at least some clingfilm and strong elastic band around the stump of her neck would prevent any unfortunate 'secretions'.

Though seeing her battered, horror stricken face glaring at him as he placed her in the last coffin had really shaken him. Thank God it was done!

All the funerals went without a hitch. He'd even been given a tenner by the 'grieving widow' who'd tried her utmost to weep behind a thick veil, but the young man in his mid-twenties who slipped his arm around her waist on the way back to the car, and then pinched her bum as she climbed in the front seat, gave the game away. They drove off smiling happily.

The set of shiny new knives was now at the bottom of the Thames several miles from Harry's bungalow together with the blood-stained milk pan. The groundsheet was now buried at the tip under tons of landfill and a suitcase full of Valerie's clothes, passport and personal effects had been thrown onto a huge bonfire on a building site. He left it for almost a week before paying a visit to his local police station to report his wife as a missing person. Harry explained about the note Valerie had left, telling him that she was going to visit some long lost aunt's house. He also told the police that some of her clothes were missing along with personal items and a suitcase. He added that he was out of his mind with worry about her.

The desk sergeant was very understanding and sympathetic,

Rest in Pieces

but he held out little hope that a forty-six-year-old woman who clearly didn't want to be traced, would turn up again unless she wanted to. He would go through the motions, of course, and add her description to the file, but there was every likelihood of her returning under her own steam with her tail between her legs and a bag full of apologies for being so daft.

Three days later, Harry bumped into Maggie Robertson and told her that Valerie had finally left after a blazing row, vowing never to return again. Maggie was soon a regular in Harry's bed, visiting every time her long-distance lorry driver husband was on a foreign trip.

Everything in the garden was rosy. Even the blackfly had finally been sprayed into submission.

"Ah, Harry. Glad you're here early as usual. We have important visitors today!" crooned Jackson. Harry had wondered who owned the strange cars cluttering up the car park. And so early too.

"What's happened, Mr Jackson? Has someone important died?" asked Harry as he took off his jacket and slipped on his working apron.

Jackson smiled like a cat who'd had the cream.

"It's better than that, Harry!" He beamed. "We've been chosen by the Coroner's office because of our facilities here. They're chock-a-block with bodies at the county mortuary, what with this summer flu epidemic. So we have been selected for the Coroner to carry out a very special post-mortem!" Jackson was glowing as though he'd been entered into the final two of *The X Factor*, as Harry still fumbled, trying to tie his dark blue work apron.

"What's so urgent about this autopsy then?" he asked, rolling up his shirt-sleeves and following Jackson as he headed through the plastic swing doors that led into the mortuary.

Jackson's smile was wider than ever. "It's an exhumation, the first you have witnessed, I believe, Harry?"

Rest in Pieces

The pathologist and his assistant had just removed the lid from the coffin as the two undertakers entered the room.

"Jesus Christ!" screamed the assistant, falling back from the open casket, a look of horror on her face.

Harry spotted it as Jackson, unperturbed, prattled away beside him. "Yes, it's a suspected poisoning, Harry. A man in his forties possibly murdered by his wife, and we actually planted him. What a coincidence, eh!?"

Harry wasn't listening.

He was staring at the extra head in the open coffin.

His eyes bulged alarmingly, his face going a deep purple hue as a strangled sob escaped from his constricted throat and he reeled away from the casket.

It was far more than the terrible shock of seeing Valerie's decomposing face.

It was the fact that she was – God help him – she was smiling! A broad, cheery smile that stretched her green, rotting lips. A smug 'I told you so' sort of smile that he'd hated so much when she was alive and which was now even more repulsive in death.

As Harry's heart finally gave out from the shock and horror, and he slumped dying onto the cold mortuary floor, his last thought was of the look in that young widow's eyes, as she'd walked away on the arm of her young lover.

It had been the same self-satisfied look that Harry had worn after killing his unwanted partner.

WALK TO THE SEA

Rog Pile

'Yesterday,' she wrote, 'something terrible happened.'

But now that she came to write it down, like the fading memory of a dream, the details of the terrible thing were escaping her. It was as if part of her mind was blocking the memory. Perhaps if she just started writing about other things, she thought, it would come back to her.

Deciding to start afresh she screwed up the sheet of paper then paused, pen in hand.

The kitchen was intolerably stuffy, and there was a bad smell. She got up to open the windows; then seeing the garden bright with colour in the sun, she decided to go out for some air. Some of the flowerbeds had been disturbed as if a fox or a badger had been rooting about here. Sitting on the step in the afternoon warmth she wondered what made her stay in this place. The cottage stood on a quiet road about three miles from the sea; on clear days its deeper blue was just visible through the gap in the hills. A sense of timelessness seemed to wrap it around like a shroud or a caul.

A caul, she decided firmly. A shroud is to wrap the dead; a caul wraps the head of the newborn. When she had first set eyes on the house she had thought that it could not have been built but must somehow have *grown*, like the tree beside it, its boughs spreading low over the roof as if for support.

She got up from the step and walked down the path to the gate; leaning on it, she looked over the road and across the fields to the dip in the hills.

Tomorrow, she thought, I will get up before anyone else is awake, and walk down to the sea.

She was awakened by the sound of the Post Office van. She turned on her back and listened, wondering if it would stop.

I'm being silly, she thought; all I ever get is bills.

Walk to the Sea

But she waited until the sound of the van faded away down the road before sitting up. Then remembering what she had promised herself the previous day, she slipped on her dressing gown and hurried downstairs.

To get to the beach she had to pass through the village. It had one narrow street. At one side of the street was a pavement raised a yard above the level of the road, and at intervals there were short flights of steps. The houses on that side were relatively modern in design, anonymous behind spiked iron railings. In all of the windows the curtains were closed. Early morning sunlight made hard shadows on the pavement.

She found herself thinking that the scene was somehow incomplete. There ought to be a cat, she thought, sunning itself by the railings. Something alive.

But nothing moved in the village.

She walked on the other side of the street where the pavement was narrow and level with the road, and where the buildings were mostly shops. She walked quickly along, glancing dutifully into shop windows as she passed.

She was the only person awake in the village; everyone else was asleep. The shops were all closed and the curtains pulled, and if one of those curtains should part and someone look out, they would think, Who is that woman walking through the village at this hour of the morning, and where is she going?

Then the thought came unbidden, a little unnervingly: what if *all* of them should open? All of them at once?

She quickened her pace, hurrying on past the monument in the square, then out of the village and along the road where gates hidden in the hedge surprised her with glimpses of the hills. She passed a house where a sign advertising 'Vacancies' had been covered with a sack. The house was strangely quiet, even for this early hour, and she wondered vaguely what had happened to the large black dog that she remembered, usually waiting at the gate.

A mile further on she came to the church. Beside it, on the

Walk to the Sea

other side of the high brick wall, was a café where she remembered once sitting at a table in the garden, looking down over the valley to where the walls of a ruined monastery were visible through the trees.

Then the road dropped abruptly, steepening with every bend, to the hotel at its foot overlooking the beach.

Steps had been carved into the rocks leading down to the sand, but the last few had worn away or perhaps never been cut at all, so that she had to jump the last few feet.

The rock seemed to press up through the thin soles of her shoes; she fancied that it seemed to be welcoming her, and she felt strangely, almost disturbingly, at home.

Quite suddenly the beach dimmed as a cloud passed across the sun, and she trembled. She felt in her skirt pocket for her cigarettes, fumbled one from the packet. The breeze blew out her first match; she cupped the second in her palm and lit the cigarette.

She was still strongly aware of the pressure of the rocks under her feet, and had to make a conscious effort to step forward. She stumbled and swore as the cigarette dropped into a pool. Hurrying on across the ridged black rocks, she avoided the dark patches of weed and felt relieved when at last her feet sank into soft yielding sand. At the foot of the cliff she sat down and slipped off her shoes; she leaned forward, clasping her arms around her knees. The sun was higher now and she turned her face up for its full warmth. As she did so, she thought that she saw something bobbing in the sea.

When she looked again, it had gone.

She didn't mean to fall asleep, but when she opened her eyes again the sun was high. With a slight sense of guilt at her laziness she realised that it must be noon; she must have slept for hours.

The screaming of the gulls had awakened her.

They were wheeling in a great cloud above the rocks, just at the edge of the sea, making the most hideous noise. She wondered if perhaps a dead whale had been washed ashore.

Walk to the Sea

She remembered that had happened once, years before. Getting to her feet, she began walking down the beach toward the screaming flock of birds.

The tide was right out now, and it was much further away than she thought. She was breathless by the time she reached the pool – but long before she reached it the screaming of the gulls had become almost unbearable.

Afterwards she was never quite sure how long she stood there, the water lapping over the rocks and around her bare feet, looking down at the thing in the pool. It seemed that while she stood there, the sun paused overhead and the birds ceased their mad whirling. A dead silence fell, and another sound came out of it, a crackling and rustling like the sound of some cosmic radio set being tuned in, whining and hissing as if stations were being found then tuned out again. Then the sun began to move again, and she heard the screaming of the birds. She thought how strange the seaweed looked drifting in the water around the thing in the pool. At first she thought it was a log; it looked just like one, lying there straight and wrapped around by the black fronds. It rose and fell slightly with the movement of the water, which entered the pool from a deep channel hidden behind a high shoulder of rock. Fine wireweed drifted around the thing, tangling with the heavier fronds that wrapped it, suggesting the hair and bandages of some strange, sea-borne mummy. But of course, it was only a log, she knew. At her most fanciful, she couldn't believe that it was anything more fantastic than a broken spar brought in by the tide.

It was too late and she had already reached into the water and pushed at it and it was rolling over, when the stench rose up and hit her. The smell made her gag, and she lifted her hand to cover her mouth and nose, trying to keep out the stink of rottenness and corruption.

As soon as it rolled over, she was sure that it had been a woman, knew it immediately, though there was no face, no real distinguishing feature left. What had been a face was now only a crude swollen mask that looked as if it was made of white

Walk to the Sea

plasticine, its mouth and eye holes streaked with the thin tar-black weed-like hair.

The dead woman's stomach bulged out of the water, black and swollen as if with some ghastly pregnancy – as if some terrible mating had occurred out there in the sea. And the rocks were sucking at Susan's feet now, holding her, insisting that she stay as company for this other lonely occupant of the beach.

She turned mechanically in the direction of the cliffs, which now seemed very far away. She began to walk and then to run toward the hotel and the scattering of shops around the foot of the cliffs. She had covered about half the distance when she paused and looked back. The place where the rock pool lay was alive with gulls. The grey and white birds covered the black rocks and darkened the sky. Then as she watched, there was a mad flurry of beating wings as the birds around the pool began to take flight. Something had startled them.

Then she saw the dark shape as it broke the line where the rock lay against the horizon. Lumpish and blacker than the rock, it moved awkwardly against the sky, long weed and hair hanging below its waist, swinging as it climbed over the ridge of rock and then down the other side.

It was coming this way.

As it disappeared into the dip between the two rock ridges, she turned again and began to hurry to the safety of the buildings below the cliffs. When she got there, she would tell people what she had seen. It would not be so bad then, she knew; a terror shared is somehow less feared. People would help. They would shine the lights of argument and sympathy. They would investigate, and the thing she had seen would fade and disappear, banished by bluff voices and reason.

Climbing the hill from the beach later she thought it might not have been quite so bad if they had simply told her that they didn't believe her. Resentfully, she remembered their blandly sympathetic, too-understanding faces. They had finally told her

Walk to the Sea

they would look in the pool, but though she had waited, watching from the hill, no one had.

She had scanned the rocks looking for a sign of the black thing, but could not see it now. Eventually she began to climb the hill, returning home.

As she climbed the sun rose higher and cars passed her on their way down; big quiet cars with sunroofs, and smaller ones with furry toys hanging in their rear windows. Far below, the beach was gaining a noisy, stolen life. As the beach disappeared from view beyond the cliff edge, she saw that dozens of dark shapes now moved there across the sand and rocks.

At last she came to the café.

The café was not yet noisy, or occupied; it wouldn't come to life until much later, when the novelty of the tiny cove had gone and the cars began to return. But it was open, and she needed to rest.

A sense of familiarity swept strongly over her as she went in through the small door and along the hall. Further along, the hall became a kind of enclosed veranda, with old coach seats set beside windows overlooking the garden. She sat in one of them and studied the view, she felt that something was different, but for a while she couldn't decide what it was. Then it came to her.

A waitress approached the table, pencil and notebook in her hand. The waitress studied the woman at the table with a slightly tired look. "You'll be wanting a cup of coffee, with a little cream," she said.

Susan looked up, surprised; it was exactly what she had wanted. When the waitress brought the coffee, Susan looked up and said, "It's very odd. I remember sitting here before, looking down into the valley. There used to be a monastery down there. I remember thinking how isolated it was, down there among the trees. Now I can't see it at all."

The waitress set the cup on the table. There was something

Walk to the Sea

automatic in her response, a little condescending. "Yes, I remember it too. But that was a long time ago, dear. It's still there. The trees have grown up and hidden it."

Susan stared at her. "But that's impossible."

She looked down into the valley again. She studied the curtains of the trees where, now that she looked harder, they seemed to mask a vague stony greyness. Was that a wall behind them? She stared harder, wondering if that was the edge of a roof, chimneys. She was aware that the waitress had moved away and she thought she heard a door close. She took out a cigarette. She lit it and relaxed slightly as she inhaled. She wondered if she'd been asleep too long at the beach; the hot sun might have caused her to see things. She tapped the cigarette in the ashtray. The cigarette smelled quite strongly; maybe it was stale. But yes, that was it; the hot sun had caused her to see things. Smell things, too. She remembered the stench while she had stood by the rock pool. She could hear the waitress moving about behind her, a soft shuffling. Then she realised that the smell was not the scent of tobacco. Not even stale tobacco.

Behind her there was the soft clink of china as someone bumped into a table.

Someone was here.

"Do you get much custom here in the off season?" Susan said, without looking round.

There was more shuffling behind her, closer now.

"I should be leaving." Susan stood up abruptly, pushing back the heavy seat, which grated harshly on the concrete floor.

The stench was indescribable now, and she heard the table immediately behind her move slightly as somebody moved against it.

Somebody.

She began to walk firmly towards the door ahead of her. Was the shuffling sound more pronounced now, as if somebody was trying to catch her up? She imagined fingers

Walk to the Sea

reaching for her back, thought she felt the slightest touch of soft, blackened digits on her shoulder.

Something. The *stench!*

The door swung shut behind her. There was a low garden gate ahead, and beyond it the road. Breathing deeply, she took in lungfuls of fresh air and garden scents.

The journey along the road home would take her half an hour; it was about two miles.

This time she did not stop by the house with the covered sign. The windows of the house were dark and there was still no sign of the dog. The animal's absence somehow disturbed her more than the lack of lighting in the house. The dog had always greeted her as she passed, jumping up and barking behind the gate. It was so big and noisy that she wondered what could have happened to it. The time seemed to be passing faster than she realised, and as she carried on up the hill from the house, she saw that it was already growing dim under the overhanging trees. Looking up through breaks in the branches she saw that clouds had begun to gather. Eventually the road brought her out on the exposed brow of the hill. At the top, it continued straight ahead of her for about half a mile, bordered by stone walls at either side that converged in the distance. Usually she enjoyed this stretch of road, taking pleasure in the waving corn reaching away to either side. On a sunny day only occasional birdsong and the sound of her footsteps broke the silence. Now as clouds banked overhead and a thick mist began to sweep in from the coast, the entire landscape darkened and all she wanted to do was get home. She heard thunder growl in the distance and buttoned her light coat against the penetrating mist and increased her pace. After a few minutes walking, she was beginning to regret her choice of light clothing and was glad to see the shape of the letterbox becoming visible ahead of her, because that meant she was nearing the bend in the road, and her home would be only a few minutes further on.

It had grown very dim now. There had been no sunset, the

Walk to the Sea

mist and clouds had precluded that; the day had passed from afternoon to nightfall without the usual grace of a summer's day. The thunder grumbled again and she felt the first heavy drops of rain land on her face. By the time she reached the post box, her legs were growing tired and she'd started to shiver. But at last the long straight stretch of road ended. She remembered the way the sun had woken her that morning and looked around as she paused at the box.

Small with distance, she saw someone walking towards her at the other end of the road.

She stared incredulously at the figure. She tried telling herself that someone had become lost on this lonely stretch of road, someone wearing a long coat as sensible protection against this summer storm. But she knew that the dark mass that swayed around the figure wasn't the shape of a coat, it was hair, tangled with weed, and it was not lost.

She began to run.

As she started running, she threw one glance back over her shoulder.

It was running after her!

Down the road and through the garden gate, she pounded up the path and feverishly fitted the key in the lock. Behind her, she thought she heard the sound of dreadfully soft feet slapping against the path, thought she heard the clicking of bone where soft rotted flesh had been worn away. The key was in the lock and she pushed as it turned and fell into the hall, kicking the door shut behind her.

The Yale lock *snicked*.

There was a soft thump as something collided with the door.

Later, she sat in the shadowy living room. It had begun to rain, and she listened to the water rattling hard against the glass. For ages she had sat there, starting at every sound. She had heard vague padding and rustling sounds from the garden. Possibly it was a fox or a badger. But she knew it was not. She dared not open the curtains, dreading what she might see staring in at her

Walk to the Sea

through the rain-streaked glass. She didn't like sitting in the dark but was afraid of betraying her presence by switching on the light. Finally, freezing in her damp clothes, she had found her way into the kitchen and made herself a hot drink by the light of matches. There was no alcohol in the house, but the ludicrously prosaic act of boiling milk had a calming effect on her.

She carried the drink upstairs to her room and got into bed. She sipped at her cocoa, but by now it had gone cold and a skin had formed across the top.

She woke the next morning to the sound of the Post Office van labouring up the muddy track. It was still raining hard. A pool of water had begun to form in one corner beneath the place where the boughs of the tree had begun to loosen the tiles. There was no post, but she forced herself to get up and start preparing breakfast. While she ate, she saw the writing pad lying on the table in front of her, and remembered that she had a letter to send.

Drawing the pad to her, she opened to a clean page. She had a vague memory as if of a nightmare, though the details wouldn't come back.

'Yesterday,' she wrote, in a neat fine hand, 'something terrible happened.'

ROMERO'S CHILDREN

David A. Riley

Senator Hardy launched an attack tonight against the widespread use of the age-retarding drug OM (Old Methuselah), in which he condemned black market sales. "No one today knows what its long term results will be. It may halt aging in the short term, but it will be years, perhaps decades before anyone can say that its usage is safe or does not have possible side effects which no one at this time can predict. People take this drug with the hope of a longer, healthier life, but they do not know if this is all they will get."

One of the last newspaper reports ever published in the United States.

The old man could hear them scratching and clawing at the outside door two floors below, trying to get in. He'd been able to hear them for the last few nights as he lay in bed, trying to keep warm on the thin mattress of the old cast-iron bedstead, with its well-worn blankets and hard pillow. But the door was strong. It would take months for them to wear it down and he felt secure enough to lie listening to them without any fear. Let them waste their energies. He was safe, if neither comfortable nor warm.

The next morning, his joints aching, Jack climbed out of bed and put on his clothes. Although the sun rose several hours ago, it was wintry and pale and gave off little heat, and the cold of the threadbare carpets, scattered like rugs on the bare floorboards, chilled his feet as he trod across them. He rooted out his boots from where he discarded them last night when he drunkenly made his way to bed, and tugged on the socks he'd stuffed inside them, then the boots themselves. He yawned, scratched for a minute or two, then padded across to the window. Its dusty panes looked down onto the street.

Romero's Children

They'd gone. Romero's children nearly always disappeared when the sun came up. They preferred the night, with its darkness and shadows. In daylight they were easily seen and picked off. Even their dim minds were aware of this, self-preservation kicking in to make them hide.

Jack put on his padded outer jacket and slipped on his gloves. Snow was on its way, though he didn't need that to appreciate how cold it was. He reached for the rifle propped against the wall, safety catch on, one shell in the breach. Although he felt secure up here at night, there were always accidents – and enough survivors had been complacent in the safety of their homes that they had ended up as meat.

Less than twenty years had passed since OM made its first appearance and still they were paying for it. And would till long after he turned into maggot food, Jack thought as he set about unlocking the series of doors that led down the stairwell to the street. He had installed them at the top of each flight, with spy holes through which he could see if any of *them* had gotten inside the building. That had only happened once so far. One night he had been too tired – or drunk, if truth were known – and left the door onto the street ajar. There was a large piece of wood still screwed to the last door at the bottom of the stairs to cover the hole he'd blasted through it – and through the head of the thing mewling on the other side, its beautiful, youthful, dirt-stained face visible through the fish-eye lens.

OM. It was hard to remember it now as anything but a curse that had destroyed everything. Brought an end to all the calamitous fears of Global Warming too, since few cars, factories or anything else mechanical or electrical had functioned for years. Yes, we sure put a stop to that all right, Jack thought to himself ironically. Something to be proud of, at least.

He pushed an eye against the spy hole of the outside door and peered onto the street. It was a rarely needed precaution. And as usual there was nothing there. Just the permanently parked cars, their tyres long since flattened, while rust ate at their bodywork. There were streaks of ice along the road. And the inevitable debris.

With a sigh, Jack unlocked the door and pulled it open. It was heavy, and shut behind him with a resounding thud, before he locked it again. He swung the rifle from his shoulder and took a careful look in every direction.

In the distance three figures were running towards him. The nearest was a girl. He recognised Candice Roe at once, a hard-bitten seventeen-year-old from the settlement. And a damned good shot with a rifle. Which puzzled him. Why was her gun clenched in one hand when she was being pursued? It wouldn't be like Candice to have run out of ammo. Like most people these days she would carry at least a dozen rounds, stuffed in bags or in her pockets – anywhere they would fit. Ammo meant survival. Especially against stinkers.

Jack hurried towards her. He could see she was tiring and it looked as if the creatures were gaining on her. They were a man and a woman, their unwrinkled faces grey with years of accumulated dirt, dried food and blood like flaking masks of mud.

Dropping to one knee, Jack aimed his rifle at the nearest, centring the cross-wires of the telescopic lens on one eye. He eased back the trigger. The shot took away most of the upper cranium in a spray of brains, bone and discoloured blood. He took out the other a few seconds later. Both lay twitching on the street when Candice reached him, gasping for breath.

"My rifle jammed otherwise I'd have taken them myself," she panted. "Must have run over a mile before I saw you. Gave me a second wind."

"Good job you did. Looked to me as if they were gaining ground."

"Persistent bastards. Comes from not having brains enough to know when you're exhausted."

Jack chuckled. "Stands to sense there must be some compensation for being brain dead psychos. That's just one of 'em."

Candice scowled. "Glad it amused you, Jack."

"It'll amuse you too as soon as you've got your breath back."

"And forgotten how close I came to becoming meat for those bastards."

"And that," Jack added, his humour dying a little. It was a danger all of them had to live with, and one that no one took lightly. They'd all seen the aftermath too often for that.

"How come you're out here by yourself?" Jack asked.

Candice regarded him edgily. "You're a fine one to ask that."

"That's my choice. One I've lived with for years. Wouldn't suit everyone, 'specially these days. But you're not a sad, dried-up old loner like me."

"No." Candice gazed down the empty street, with its stone-clad apartments, shops and offices, all of them derelict. "I just needed some time by myself for a while, that's all."

Deducing it was probably something to do with a boy and none of his business, Jack shrugged. "Okay by me. You can hunker down here for a while if you like. Leastways, I can help fix your rifle. And lend you a handgun. You should always have one as backup. Me, I have a Colt automatic. Stops 'em dead in their tracks every time. I'm not much of a shot with it, mind, but at close range I don't need to be."

"I usually have something. I just wasn't thinking today."

"Not thinking is what gets you killed." Jack gazed down the street, aware suddenly the cold had begun to sink into his bones. "I'm off after some fresh stores. D'you want to lend a hand?"

"Suppose that's the least I could do," she said, an uncertain smile twitching about her lips. "What's it today? Wal-Mart?"

"As always. Canned section."

They walked down the street in silence for a while till they turned onto the car park at the nearest store, with its abandoned cars and the skeletal remains of several hundred bodies, a grim reminder of just how turbulent times had been when the after-effects of OM showed themselves.

"How come you never took OM?" Candice asked as they passed the first of the bodies. "There aren't many people your age around these days. Almost everyone of your generation took it. Why didn't you? Religious reasons?"

Jack shook his head. "My wife. We were both in our fifties when OM hit the headlines. She'd already started with Alzheimer's by then. What good is a drug that'll retard ageing to someone with that? Putting off old age indefinitely isn't much of a lure for someone whose brains are turning to mush. Me, I couldn't take it while Rachel was like she was. Didn't seem hardly fair somehow. An extra forty or fifty years of life didn't appeal to me then. Hell, even suicide wasn't far from my mind when Rachel passed on, that's how bad I felt."

"You were lucky."

"You could say that, though I don't reckon as I would necessarily agree. This isn't exactly how I saw my Golden Years." Jack gazed across the car park. "It was bizarre how greedy folks were for it," he said a moment later. "It was never licensed by the government, you know. Most of it was sold on the black market – a black market that became huge quickly, the demand was so big. Things went insane. Everyone wanted it, especially those who'd passed their thirties. Made the profits during Prohibition small potatoes, believe you me. Made some criminal empires enormous. For a while, at least."

"Till its after effects destroyed them too."

"Destroyed everything – almost. There'd been warnings, of course. Some scientists spoke out against OM. But they were ignored. Immortality was too big an incentive for anyone to wait till all the tests had been completed – tests that would take years. Too many years for most folk. Hell, if OM had come along earlier, when Alzheimer's was something that happened to other people, not to us, I expect that me and Rachel would have taken it too. Why not? We'd have leapt at the chance of putting a stop to ageing and gaining all that extra time."

"And you'd have ended as stinkers too."

"Without a doubt. Never heard of anyone who took OM without that kicking in seven, eight years down the line. Made Alzheimer's look like a dose of flu. You think we've got it bad, girl, you should have seen what it was like when there were millions of the bastards going off the rails. Looking back, it's hard to imagine how any of us survived. If'n they hadn't been such dumb bastards I don't suppose we would. Luckily, they were more often as interested in tearing each other to pieces as attacking us. Cut their numbers down a lot in the first year till some of them started working together, those that were left. The *smart* ones."

"I can't remember any of that," Candice said. "I was only a baby then. Lucky for me, Mom was only eighteen when she had me and hadn't thought about taking OM then. Before she could, it all went to Hell."

"How is your mom?"

"Okay. Feeling her age these days."

"If she's feeling her age, imagine what I'm feeling." Jack gave her a sideways grimace, then tucked the rifle under his arm, ready to fire. They were only a few yards from the main entrance to the abandoned store. Its doors had long since been reduced to splinters. The dark interior was a vast array of tumbledown shelves and scattered produce, filled with shadows. "I don't expect to come across any stinkers here. They tend to prefer somewhere less well-trodden to hang out during the day, somewhere less likely to get them shot."

"They know that well enough," Candice said sourly.

"Those that've survived this long know it. There were a lot in the early days too dumb for that. I suppose it was survival of the fittest. The dumbest were culled early on."

"So we've the brightest, eh?" Candice laughed. It was a sound that helped to lighten Jack's spirit somehow. He hated scavenging through derelict stores for the few undamaged cans of food still left in them. It depressed him. Candice's presence helped take away some of his gloominess. Perhaps he'd made

Romero's Children

too much of his preference for solitude. Now he was getting older perhaps it was time to enjoy some company for a change; maybe even join the settlement. They'd asked him often enough over the years.

You can't do penance for having outlived her forever, he told himself as he looked back on the last few days of Rachel's life. Ironically, her passing had coincided with the first of the stinkers. Romero's children.

If only they'd known how widespread it was going to be, all those politicians and scientists who had appeared on television, discussing the first cases of violence wreaked by the stinkers. The irony was that most of these people became stinkers too in the next few months.

Romero's children had sounded like a joke at first. Except these creatures weren't movie zombies. Not the shambling, ugly, walking corpses the great director had portrayed them as. They were neither shambling nor ugly. Nor dead. Far from it, Jack thought. But they were deadly all right. Just as deadly as anything ever dreamt up in Hollywood.

"Careful," Jack cautioned as they stepped inside the store. He eased some of the tension from his trigger finger as he scanned the poorly lit interior. He had been here often in the past. Knew almost every untidy pile of mouldering food that had been spilled onto the floor from burst bags and ruptured packets. In a few years there'd be nothing left worth scavenging. The alcohol went long ago. Fortunately he had another source for that. One no one else had stumbled on yet.

Something scuffled deep inside the store, and Jack swore softly as he automatically fell into a crouch, gun at the ready, his eyes scanning the gloom.

"What was it? A rat?" Beside him, Candice held a knife in one hand.

Jack shook his head. "I don't know. There are enough vermin about. But that didn't sound like a rat to me." He passed her his Colt, then crept along the aisle, his head twitching from side to side. If there were stinkers present, he was confident of taking two or three of them easily enough. But there was always the chance a nest of them had decided to camp here. He had on occasion come across a dozen or more – though that was rare. The sensible thing would have been to get help. But that wasn't Jack's way. He'd been a loner too long to break old habits easily. And with Candice as back up, he felt sure they could handle up to four, maybe five between them without breaking into a sweat.

"Over there," Candice whispered. She jerked two fingers leftwards. "Behind the freezers. I saw something there. It's watching us."

Which was damnably odd behaviour for a stinker, Jack thought.

"You sure it's watching us?"

"Looked like it to me," Candice whispered back. He could tell she was disturbed. She had been brought up dealing with creatures like this and probably knew their behaviour as well as him. "Perhaps it isn't a stinker."

Jack didn't know. Could be someone else scavenging for supplies. But why hide? It would have been obvious who Candice and he were the moment they stepped inside the store. For a start off Stinkers didn't carry guns. Stinkers didn't talk either.

Coming to a decision, Jack stood up and advanced towards where Candice had pointed.

"If'n you're one of us step out," he said. "I'll hold my fire. We only shoot stinkers."

Even though the face had recently been washed, Jack could not mistake what hesitantly stepped out of the shadows in front, its hands above its head in an awkward gesture of surrender. It would take more than a few wipes with a wet rag to remove the years of ingrained grime from the creature's face.

For a moment Jack faltered. He knew he should aim and fire. He could have done that in a split second. Instinct tugged at nerve endings, urging him on. But he didn't. He couldn't.

Romero's Children

He waved Candice's weapon down when she stepped up beside him.

"Why?" Her question was half bewilderment, half accusation.

Jack shook his head, uncertain. "Something odd about this thing," was all he could think to say as he stepped towards it, his finger still hooked about the trigger of his gun, aimed at waist level ahead of him.

"Who are you?" he asked.

Her clothes were tatters, held together by grease and dirt, which clung like a grimy, obscene skin to her scrawny body. The woman took a cautious step from where she had been hiding. Her fingers were black with crusts of blood and grease, the accumulated debris of a thousand meals eaten raw. She was a stinker all right. Jack was certain of that. But her face, especially her eyes, was wrong. There was fear in her eyes. And confusion.

"You hold it right there," he told her. "One more step and, like it or not, I'll fire."

The woman came to an unsteady halt. She was trying to speak. Jack was certain about that. But her tongue and jaw muscles moved awkwardly as if from lack of practice.

"What the fuck is it doing?" Candice asked.

"Damned if I know." Jack squinted through the gloom. Like every stinker he had ever seen she looked youthful. However old she may have been when she first took OM it had stopped the years from gaining on her, even though nearly two decades had passed since she took it. The drug may have messed up her brain, but beneath all the accumulated filth her body was as perfect as the day she took it.

"Awake…" The woman spoke in a stutter, her voice thick, as if her tongue was too large – or unaccustomed to the motions it was being forced to make. "Night … mares … gone…"

"You're the fucking nightmare," Candice grumbled, her eyes venomous as she stared at the woman. "We should cap that thing."

Gently, Jack touched the girl's arm. "Easy now," he said. "Stinkers don't talk."

"Then what is she if she isn't a fucking stinker?"

"That I don't know," he said. "But stinkers don't talk. I know that, if I know nothing else."

The woman swayed. She looked as if she hadn't eaten in days.

"Awake…" she repeated.

*

While Jack heaved a sack of canned goods on his shoulder, most of their labels unreadable, Candice led the woman back to his place. The stinker's hands had been tied together in front of her. Jack had relented on this precaution. If he hadn't he suspected Candice would have used the slightest excuse – an unsteady step or an odd movement – to open fire and kill the thing.

"You're taking one hell of a risk taking this thing back to your place," Candice grumbled.

"We'll see," Jack said, unsure why he trusted the woman. But somehow, though, he did. Perhaps it was the pain, the confusion and the look of horror in her eyes that convinced him. He didn't know. Less than an hour after discovering her, though, she was sitting in a bath of warm water in Jack's apartment. Apathetically, she let Jack, and then Candice set to work scrubbing decades of grime from her thin body. For the most part the woman was placid, either through exhaustion or fear or both. After a short time she looked almost human again. Or would have except for the fact she was unnaturally youthful and too mature at the same time despite the tiredness and fear on her face. The woman's hands, especially her fingers, had blackened lines of grease and blood that would take more than soap to remove. Like Lady Macbeth, Jack thought to himself, her sins would haunt her in her hands for years to come.

Romero's Children

He gave her a pair of trousers and a jumper to replace the shreds of clothing they had peeled like layers of diseased flesh from her body. The mess had reeked so much Jack had been forced to open one of the windows and toss them out into the street, though the apartment still had the unmistakable stench of Romero's children. They weren't called stinkers for nothing, he thought.

"What next?" Candice asked after the woman had been led into one of the bedrooms to rest.

Jack shrugged. "See if she'll eat some of our food. That's the ultimate test. Stinkers aren't interested in normal food."

"Just off the bone with the pulse still pumping," Candice said, more than a trace of bitterness in her voice.

"Never seen one eat cooked food, even when it was available."

"So if she does, she's cured? Is that what you think?"

"Maybe."

"Would you trust her then?" Candice glanced at the closed door to the bedroom the woman was in.

"I don't know," he said. "I'd have to hear her talk. Hear her story. See what she's got to say for herself. Weigh it up."

It was dark by the time they were sat about the table. Jack had prepared a thick stew from some tinned potatoes, beans and meat they'd brought back from the store. He placed a bowl of it before the woman, along with a spoon. There was a feeling of tension as she stared at it for several moments, and Jack saw Candice's hand stray towards the Colt still tucked inside the belt of her jeans. Uncertain, the woman grasped the spoon. It shook as she awkwardly held it between her fingers, then dipped it in the bowl, before slowly lifting it towards her mouth, spilling half its contents. She stopped as the edge of the spoon touched her lips, as if she was struggling to remember what came next. Then she pushed the spoon into her mouth. Some of the stew spilled down her chin but she barely seemed to notice that. For a moment what was left of the food rested inside her mouth, and it looked to Jack as if she was tasting –

or testing – the oddity of it. Or trying to recall when she last had food like this. Cooked food. Seventeen, maybe eighteen years was a long time to remember. Could he remember what the food he ate back then was like?

After gulping what remained on her spoon, the woman surprised him by going on to clear her bowl with an appetite that made Jack wonder how long it was since the last time she ate, though he tried not to think what that meal might have been. That was her past. This was her present. Her different present, he hoped.

When they'd finished eating, Jack eased his chair back from the table and regarded the woman. Her complexion looked better now – more normal, he thought. Almost.

"Do you recall your name?" he said.

Though physically she looked no more than thirty, Jack knew she had to be fifty at least. Nearly twenty lost years of madness lay between the last time she'd used her name and now. It was easy to forget this when looking at her youthfulness.

"They – they called me – Lucy – once."

It was painful to hear that voice. It jarred with her face. A fractured, husky whisper, it made Jack's hair rise on the nape of his neck. He could see the same reaction in Candice. Which was worrying, he thought. Maybe practice would ease a more acceptable sound into the woman's voice.

Jack nodded to Candice. He introduced her to the woman. "My name is Jack."

Lucy repeated their names as if to memorise them.

"How long have you been back with us?" Jack asked. "Since the nightmares ended, I mean."

"Days – nights. I was – frightened. I hid."

"What do you remember?"

She closed her eyes and shuddered. "Nightmares. On and on … endless … nightmares."

"Before then, before the nightmares started?"

For a moment Lucy opened her eyes. She stared at him as if

struggling to search back through the decades, then burst into tears. They streamed down her face unchecked. Even Candice looked concerned.

"Easy now," Jack said, quietly. "No need to struggle. If you can't remember, it doesn't matter. If those memories are there they'll come back with time."

"If you want them too," Candice said.

That night, while they lay in separate rooms, Jack heard the scratching outside again. Lucy might have come through whatever Hell she had been to, but others were still living it.

Eventually, though, he slept.

It was three, perhaps four in the morning when he awoke, aware the sounds outside had stopped. Realised they were wasting their time, he thought, though those bastards had time enough to waste, he thought to himself, aware of the irony.

He felt a chill in the air, and he wondered if the window had slipped open. But he was reluctant to leave the warmth of his bed and walk to it, knowing how bitterly cold the air would be. He opened one eye and was surprised to see how light it was. It had snowed overnight, and the building across the street was coated with piles on every ridge and window ledge, reflecting moonlight into his room. It was then he heard something move. Instantly he was wide-awake. He reached for the rifle he had left against his bed. It had gone. Prickles of alarm shivered through his body as his hand reached into emptiness. He moved his head and scanned the room. He saw a figure by the doorway, staring at him. It was Lucy. He recognised her even in the gloom. She was holding something in one hand. It was dark and round. In her other hand he saw the glint of a blade. It was broad like one of the high tech butcher's knives from his kitchen. His breath caught in his throat as his eyes adjusted to the gloom. Beyond her he could see two other figures in the open doorway. At the same time he recognised the smell that wafted from them. Had she gone downstairs and opened the bottommost door to let them? Her fellow 'children'. Down the front of her clothes Jack saw the vomit that had begun to dry, of the stew she must have thrown up as she lay in bed as the nightmares came and took her again.

Jack swung out of bed, though he had little hope without his rifle. But in the top drawer by the window he kept a handgun. If he reached it he would have a chance. But the thing, that had briefly been Lucy again, flung the object she held in her hand across the floor at his unshod feet, tripping him. Sprawled helplessly on his back, Jack cried out as he recognised Candice's face staring up at him from between his feet.

Lucy moved towards him, her grease-stained fingers hooked like claws.

THE GREEN BATH

Paul Finch

They set off at four o'clock that morning, to make good time on the crowded summer motorways. It worked. They'd reached Birmingham by six o'clock, and the Cotswolds by seven. By the time they were into the West Country, the hot mists of the July dawn were only just starting to clear. They breakfasted on the edge of Dartmoor and were in Cornwall by mid-morning.

The winding country ways slowed them down a little, but that was fine. They'd broken the back of the journey and were only due to take charge of the villa in late afternoon, so there was ample time. Besides, neither Pete nor Sarah had any desire to rush. The thickly blooming hedgerows and ridged pastures, with their distant tors and clumps of gorse, were an essential part of the Cornish experience. Why zip through it? Especially on a sun soaked morning like this.

Even Pete found himself relaxing. The further he drove from Manchester, the easier it was to forget about things back home. Not that you could ever completely forget being summoned to your MD's office the day before you were due to take your annual leave, and being told that from next March you were expendable, and that everyone was sorry, and that if it was any consolation you wouldn't be the last, and that the economic climate was mainly to blame but that a generous package would still be put together for you. I mean, after all, you'd been there ten years or more, so…

Sarah touched his leg and smiled. Pete tried to smile back, but failed miserably.

"We can still afford a holiday, you know," she said gently. "I wouldn't worry."

"I just think I should be back home now, trying to find something else."

"Don't let it spoil everything, Pete. You deserve the break.

The Green Bath

We both do."

"Those bastards!" he snapped. "Eleven years, I gave that newspaper."

"I know."

"There've been lazy, bone-idle sods swanning around in Accounts and Admin, not doing a tap, for years and years. But they're okay, aren't they? Oh yeah…"

Sarah looked out of the window. Now, other vehicles were appearing on the roads, their roofs stacked with surfboards and baggage, hauling boats and caravans.

"Perkins said that if you made a play for it, you might still land the new editor's job," she said, expecting an explosion – they'd already had this conversation six times since the bombshell had been dropped, and she knew that her husband was growing tired of it.

"I'm a design-sub, Sarah. I'm no bloody editor."

"It's a lot more money…"

"I know, and I'm not ambitious enough, and I've heard it all before, yawn yawn."

"Perkins virtually invited you to apply for it. He said they wanted somebody good in charge."

"Perkins is a fat wanker, and now he's an embarrassed fat wanker! He got lumbered with the hiring and firing job, and the only way to save face each time he blows somebody out is to invite them to apply for another post. It's a load of crap. You know perfectly well that I've no more chance of landing the editor's job than one of the tea-girls."

"That's rubbish," Sarah said under her breath, gazing outside. A cloud had appeared from somewhere, and cast a shadow on the patchwork landscape. She wished her husband had more confidence in his abilities. Despite his big, rugged appearance, Pete was a sensitive sort of man, unnerved by responsibility.

"Anyway, like you say, let's not spoil the holiday," he added, placing a hand on her thigh. "I can't stand it when outside pressures turn us against each other."

The Green Bath

She nodded and smiled. Ahead of them, the sun sneaked out again.

*

Penzakhy was a scenic blue-water bay located just west of the Lizard, and, though a fishing village turned resort, it wasn't a busy one by normal Cornwall standards. A handful of hotels stood along the front, but these were small, family-run affairs, in keeping with the quaint local architecture. Pete and Sarah had taken a villa. It was outside the town centre, at the end of a seafront cul-de-sac, on a high point where the sands gave way to rocky cliffs, and a pebbly footpath snaked away through sweeping meadows of tussocky marram grass.

The villa was a double-fronted Victorian Gothic, massive and whitewashed, and standing in heavily overgrown gardens. It was an impressive building – Pete imagined you'd be able to pick it out from St Jute's Head on the far side of the bay – but it had an atmosphere of neglect. They crept past it once in the car, before turning round and cruising slowly back. Thick green moss covered its walls, while much of its guttering was stuffed with grass and weeds. Yet it still held a certain holiday appeal. The enormous front windows, both upstairs and down, bespoke big, airy rooms with magnificent sea-views.

The only other building on the cul-de-sac was the hotel next door, the *De-Luxe*. This, Sarah had been assured when first booking, would not interfere with their privacy. The *De Luxe*, which actually owned the villa, was not operating a full vacancy service at the moment, owing to refurbishment. Things would be quiet.

In truth, they looked like they'd be *very* quiet, Pete commented, as they parked their Toyota.

The *De Luxe*, which was only separated from the villa by a hedge of densely matted vegetation, was almost derelict. This too sat in dilapidated gardens, though in this case the gravel drive and footpaths were hidden by carpets of luxuriant

The Green Bath

foliage. Some of the hotel's windows had been boarded over, slates were missing from several parts of its roof, and much of the rendering had rotted and fallen away. The only sign that anyone still lived or worked there was the open front door and a curtained bay window to the left side of it.

Sarah and Pete sat in the car. They were stiff and tired from the long drive, but that glorious feeling of arrival had not yet surged over them. The sight of the *De Luxe* didn't help.

"It's horrible," Sarah said flatly.

"Well at least that lady we booked with … what was her name, Miss Trelawny … at least she wasn't lying," Pete replied. "No one'll disturb us."

Just then there was movement. They turned and saw a smoke-grey Jaguar reversing slowly out from the drive of the villa. It turned and parked. A man climbed from it and adjusted the baggage strapped to the roof. A second later, a woman joined him from the drive. She was carrying two plastic bags filled with crisps and bottles of pop, which she placed in the rear seat. They were both middle-aged and heavily built, but clad in bright holiday clothes. The man was red-headed and had a tough, no-nonsense look about him. He adjusted the straps and ropes with practiced and speedy efficiency.

"If those are the previous tenants, they were supposed to have checked out this morning," Sarah said.

Pete shrugged. "No real rush, is there? Might as well give 'em a hand."

He climbed out and wandered along the pavement, stretching his legs. The middle-aged couple spotted him and fell silent as he approached. Pete was surprised to see worried looks on their faces. The man couldn't seem to meet his gaze, while the woman stood rigidly, holding her breath. Up close, she had dark rings under her eyes; she looked positively drained.

"I wondered if I could help," Pete said uncertainly.

"Thanks," the man replied, indicating that the woman should get into the Jag. "But we're okay." He had a strong Midlands

The Green Bath

accent, but a weak voice which didn't go with his bullish appearance. "I'm sorry we're … er, still here. But the wife's not so well, you see. Neither of us are. Took us a while to get things together."

He opened the driver's door as if to climb inside.

"Don't zoom off on our account," Pete said. "We've only just got here. We've got loads of time."

The man glanced back at him, and was about to speak when he spied something over Pete's shoulder. His expression blanked, and, without saying anything else, he climbed into the Jaguar, gunned the engine and drove away.

Pete turned to look and saw that a figure had emerged from the front door of the hotel. It was a woman, very tall and shapely, with flowing tawny hair. She wore a tight, flowered dress, which fitted her hourglass figure snugly, and a black net shawl.

Pete waited, as she came gracefully down the footpath towards them, picking her way through the weeds in backless, heeled slippers.

She was exceedingly pretty, with bright green eyes and a healthy golden-brown complexion. When she was standing directly in front of him, Pete had trouble avoiding looking at her cleavage, which was deep and inviting. He was vaguely aware of Sarah climbing out of the car behind him.

"How do you do?" the woman said with a West Country lilt. "I'm Miss Trelawny." She offered a hand with long, white-lacquered nails. "You must be the Jacksons?"

"Er, yeah," Pete said. Her perfume was intoxicating, redolent of tropical flowers.

"I hope you enjoy yourself here. The villa's ready for you." Miss Trelawny glanced along the road after the Jaguar – its sleek grey shape was just turning out of sight. "I'm sorry those people were still here. There's always someone who drags their heels, outstays their welcome. I hope it hasn't spoiled anything for you?"

"No," Sarah said. "Not at all."

The Green Bath

Miss Trelawny smiled at her. Her mouth was very full, the lips pink and plump. "Well ... I'll not keep you. The villa's open and the keys are inside. No doubt you'll want to get on with your holiday, and see as little of me as possible."

"I wouldn't say that," Pete muttered as she sashayed back to the hotel's entrance.

Sarah dug an elbow into his side.

"If you need me for anything, I'm always here!" Miss Trelawny called from the hotel steps.

"It's okay, thanks," Sarah replied. "I'm sure we won't."

"Something else about the place you don't like?" Pete chuckled, as they climbed into the Toyota.

"That has to be the most over-the-top woman I've ever seen," Sarah snorted. "Don't tell me she turned you on?"

"She's got something."

"Probably a 'Made in California' sticker on the sole of her foot."

Pete bellowed with laughter as he drove onto the drive. It wasn't a genuine laugh, though. Rather to his surprise, he had a solid erection in the front of his jeans, which he was hoping Sarah hadn't noticed.

*

If the villa's owner hadn't been everything they'd expected, the villa was. They spent an hour unpacking, and another one exploring a house that looked as if it had been designed to accommodate a coach-party. The central living area – a lounge, dining room, kitchen and washhouse – was located on the ground floor, but the next two floors, accessible by a grand staircase, were made up entirely of bedrooms, most of which had once had separate locks on them. All were now open, carpeted and fitted with double beds, wardrobes and showers.

They had been right about the seaside atmosphere. Pete stood in the front bay window of the bedroom they eventually chose. It was filled entirely by a close-up view of the Atlantic,

The Green Bath

pebble blue and rolling gently in the afternoon heat. The horizon was broken only by the distant rocky hump of St Jute's Head.

"It's incredible!" Sarah said from another part of the house.

Pete glanced sideways, and realised that he could see clear over the tangled hedge. From this angle, only the extreme front projection of the *De Luxe* was visible, but on its lower nearside wall there was a narrow window, and, for a fleeting moment, he fancied he saw Miss Trelawny framed in it as she drew the curtain – framed in it naked.

He blinked, and the curtain closed. But the image was burned on his brain: waves of tawny hair, a golden body, voluptuously curved.

"Hey Pete ... come and look at this!"

Sarah suddenly sounded excited. So excited that he was able to break from his temporary erotic fix. He found her in what he'd first taken for a closet just to the side of the stairwell, but which actually was a bathroom, and a spacious one at that.

Sarah hopped up and down on the green-tiled floor. She indicated the bathtub. "Isn't it amazing?"

Pete stared at it, puzzled, thinking that it looked like any other bath. But then he realised how large it was: perhaps seven feet long and three feet deep. That was big, he had to admit. It was long and narrow, as a bathtub should be, but oval in shape rather than rectangular.

"You could go for a swim in that," Sarah said, as she bustled back out to the bedroom. "I can't wait to try it. Pete, I think I'm starting to like it here."

He glanced around the room. The tub was probably worth a fortune. It was an old Victorian model, hand-made in curved cast-iron. Its taps were massive and ornately carved. Mind you, its current owner was doing her best to lower the value. Damp wooden panels reached from the floor to the tub's rim, which might have caused corrosion underneath, while the metal itself had been painted a hideous lime-green. That was to fit in with the decor presumably, though the rest of the room had faded a

The Green Bath

little. It was tiled alternately in grey and white, but the grouting had flaked out from between many of them. A grey patch over the green washbasin showed where a mirror had once been fixed, while the windowsill was littered with dead flies. Beyond the frosted glass pane, tendrils of ivy hung down.

Pete wondered if Miss Trelawny had ever been in here to bathe. He imagined her in some tacky centrefold scenario; tawny locks piled high, huge breasts heavily soaped.

When he went back into the bedroom, Sarah was chattering away as she laid her scanties on the bed. Pete watched her carefully. She was a pretty little thing, his wife, with short dark hair and a tanned, trim figure. As always, she was dressed simply but sexily. This time she wore a lacy halter-top, white shorts and pumps. He eyed her as she talked, wondering what was drawing his attention to her. Then it struck him – no knicker-lines. She wasn't wearing any underwear.

God, it turned him on when she did that.

Without a word, he reached out and yanked her shorts to her ankles. Sarah jumped with shock. She slapped at him playfully, trying to pull them up again. "You mucky beast," she laughed. "Not with the curtains open!"

"Sod the curtains." He picked her up and threw her squealing onto the bed. Leaping on top of her, he unbuckled the front of his jeans. Sarah wrapped her legs around him and planted a big moist kiss on his mouth.

"So long as it's me you're thinking about and not 'Miss Boob-Job 2010' next door!"

Pete didn't answer.

*

They made love four times that evening, only falling into an exhausted sleep around nine o'clock.

The following morning they were up sharp and early. They showered, breakfasted, and then crossed the road to the beach, hoping to get an hour in before the crowds gathered. It was

The Green Bath

another glorious morning, the sky gas-flame blue, the sea lapping on soft white sand. Sarah stretched out, her bikini-clad body gleaming with lotion, eyes closed behind her shades. Pete wasn't much for sunbathing, but Sarah insisted that he should at least try to unwind, so he stripped down to his denim cut-offs and lay beside her, working his way through a detective novel.

Inevitably, an hour later, he was sufficiently restless to get up again, pull on his T-shirt and return to the house. He wanted to check on something, he said. As he followed the footpath back, it struck him as odd that the beach was still largely deserted. One or two people had appeared, but for so idyllic a spot in high summer it was very quiet. Even the ever-present Cornish gulls were noticeable by their absence. Well, Miss Trelawny had said that it would be like this.

Miss Trelawny, he thought.

He couldn't get that naked form, glimpsed through the dusty window, out of his mind. She *had* to have been putting on a show for him. Either that, or she cared nothing for decency. Either way, it was a tantalising prospect that he was due to spend the next week here.

Pete wasn't unfaithful by nature – he hadn't been in seven years of happy marriage – but in this case the temptation to see what the next step might bring was overpowering. Before he knew what he was doing, he'd veered away from the villa and was heading for the hotel. He stopped at its gate, glancing guiltily over his shoulder, expecting to see Sarah. There was no sign of her, and after a moment's brief uncertainty, he pushed the gate open. He was still sore from the night before, but already felt new blood flowing into his groin. The hotel entrance seemed to beckon. As he strode towards it, he wondered what he was going to say.

Not that the *De Luxe* was the most auspicious place for illicit love. Now that he was here, he saw that the gardens weren't just overgrown – they were a jungle. The hedge of foliage separating the hotel's grounds from the villa's led back

The Green Bath

between the properties, at which point it seemed to explode in colossal sprays of shoots and stalks, so tangled and profuse that they appeared to connect the two buildings together. Loops of leafy vine were suspended between them. Rampant greenery, clearly sprouting from the same roots, ran in rivers up both sets of crumbling brickwork to the eaves, where more swags of vegetation hung down. But despite both structures falling prey to the same predatory plant-life, the hotel still seemed to be getting the worst of it. Its windows were either cracked or boarded, the woodwork around them long perished. Fissures gaped in its walls. Beyond its open front door, darkness hung like a curtain. A rank odour seeped out.

Pete halted. Did Miss Trelawny really *live* here? He supposed the only way to find out was to go inside, but he was hardly dressed for it. He suddenly felt like a holiday buffoon: bare legged, sand between his toes, his paunch hanging out over his waistband.

When a woman suddenly emerged from the entrance, he was not at all prepared for it. However, she was not Miss Trelawny.

"Oh, er … hallo," Pete said, smiling awkwardly. "I'm sorry, I was looking for the proprietor."

The woman didn't smile back. She had the sort of face that looked as if it couldn't smile. She was only about sixty, but wizened like aged wood, straggles of white hair hanging to either side of her pinched features. Her emaciated frame was wrapped in a heavy black shawl, and under that a shapeless, flower-patterned dress.

Pete cleared his throat. "I'm…"

"You're Mr Jackson, I know." Her accent was Cornish, but her voice was creaky, as if she rarely used it.

"Ah. Well, as I say, I was looking for…"

"I'm the proprietor, Mr Jackson." The woman's beady eyes had fixed on him. "Can I help you?"

"You're…?" Pete tried not to show his surprise. "No, I'm sorry … I was looking for Miss Trelawny."

"You've found her. I repeat, can I help you?"

The Green Bath

Pete wasn't sure what to say.

"I imagine," she added, "that the person you're actually looking for is my daughter, Carla?"

Pete nodded. Now that she mentioned it, there was a faint family resemblance. However, the years had taken a severe toll on the older Miss Trelawny.

"I was under the impression you were married, Mr Jackson?"

"I am, but…" His words tumbled out as he struggled with so surprisingly blunt an observation. "I was only … well, I … that is we, myself and Sarah … we were hoping to do some touring. You know, take in the sights … as it were."

It didn't sound convincing, even though it was partly true. This was the line he'd been planning to use to open conversation with the beautiful younger Miss Trelawny.

"I believe I can be at least as helpful as my daughter in that respect, Mr Jackson."

"Of course … please. Anything you can tell me."

So she began – the unabridged guide to what to do and where to go in Cornwall, listing every conceivable tourist attraction from the surfer's paradise at Newquay to the cliffs and caverns of Land's End, and all delivered in curt monotone. By the time she'd finished, Pete was feeling the heat, nodding repeatedly, sweat pooling on his brow.

"The only place I advise you avoid is St Jute's Head." She nodded across the bay towards the distant promontory. "The ferry crossing is longer than they advertise at the jetties in town, and, like many of these remote religious sites, there really isn't a lot to see once you get there. I can't tell you the number of guests I've had who've complained about wasting whole days visiting it."

Pete, who was now retreating towards the gate, assured the old lady that he and Sarah would not be making that mistake.

*

The Green Bath

"I told you it was one of the places I wanted to go to," Sarah said later on, as they climbed aboard the St Jute's ferry in Penzakhy harbour.

They found seats on a hard wooden bench, squashed between other tourists, the sun beating down on them. Pete explained once again, very patiently, what he had been told.

"I thought *you* were the one who didn't like lying on beaches all day?" Sarah said.

"It's just what I've heard."

"Well I've heard differently. It's supposed to be fantastic."

Pete held his hands up. "It hardly matters. We're going anyway, aren't we?"

Sarah pouted beneath her wide-brimmed straw hat, an expression that she knew Pete found irresistible. After a moment, he placed a hand on her thigh. She'd changed her bikini for a more sensible pink T-shirt and denim mini-skirt, but there was still plenty of leg on offer. Earlier on, he'd noticed the two boatmen who'd helped them aboard leering at her from behind, and he wondered how they'd have reacted if Carla Trelawny had arrived dressed in such provocative fashion. His heart began to thump, and he tightened his grip on her leg.

She regarded him coolly. "Didn't you get enough last night?"

"I'm desperate," he whispered.

Sarah edged primly away. "Well you'll have to be patient. Good things come to those who wait."

*

Saint Jute was an Irish monk who had allegedly arrived in Cornwall in 564 AD. He'd made his hermitage on the first place he'd set his holy feet – the rocky spur of land jutting out into Penzakhy bay, now known as St Jute's Head. A boathouse and an English Heritage-run gift shop and restaurant were located in the small cove serving as its harbour, but aside from

The Green Bath

that, it was a completely natural attraction. Steep paths wound around it or up to its precarious summit, where magnificent views could be had of the coastline. Internally, it was riddled with caves.

Pete and Sarah ate a simple but expensive meal in the restaurant, and spent the next two hours exploring the islet. It was certainly atmospheric. The higher paths were perilous, steep and crumbling, the overhangs above them tufted with cormorant nests. The caves were deep and echoing, and smelled strongly of the ocean. On one occasion, Pete glanced down a tunnel to its far end, and thought he saw a tall female figure etched against a backdrop of sunlight and waves. Curious, he wandered down there, only to find himself alone on a strip of shingle at the head of a narrow inlet. The sea inside it swirled darkly, foam hissing and frothing on the surface.

Later on, in the gift shop, Sarah bought a few trinkets.

"It's a nice place but I can't imagine why Saint Jute wanted to spend the rest of his life here," she said, handing Pete a small, flat sliver of granite that had been shaped like a cross and was now attached to a leather thong.

"Probably didn't cost him as much as it cost us," Pete replied. "What's this?"

"Good luck charm." She wrote a cheque for the woman behind the counter. "Rather nice, don't you think? Apparently it's carved from the very stone Saint Jute first stood on."

"The locals swear by them," the counter lady chipped in. She was rotund and middle-aged, and clad in a woolly cardigan despite the weather. She had a mass of grey-blonde curls and a kindly face, which wrinkled all over when she smiled. "Saint Jute is considered a very powerful saint, despite his being confined to this islet."

"Confined?" Sarah said.

"Legend tells how he wanted to come ashore, but was never able." The lady beamed. "Typically, it doesn't say why. Of course, this coast was uninhabited then, and very wild. Most of

The Green Bath

the country was pagan."

"How fascinating," Sarah replied.

"Yeah," Pete agreed, turning and ambling outside.

Sarah joined him as they stood on the stone quay facing into the little harbour. Other tourists gathered beside them. The ferry was just rounding the headland.

"I want you to put that crucifix on," Sarah whispered.

Pete grimaced. "Oh, give me a break."

She kissed him on the cheek. "Just for me, please. Who knows, your luck might change."

Grudgingly, he dug the charm out of his jeans pocket, looped it over his head, and tucked the pendant beneath his T-shirt. "Satisfied?"

Her delighted smile showed that she was. She licked her lips to moisten them.

Pete felt his cheeks flush.

Ten minutes later, they were back on the ferry, chugging towards Penzakhy. As before, they were squashed together on a hard wooden bench. As before, Pete was acutely aware of his wife's curves, and she apparently of his, because, when nobody else was looking, she casually placed a hand on his crotch. Instantly, he stiffened inside his jeans.

"Oooh," she said quietly. "What a reaction."

"Christ, Sarah," he muttered.

She took her hand away, and leaned against his ear. "Guess what I'm not wearing today."

He looked slowly round at her, and then down at the denim mini-skirt. "You're joking?"

Her eyes gleamed.

"All day?"

She smiled wickedly. "I told you your luck might change."

Pete thought he was going to burst out of his pants. It seemed to take an age to get back to Penzakhy, never mind back to the villa, but once they were inside the front door, Pete shoved his wife roughly against the wall, his mouth planted on hers, one hand under the short skirt, his fingers rolling in her

The Green Bath

moist, naked pubis. A second later, she'd released him from his jeans and he speared her to the wooden panelling, hammering her loins with bestial force. Sarah was normally quiet during love, but now she cried out hoarsely, again and again.

It went on for several hours and multiple orgasms.

They had each other on the hall carpet, on the stairs, over the banisters, in the kitchen and lounge, and finally in the bedroom, rolling on the mattress, bucking so hard together that at one point the headboard struck the wall with a deafening 'thwack' and the plaster cracked.

*

It was late evening before Sarah climbed wearily to her feet and drifted from the bedroom. Pete turned over, pulling the duvet to his ears. He was spent: totally exhausted, every muscle cramped, his cock shrivelled like the stub of a melted candle. He heard the sound of a bath running – distant thunder as hot, clean water struck the bottom of the tub. Slowly, he tumbled into a void.

It wasn't quite dawn when he awoke, lying in the half-darkness, sweating feverishly, one hand clamped on a painful erection. At first he didn't know where he was or what was happening. Then he remembered the dream he'd just had – or at least part of it; the part where Carla Trelawny, clad only in bra and heels, had squatted and lowered her open sex onto Sarah's willing, wet-lipped mouth.

Pete staggered to his feet and moved to the window. Beyond the thin curtain, a milky mist hung over the sea. The beach and footpaths were deserted. It crossed his mind that this was unnatural, that he must have shot his juice four times the previous night – yet he was agonised with arousal. Raw though his manhood felt, he had to fuck again; he just had to. His balls were tight as duck eggs. His tip was wet with pre-ejaculation fluid.

The Green Bath

"Sarah," he mumbled, moving back to the bed.

But Sarah wasn't there. Her indentation was cold and crumpled. By the looks of it, she hadn't been in bed for some considerable time. Pete's desire ebbed a little. He straightened up, confused. Wandering out onto the landing, he saw that all the lights were off. There were no sounds from the kitchen or lavatory.

"Sarah!" he called. Still there was no reply.

He began to search, one bedroom after another, wondering if in her stupor, she'd inadvertently gone back to the wrong room. He tried to remember what their last movements had been, though all he could recall was the musky smell and hot, wet grip of her vagina. He stiffened again, and he cursed under his breath. Where the hell was the woman when he needed her so badly?

That was when he heard a faint sound of water.

He stopped and listened.

It came again: a soft *splash*, like a drip landing in a full bowl.

Now he remembered – she'd been having a bath.

Pete turned and saw the door to the green bathroom yawning open. It was dark inside. No further sounds came out. A truly horrific thought struck him. She hadn't fallen asleep? Not in a bath that size!

"Christ, no…"

He blundered quickly in, yanking the light-cord. There was an electric hum, a flicker, and the bulb came on. The bath was almost full, and Sarah was in it, eyes closed. She hadn't slid under but was lying at one end, her head and shoulders propped up so that she was only submerged to the chin. Pete scrambled forwards. As he did, Sarah groaned and moved slightly. Relief hit him. He sank to his knees.

By the looks of it, she'd been sleeping in here all night. When he shook her, the water lapped over his hands – it was cold and clammy, with a greenish, scummy tinge.

"Sarah, snap out of it," he said irritably. "You'll catch your

The Green Bath

death." Groggily, she awoke. As he helped her out and led her to the bedroom, she leaned heavily on him. "You're lucky you've not drowned."

His erection was still firm, pressing against her cold, damp body, but she was almost comatose, and it quickly became clear there'd be no further fun and games that night.

"I feel awful," she mumbled, as he laid her on the bed.

"I'm not surprised." He towelled her down. "What the hell were you thinking?"

Sarah made no reply, just pulled the duvet up and rolled over.

Pete padded back into the bathroom, and stood looking at the tub. He'd once read that it was impossible for an adult to drown in a bath by falling asleep. Supposedly, the act of immersion would immediately wake you up. Even so, he felt that Sarah had been lucky. He imagined that a horse could drown in this bath. It was the biggest he had ever seen. In addition, judging by the colour of the water in it, it needed re-plumbing. He unplugged it and stood watching as the stained liquid gurgled down the hole at astonishing speed. It swirled away in less than a minute, the last drops draining from sight with an echoing 'slurp', which sounded almost organic.

*

Pete awoke several hours later to find Sarah sitting up stiffly. When he opened the curtain, she shielded her eyes against the brilliant daylight. Her pallor was ashen.

"Did we get drunk last night?" she croaked.

"Not as I remember."

She stood up weakly. "I'm having a bath. I feel terrible."

"Haven't you had enough baths for one holiday?"

She gave him a quizzical look.

"You don't remember?" he said.

She waved his question away, and stumbled out onto the landing. Soon he heard water thundering in the green

The Green Bath

bathroom.

"Sarah," he shouted. "I wouldn't use that one ... there's something wrong with the plumbing."

She gave no answer. He heard the sloshing of water as she settled into it.

"Up to you, babes," he muttered. "Don't listen to me. I'm only the one who saved your life last night."

Pete couldn't help feeling a little peeved. He hoped this 'not feeling well' routine didn't mean no more mattress sports for the holiday. Not when he'd suddenly found reserves of sexual energy that he must have been saving up since his youth.

Eventually, he put his shorts and T-shirt on, and went into the bathroom. The air in there was hot and steamy, the green-tiled walls streaming with condensation. Sarah was still soaking in the tub, her eyes half closed. Strangely, the water looked clean and fresh, albeit covered with suds. His fantasy about Carla Trelawny, up to her breasts in bubble bath, came back to him.

"You okay?" he asked.

"No," Sarah groaned. "Every part of me's aching. I'm sorry Pete ... I think I've got the flu or something."

"Bath not helping?"

"It's making me feel all numb."

He was tempted to ask her why she didn't get out of it then, but something stopped him.

Instead, he went back to the bedroom, and stood by the bay window, watching the *De Luxe*. It looked as gaunt and decayed as before. The overgrown gardens were lush and still, basking in the heat. There was no sign of either of the two women, though the front door, as always, stood open. It took him several seconds to make his mind up. He pulled his trainers on and made his way downstairs, calling to Sarah that he was nipping out. Her semi-audible reply confirmed that she neither suspected anything nor cared.

His mind was awash with thoughts and fears as he left the front of the villa and set off down the drive. It was just a

The Green Bath

physical need, he told himself. It didn't mean anything. He loved his wife, but he couldn't get Carla Trelawny out of his mind. Good grief, she was the most desirable woman he'd ever seen, and if those goods were genuinely on offer, as he suspected, it was a crime not to sample them.

When he reached the entrance to the *De Luxe*, he hesitated. He wondered if it would be politick to call out, to ask if there was anyone at home. If the old woman answered, he could hit her with some excuse, like he had before. On the other hand, might calling out alert her to his presence when there was no need? Suppose she was in, but asleep or busy in another part of the building? If he got inside *furtively*, he could perform sex acts with her daughter while she was in the next room. How horny an idea was that? The mere thought set him straining at his flies.

Shivering with excitement, he ventured inside.

The passage, which was dark and cluttered with planks and waste paper, branched almost immediately. To his right, it led into what looked like an old bar area. Pete gazed in. The carpets were black with dirt, strewn with up-ended tables and stools. The bar counter was draped with cobwebs. Behind it, empty shelves gathered dust. A central section of the wall was bare, where a mirror had been removed. Blinds were drawn on all the windows.

Once again, Pete felt his ardour cool. If this place was supposedly being refurbished, it had a long way to go yet. He turned left and found access to the next area barred by a musty drape. He listened at it, but, hearing nothing, pulled it aside and stuck his head through. By his reckoning, he was now looking into the part of the ground floor which the two women used as their living quarters, but what he was seeing could hardly be right.

If anything, this part of the hotel was even more dilapidated than the rest. By the mildewed remnants of armchairs, it had once been a lounge, but now it was more like a cave. A saline, fishy stench was everywhere. The walls were green with age

The Green Bath

and damp. Vegetation grew up through the rotted floorboards, which were littered with garbage of every description – empty bottles and cans, dried husks of fruit. Strips of creeper dangled down through numerous rents in the ceiling.

Pete wondered if he was hallucinating. This was the sort of thing you saw in buildings that had been abandoned for decades. It surely wasn't possible that anyone could be living here. He remembered the hotel's proximity to the rampant vegetation outside – the way it festooned the walls and eaves like some kind of parasite. The farthest end of the room had literally been inundated. It was dense with greenery – greenery that was twitching, as if a breeze was blowing. Or as if something concealed inside it was slowly emerging.

For all that it smelled of the sea in here, the room was close, the air hot and stagnant. Suddenly, Pete knew that he had to get out. The reek was overpowering, the muggy heat unbearable.

He staggered outside and down the path. Even in the cooler confines of the villa, the sour stink hung about him, the sweat stayed sticky on his brow. The thought that he'd been inside that squalid pit next door made him itch all over. Scratching himself, he went up the stairs, glanced once into the bedroom, where Sarah, having bathed yet again was now back in bed, fast asleep, then moved into the green bathroom, which was still damp and warm, and turned on the taps. Clear water gushed into the tub, sparkling with sunlight.

Stripping his greasy clothes off, Pete climbed into it. It was deeper even than it looked. Though it was only half-full, he lay back and found the water level as high as his chin. He closed his eyes, but relaxation didn't come quickly. It wasn't as easy to wash away the guilt of what he'd almost done, as it was the sweat and grime. He noticed that his chest and neck were chafing him. Reaching up, he was surprised to find that he was still wearing the tiny granite cross from the gift shop on St Jute's. He clung onto it, in two minds whether or not to take it off. Slowly the muscle in his arm loosened, and his hand

The Green Bath

dropped back into the water.

There was a low hiss, like an intake of breath.

Pete's eyes snapped open. Was somebody in the bathroom with him? It was so clouded with steam that for a moment he couldn't see. But then a dim outline became clear.

"Sarah, what're you…" But his words faltered as the intruder stepped into view.

It was Carla Trelawny.

Her hair hung over her shoulders in a tawny cascade. She wore only a filmy nightgown, through which he could clearly see the firm globes of her breasts, their nipples prominent against the thin material, and down below that, between her thighs, a dark triangular patch.

Pete's throat went dry. The hair prickled his scalp.

And suddenly she wasn't there anymore.

Shaking himself, as though from a mid-day snooze, he rose quickly to his feet, scanning the billows of steam. The various corners of the room came in and out of view intermittently, but nobody else was in there with him.

He remained standing, unsure about what he'd just seen. One half of him wanted it to have been real; the other was relieved that it hadn't been. He climbed from the tub and peeked around the bathroom door. Outside, the landing was deserted. From the bedroom, he could hear Sarah's soft breathing. His wife wasn't well, he realised, with another pang of guilt. She wasn't well at all. Then a crazy thought occurred to him about why that might be. A *totally* crazy thought…

"Peter," a soft voice said.

He turned sharply.

He hadn't been dreaming after all

Carla was framed in the doorway to the next bedroom, stark naked. Not even wearing that indecent nightgown. She watched him coyly, hands clasped behind her back, schoolgirl style.

"Like what you see?" she asked.

Pete didn't need to answer. She glanced at his manhood,

The Green Bath

then back to his face. Her eyes glittered like emeralds. Again he said nothing, though he could hardly conceal his hunger. She came lithely up to him.

"Awww ... don't you want me?" she asked, sounding disappointed that she'd had to make the first move. One of her hands crept onto his shoulder. The other drifted down over his belly. "Well?"

Still he said nothing.

She seized his member, her grip tight and cool. "Show me!" she hissed. "Show me how much you want me!"

Unable to resist any longer, he pulled her to him and smothered her mouth with his own. She responded hungrily, rolling her tongue around his, sinking her claws into the flesh of his shoulder. They kissed with a passion so intense that it was almost painful. She pushed him backwards – until they came up against a door. It opened. For an alarming second, Pete thought she was steering him into the bedroom where Sarah was sleeping, perhaps thinking they were alone. Only for the familiar heat and steam of the bathroom to envelop them.

The kiss lingered, Carla's sweet tongue snaking into every corner of Pete's mouth, finding depths he hadn't thought possible. He ran his hands down the contours of her back, to the cleft of her buttocks. She opened her legs slightly, to allow him access to her secrets. Now the rim of the tub was pressing into the back of his legs. He could feel the heat rising from the deep water directly behind him. Was that the greenish tint of metal he saw in it? Or something else?

The stone cross itched at his throat.

Thoughts of Sarah lying ill in the next room rushed back to him. Ill because of this bath, which now that he thought clearly about it, was not shaped much like a bath at all – but more like a mouth; a gigantic, gaping mouth.

Carla pulled back from him, saliva stringing between their lips. She smiled lasciviously, before grabbing at his crucifix, and wrenching it loose from his neck. Pete reacted instinctively, snatching hold of her wrist. She laughed to see

The Green Bath

the startled look on his face – and it wasn't a pleasant laugh. There was cruelty in it, mockery. She tried to kiss him again, but this time he resisted, and, absurdly, found himself wrestling with her, both their feet sliding on the wet tiles.

With more effort than he'd have believed possible, he managed to yank the crucifix from her grasp.

"Pete?" he thought he heard Sarah mumble in the next room.

Carla laughed again, loudly.

"For God's sake, shut the fuck up!" he hissed.

Carla reached up for his cheek. He thought she was going to stroke him, but instead she clawed him, drawing three bloody trails with her long, lacquered nails.

Gasping, he tried to push her back, but she didn't move and now reached for the other side of his face. This time he caught her hand, and pressed something into its palm – the crucifix. He wasn't sure whether or not he genuinely expected the flesh to start smoking, and Carla to shriek in pain and despair, but he didn't expect nothing at all to happen. Nor did he expect her to suddenly grab at his throat, and catch it in a vice-like grip.

Gargling for breath, Pete felt himself tottering towards the bath.

"You can have this body, this fleshy puppet," she snarled. "If that's what it takes. And that's always what it takes ... but no matter. It's no cost to me, and I *will* drink of you..."

"Pete ... what's happening?" Sarah moaned. She was just outside the bathroom door. "What are you doing?"

Pete's throat was too constricted even to draw breath. He was a big guy – six feet and three inches tall, over fifteen stones in weight – yet this woman (puppet?), was not only shoving him backwards towards the bath, but, with one hand, was choking the life out of him. Again he pressed the crucifix against her, this time on her wrist. Again it failed to sear her. So, thinking more practically, he turned it on its end, and this time *dug* it into her – using all his strength.

Carla grimaced as blood welled up in a globule where the

The Green Bath

skin on her forearm was suddenly brutally punctured. She yanked her arm away, screaming – but with rage rather than pain, and Pete caught her with a right hook, which sent her staggering sideways.

"Old Saint Jute wasn't strong enough to resist, was he!" he said. "At least … he didn't trust himself to resist. Which is why he stayed put!"

She glared at him, froth seething from her mouth, before throwing herself forwards again. Her breath turned fetid as she grappled with him. Again, her strength and ferocity were enormous, but her feet slid on the floor-tiles, and she lost her balance, half-falling. Pete manoeuvred himself behind her, crooking one arm around her neck, yanking her head back.

She slashed at him with her nails, leaving more livid wounds on his ribs. Sweat-soaked hair filled his mouth. It tasted like seaweed. They crashed against the tub, and rotted wooden panels sprang free, a mass of sodden vegetation rolling out in dark and glistening coils.

Now it was Pete's turn to slip on the tiles. Carla twisted free of him and spun around, spitting something unintelligible, her talons raised above her head – only for Pete to lower himself and charge, barrelling into her midriff, sending her backwards into the tub, plunging her beneath the water.

She rent at his arms and chest as she went, but he launched himself in after her, pressing her down with all his weight, pinning her to the cast-iron bottom.

The water began to boil, turning acid-green.

Carla continued to fight, raking and tearing but gradually weakening. At the same time, Pete, with his hands locked on her throat, felt an energy surge through him the like of which he'd never known. His sinews knotted as visions swam before his eyes: awesome oceanic depths, rumbling chasms, surf crashing and roaring, and then, through a haze of spume, a jagged, rocky coastline, thick with primeval woodland.

The force of it rocked him and years were sloughed off him. He laughed and cried at the same time as youthful strength flowed though his body like wine.

*

Minutes passed before he realised that Carla had given up the fight.

He glanced down, his brow beaded with sweat, his muscles standing out like wood. She lay on the bottom, glaring balefully at him through the clouded surface. It went without saying that she now looked very different, and frankly, he didn't want to see the details.

He rose and mopped his face. The tangled mat of herbage that had spilled out from under the bath was already mottled and dying, but Pete ignored it. Briefly, he examined the gashes on his arms and body, before going out onto the landing. Sarah was lying in a swoon on the carpet. He picked her up, and took her through to the bedroom, where he laid her on the bed. It came as no surprise to see strands of vegetation poking through the split in the plaster caused the night before by the headboard. Like the foliage in the bathroom, it already appeared to be withering.

Sarah now opened her eyes. She looked pale and washed-out. "Why ... you packing?" she asked weakly, as Pete threw clothes together.

"We're going home," he said. "You're not well ... and I've an idea the key is getting you away from this place. Don't worry, I'll sort things out."

After he'd collected everything, stuffed it into the cases and closed them, he helped her from the bed and began to dress her. He paid no attention to the shivering, dripping form, which slunk quietly past the bedroom door and down the stairs.

Ten minutes later, Sarah was in the car, still half-asleep but fastened securely into the front seat. Before climbing in himself, Pete walked up the hotel path. The fibrous jungle which had once linked the two buildings together had reddened to an autumnal hue – leaves had fallen, young shoots drooped

The Green Bath

and desiccated. He felt no remorse as he gazed at it, no pity or sorrow, and definitely no fear. He regarded the darkened doorway. As always it hung open, but now a trail of slime led into it.

"These belong to you," he shouted, tossing in the villa keys. "I don't know who or what you are … plant, animal, both. I don't know how many faces you can present to the world. I don't even know how you came to take root here when you obviously come from somewhere very different. But, if you can always stir these things in people that make them so choice for you, I suspect you're home from home. Don't worry … I could go out and warn folk, but who would believe me? Perhaps it's best if they discover for themselves their strengths and weaknesses. In that respect I don't need to wish you good luck, because I don't think you'll need it."

He walked back to the road, climbed into his car and switched the engine on. He didn't notice the shrivelled, green claw in the hotel side-window, weakly adjusting the curtain. If he had, he wouldn't have worried. Pete now had important reasons for getting home. Apart from Sarah, there was the matter of work. He needed an urgent meeting with Managing Director Perkins – about that editor's job.

Good Christ, some bastard had to get a grip up there.

TELLING

Steve Rasnic Tem

Before he met Maggie, he thought he understood the difference between sense and nonsense. By the end, and he could smell it coming – redolent of fish and sweaty sheets – he could hardly tell the difference between breath and flesh.

They had visited three, four hundred houses for sale. They had driven down every street in the county, every nameless lane. They had done this in late October, with a layer of ice-capped snow on the ground, the wind low but steady enough to scour the back of your throat until you were made inarticulate.

Wayne did not complain, but it was painful, creeping along, enduring the stares of suspicious neighbours, as in the shaded lanes the ice cracked and exploded beneath his tyres. It might have been better if he'd had any idea what she was looking for, but she did not share her criteria. Wayne supposed that was what artists were like. But it exhausted the people who loved them.

In most cases a relatively slow drive-by was sufficient: the house would apparently be in the wrong architectural style, or too tall, or too wide. He wasn't permitted to say anything – he couldn't even hum while he was driving. And now and then she would insist that they step inside, or walk around, or lie on the floor and gaze at the ceiling. Wayne had been unemployed two years, but he did have his real estate license - for once that made him feel useful.

Wayne didn't enjoy any of it. He especially didn't enjoy lying on those dusty floors, looking into those crusty ceilings, inviting dust into his eyes, dust into his mouth, where it tasted aspirin bitter, like all that was left by the end of the day, like the end of life itself.

He had no idea why they were doing it, except Maggie said it was something she needed to do before she could choose the right house. And as much as she annoyed and infuriated him,

Telling

Wayne adored Maggie, and would do anything she asked.

"This is the one," she said. "Finally, this is the one. I can feel it."

The house was in worse shape than most of the others. Unpainted grey boards pushed through tatters of off-white colour. Inside, the walls were thin as paper. Wayne imagined he could see the colours of the next room bleeding through.

"If you dropped something you'd hear it in every room of the house." As if on cue, vague, hesitant sounds travelled from the other end of the house, or farther.

Maggie hadn't heard, or ignored them. "But that's a good thing, isn't it? Nothing can ever sneak up on you."

The fact that something sneaking up was even a consideration appalled him. "It smells funny in here," he said. "Are you sure you can live in a place that smells funny?"

"They make paint with chemicals that kill the odour."

And that was that. She'd made up her mind. He supposed she didn't care how the place smelled. For him it was as if he'd crawled inside a loaf of old, damp bread. The rich stink filled the nose and spilled over into the mouth. He imagined a sponginess in the wood open to rot, mould, mildew.

Sun glare flashed through the window glass. A suggestion of double-exposed imagery floated across the wall. But when he shifted his head slightly it had gone. Maggie had chosen, and he had to make the best of it. It was her money.

The day after they closed, Wayne had their bedroom ready. By evening they had the appliances arranged in a rudimentary kitchen. He spent a difficult weekend stocking Maggie's new studio with paints, canvases, and a myriad other supplies.

In her studio he watched as she put the finishing touches on a new painting. Maggie never seemed to mind his visits to her workplace – often she invited him. It didn't seem to matter how unfinished a piece might be.

But then she always acted as if he wasn't there. Her focus could be disturbing, the way she stared at the canvas, aggressively applying paint, not even bothering to check her

Telling

pigments, holding her breath, unable to do anything else until the canvas filled with colour.

It was one of her house paintings. Almost all of her paintings were of houses, at least as long as he'd known her. Those paintings had proved surprisingly popular in the galleries – they were the reason they could afford to buy this house, and pay for everything else. "They work because the right house will remind us of other houses important in our lives," she explained. "They resonate. You look at certain houses, and you can just imagine the lives of the people inside, trapped by those walls, or lovingly embraced. Their experience is also our own."

When Maggie painted it was always an attack upon the canvas. She thickened the acrylic paint until it was the consistency of brilliantly coloured liquid clay. She shovelled the colour onto the surface, then worked quickly to create vegetation, planks, timbers, brick, doors, windows, roofs, sky. He was always surprised when her fury suddenly turned a chaos of swirling thick colour into something recognisable.

But what was even more surprising was that something extraordinarily appealing resulted from this process. These were the prettiest, most intensely welcoming houses he'd ever seen.

"So what do you think?" she asked.

The painting *was* like all the others, but he could sense subtle differences. "The lines around the door, the porch roof, that window, it's like *this* house, isn't it?"

"In better days, yes. Or maybe the way it will be, after we finish fixing it up."

"So this place is the model you were looking for?"

"Maybe I've been painting it since the beginning, the spaces, the lines. It's like I was trying to recall it."

"Then you've been here before?"

"No – I'm sure I haven't."

"Maybe with your dad?" It was a risk – her father had always been a sore point.

Telling

"No – I don't think so. The house he moved into after the divorce may have been similar. I stayed there summers until I graduated from high school, a few years before his death."

"It would have helped if I'd known what we were looking for."

"I couldn't have put it into words before now. I'm a picture person, not a word person. I had to see it, be inside it, and then start painting it. That's the way I've always found out things about myself. I've never been here, Wayne, but maybe someone like me lived here, or at least nearby. Someone I'm in sympathy with."

"So – living with your dad, that was hard?"

She nodded silently, then the tears began to drop. He started toward her but she held up her hand. "Sorry. I don't know why I get like this. It was a *sad* time, but you know how kids are. You can't think of much outside yourself. I'm not aware of hating that house, but I don't remember ever actually *being* in it. I remember saying goodbye to my mom, and starting out on this long bus trip, but I can't remember ever arriving, living with my dad, or anything about his house. I do remember telling my mother I could never go back, and my mother telling me I *had* to go back."

He listened, but he couldn't take his eyes off the new canvas. There was an out-of-place shadow peeking out of the upstairs front window: faded, sepia-coloured, uninvited.

Maggie worked late into the evening. Early the next morning Wayne left the house so as not to disturb her sleep. It was cold for working outdoors, but he could at least clear some of the dead vegetation out of the back yard.

He removed a large quantity of dead brush before he could see the ground. And even after he'd got rid of the taller plants he'd get the occasional slap, the random clawing from some unseen branch or stalk, like an untrimmed fingernail tracing the skin. Nothing terribly serious, but enough to well the blood.

A blurred shadow loomed beyond the last sweep of netted

Telling

branches. With his sleeve he brushed a gritty paste of chaff and blood from his face. "Maggie? You're up?" But when his vision cleared no one was there. He exhaled in exasperation. The fogged air hung suspended, as if poised.

As he removed dead flowers, the stray remains of potatoes, an onion or two, he began finding ash spread under everything, and bits of foundation from an old wall. An impatient weight crouched nearby, waiting for him to look up, which he eventually did, and found nothing. That was when he heard Maggie yelling from inside the house.

*

She was on her hands and knees in her studio. He dropped beside her and laid one hand gently on her back. "What happened?"

She shook her head, ran a finger up and down one of the wide gaps between the floor planks. Extensive sections of the ceiling below were missing, so that he could see most of the living room on the first floor.

"I don't know what time I got to bed last night, but when I woke up I was anxious to get back to the painting. Then as I was picking up the brush I smelled something – I don't know – smoky, but terribly sour as well, like overpowering body odour. I felt threatened, as if the stench might smother me. I looked down, and there was this person standing under me. His clothes were dark, dripping and greasy. And then he shifted, and he was looking at me. Two white, shiny spots staring up at me, but *Wayne*, no pupils."

It took him minutes to check the house and yard. He rushed in to tell her he'd found nothing. She was still sitting on the floor, shaking. "You say you just woke up. It was probably just a shadow, the light confusing you."

She shook her head. Then Wayne noticed the new painting. Despite the obscuring strokes of shadow and translucent mist it was still recognisably the same house, but done in a much

Telling

darker colour palette: greys, burnt umber, deep purple, shades of black and the evening blues. Deepest night. Deepest dream.

"I probably won't be able to sell my usual clients this one."

"Unwelcoming is the word, I guess."

"It terrifies me."

"Then stop working on it."

"I really don't think I can paint anything else until I can finish this one."

It *was* powerful. A series of vaguely realised trees led you to the front porch, caked in soot, deteriorating under the assault of some oily disease. A gauze of fog hung from the porch roof. But something more: a blurred presence seemed to be arriving out of the darkness from the back of the porch. Wayne wondered if it might not be the figure from the upstairs window in the previous, daylight painting, now come down for the evening, and come out.

"I don't know why we came here."

Wayne grabbed her hand. "It's like you said, houses and people resonate. You're here because of someone who lived here before. You're here because of whatever happened to them."

*

Every evening Maggie worked on the new painting into the early morning hours. Wayne had never known her to take so long with an individual work – usually she finished them in a couple of days. But she revisited the same areas of canvas again and again, applying additional thin layers of sombre colour, constantly revising lines and shades as she apparently grew closer to her vision.

Each morning when Wayne got up he checked the painting: the blurred figure slightly more resolved, its position slightly shifted on the porch, as if it were pacing. After a few more nights it had left the porch, and was making its way up the sidewalk.

Telling

Wayne moved forward on repairs to the house and yard, although concerns over Maggie slowed him. He put a ceiling up in the living room, hoping it might comfort her that she no longer had that god's-eye glimpse into their downstairs. The backyard didn't look so much like a refuse pile anymore. The uncovered foundation proved to extend to all points in the yard – the building it once supported the size of a full house. He also uncovered bits of an old flagstone walk leading back to the alley that ran behind the long row of neighbouring houses.

A night came that Maggie collapsed early, and for once he was the late one up, reading, listening.

At first he thought the breathing he heard might be his own – the book, about secrets and lies and misunderstood identities, had made him tense. But when he put it down and laid his hand on his chest, he realised the rapid panting was more distant – somewhere down the hall and up the stairs. As he made that journey the panting grew louder, and the loudness of it made him think of a dog, the way a dog breathes with his entire body, especially when in pain, heaving and exhaling, unlike people who tend to breathe shallowly from their chests.

The pale little blonde girl lay with her back to him across two steps near the top of the stairs. Her body heaved like an injured dog's. Shadows gathered along her spine: hand-shaped bruises, ending in a crown of yellow curls streaked with dark blood.

Something burned his nostrils – an acrid stench of urine. But he could find no signs of a spreading stain beneath her.

He wanted to say something, but was afraid. And he dared not touch that tender, panting shape. Suddenly coughing violently, she faded into deep shadow, then lit up again with each new intake of breath. What could he do for her? Spying on her in her old distress was some kind of violation, so he slowly crept backwards down the stairs. At the last moment her head jerked up, staring at the door at the top of the stairs. Her body started to slide toward him as she made ready her escape, but he turned and made his way downstairs and to bed.

Telling

*

"Wayne! Wayne, I want to leave!" He awakened with Maggie's face a collapsed moon hanging over him, her fingers clawing his shoulder. "Now! We have to leave! Please, Wayne."

"Of course." He jerked himself from bed, dragging at his pants. "Just let me get a bag."

"No!" she screamed. Shocked, he stumbled backwards onto the bed. "We have to leave! We have to get into the car! Please!"

"Okay, honey. I'm getting my clothes on right now."

She was unsteady on her feet. They stumbled into the hall. Then she cried, "Wait! Wait right here so I'll know where you are." Then she raced away.

Wayne was just outside her open studio door. In the painting the shadow-wrapped figure was almost to the end of the sidewalk, ready to step out of the canvas. The floppy hat was pulled down over his face. *That's his house in the yard. That was his poor child on the stairs. They're why we're here.*

"Ready! Let's go, Wayne!" She carried a pillow and blanket under one arm, a butcher knife raised in her other hand. He hurried over, pushed down the arm with the knife. "I need the knife! I have to protect myself!" They started down.

She insisted on sitting in the back seat, the pillow in her lap, the blanket over her, the knife ready in her hand. Wayne didn't ask where they were going, just pulled away from the curb.

He knew immediately that things had changed. Roads and houses, fences and fields, rearranged. When he got halfway down their street it ended in a left-hand turn, with nothing ahead where street used to be but a hayfield studded in bales. He didn't know what else to do but follow the turn.

After a short distance he had to turn again. The road narrowed, the pavement deteriorated. Soon they were on a dirt road, and headed back in the direction of the house. Maggie

Telling

stared out the window intently.

She must have realised about the same time he did that they were actually in the alley that ran behind their house. But it was dirt now, and the houses faced it. She began rocking the pillow in her lap, making soft soothing sounds. "Did you see the little girl, Wayne? Did you see her? She was just like I used to be. We have to tell someone!"

Before they reached their own house, he realised something large was blocking their view of it. Then he understood the buried foundation had suddenly grown an old dilapidated house.

Maggie started wailing when they saw the hulking dark figure by the edge of the road. Their headlights caught a glimpse of an old see-saw, the pale children teetering there, wide eyes reflecting like cats'.

"Oh, Wayne we have to tell, we have to tell! That poor little girl!"

"We will, honey, we will," he promised, although there was no one left alive to tell.

When the man began lifting his face out from under that floppy brim Maggie was screaming so loudly Wayne couldn't think, and when they'd finally driven past, and made the next turn that would drag them around that house again, Wayne couldn't imagine how they would ever get off that road.

SWELL HEAD

Stephen Volk

My daddy's name was Jarvis, but they called him Rudy and my mother's name was Gillian, but they called her Jake. Don't know why, but that's the way it was. I was born in 1927, which put me between two World Wars, and pretty much that's the way I'd a wanted it.

Skinny ass up on a tractor. Come here, my daddy calls. I was ten, give or take. Not a whole lot going on in my mind except getting that plough line straight as a dead dog's tail. Come on, he said, we're going to the hospital. And I knew my momma was there so I thought something bad had happened, and he seen the fretting on my face and says, Hell, you got yourself a baby brother. What do you think of that? I said I didn't know, and that was the truth. I didn't.

The doctor said, You can't see him just yet. There's been complications.

My daddy asked them what that meant and they said, Like we say, complications. Come back tomorrow.

So we did.

They looked even more uncomfortable then, looking at each other like neither one of them wanted to do the talking. One said, Look, er, sir, you know there's been complications?

My daddy said, Uhuh, I got that. What kind of complications?

So then I guess they told him because they took him into a little room for a while and then down the corridor. I stayed with the lady at the desk. She smelled of perfume. Daddy come back and I asked if he seen him.

He looks okay, he said.

Anyways my baby brother didn't come home in a hurry, and my daddy wasn't cut out to be no cook and he knew it. Our belly rumbles were like cries for my momma to come back, which in time she did, and that's when I got my first glimpse of

Swell Head

him, all swathed in his baby-blue blanket and cooed over as she crossed the threshold, then later when I craned over the crib.

Daddy? Daddy, what's wrong with his head?

Nothing. Nothing's wrong with his head.

He's beautiful, said my momma.

It's ... real big.

No, son. All babies look like that. It's disproportionate, because they got all that growing ahead of them. You'll see.

Course, I didn't see.

That was the complication. The one the doctors had told him about. My brother had a big, big head. When he came into this world, thirty percent bigger than normal. And, this was the worrying part – getting bigger every day.

Pretty soon, three months, four months on, momma couldn't go on disguising the fact, even though she persisted in calling him beautiful. To her he probably was. After all, I'm no oil painting and she loved me fine. That's the deal with mothers. Nature puts that in them. She probably couldn't see him for what he was.

Six months old, he had a body the size of a regular six-month-old baby. Trouble was, his head was – what can I say? Large.

Like somebody was creeping in at night and taking a bicycle pump to his skull and just inflating him all up.

Like a big old soccer ball on the pillow.

Weird thing was, as we observed week in week out, it was like all the feeding and growing went above the neck, while the rest of him stayed the same.

On his first birthday he had the body of a six-month-old attached to the head of an eleven-year-old. This I know because I compared his cranial dimensions to my own with a tape measure stolen temporarily from my momma's sewing box.

She simply put more pillows under him as he grew. Said he had more of a weight to carry than the rest of us.

Swell Head

My, she said, Just wonder at the thinking he'll get to doing. Why, I'll lay money he'll be some kind of doctor or professor, with a brain that size. I'd say that's rare. I'd say we've been blessed.

I, meantime, grew like most kids, skinny and normal.

And he didn't. Well, except for his head, that is. And how.

Not that he complained about it. No, sir. Never did hear him cry or whine about his lot. He just didn't. Maybe he was biding his time for the tragedies to come. Maybe he did know they were coming. If he did, he wasn't telling.

Anyways, momma sung to him real pretty. She had the voice of an angel, my daddy said. When kiddo was bouncing on daddy's knee he kind of – lolled. And instead of cradling him like regular parents do, they cradled his head and let his tiny body, well, dangle, the way a sock hangs off a foot. As an afterthought.

His features were rounded, but not ugly. Kind of soft. Pliable. Open to wonder, the way babies are. Yet the body attached to it remained the size of a Kewpie doll.

I asked my momma if they were going to send him to school. As the day grew near I feared what was expected of me, and what they would make of him. My friends, that is. The ones who had no idea I even had a brother because I sure as hell hadn't told them. Did I have to tell them now? And what would they do when they found out? I'd like to say I was worried on behalf of my brother, but I wasn't. I was worried on behalf on me.

No, he doesn't have to go to school, son, said my momma. We think he's fine right here. And she took my daddy's hand in hers, and I was safe.

After school I'd creep into his bedroom and read to him. Telling him what we did in class that day. His big squidgy head would roll on the bed, staring at the ceiling then lying on its side till he fell asleep, sometimes with my words ringing softly in his ears. The small clothes, baby clothes, even though he was six now and every hat size behind him.

Swell Head

I read *Treasure Island*. He liked that. He liked adventure. Jules Verne. H. G. Wells. He liked travelling to the moon.

Of a night not seldom he used to gaze out his window at the man in the moon up there. Guess he was thinking, look at that feller way up in the heavens, with his big old round head just like mine.

Momma would take one ear and me the other and we'd turn him, so that he wouldn't get bed sores on his chin, and we'd bathe him, wrapping him in towel after towel and dry his hair and momma would comb it neatly with a parting. And sometimes we used to have to keep an eye which way he rolled in his sleep because we thought he might crush his own body under him. We tried to get him to sit in a high chair and join us to eat, but the weight of his head just got too much and the strain of holding it up exhausted him and made him cranky. So we started taking him food to his bed and pretty soon he didn't want to leave that bedroom or that bed, period.

It didn't shock me any more – this head just sitting there, wide as the mattress, tall as I was when I sat there next to him, book open on my lap. No attached body to speak of, just a set of limbs and torso that just seemed to get in the way.

Me and him played games on wet afternoons or when there was no school. Gin rummy and poker for matchsticks. I got riled when he beat me. And he'd poke out his big fat tongue as he clawed up the winnings with his teeny hands and I'd smack him and we'd fight, cat and dog. Oh, yeah.

I wasn't no angel, I admit. He got himself a stack of attention because he was different. And I didn't like it one bit. I resented it. Wasn't very charitable and wasn't very nice, I see that now, sure. But kids are kids, and they see the world like that and that's the way I was.

I said bad things to him on occasion. Occasion, I made him unhappy. Ain't proud of that. Far from it.

But that was a long time ago.

Gotta live with it, and I do.

One time I wanted to go play down by the creek with my

Swell Head

friends and Daddy said no, you got to play with your brother. That got me so mad that I didn't want to be there I pushed him into the fire. Rolled him right into it, jamming him in the orifice like a big damn cork in a bottle. And he hollered. Boy, did he holler. But I held him there and cussed him and said I hated him and called him all the names under God's sun. I even smelled his hair burning.

Got a whupping for that.

Told my Daddy it was all his fault, 'cause he wouldn't let me play in the creek. Said I wished I hadn't got no brother. He said, Hush that right now and remember the Lord Jesus Christ can hear every word you utter, boy.

I said, I ain't bothered Jesus hears nothing.

He said, well you oughta. And consider what you got and that young un ain't. Consider that once in a while.

And I did.

He didn't get hurt. Not permanent. But not a day goes by I don't think about all the nasty things I said and done to him because I knew no better and sometimes I wanted a little helping of the love he got dished up to him every day.

Once a Bible salesman come to the farm and momma gave him tea and the next day in school a kid who was the kid of the Bible salesman asked me, You never told us you got no freak brother, freak.

I said, Yeah, that's 'cause I ain't.

Well, my poppa seen him and he say he so ugly he make the Lord weep. He say he got a head bigger'n the biggest watermelon you ever did see. Bigger'n the stone they rolled to seal Jesus's tomb. He say, such abominations didn't ought to be 'llowed to live.

I said, Give a dang, 'cause I ain't got no brother.

That night they threw stones at our windows. I knew who it was out there.

They yelled out: Swell Head! Swell Head! Swell Head!

And I covered my ears till I couldn't stand it no more. And I looked at my brother and I started shouting at him too: Swell

Swell Head

Head! Swell! Head! Swell Head! And in my bare feet I ran out of that house and down to the kink in the track with the bushes where the voices were coming from. And I stood there with my friends shouting: Swell Head! Swell Head! Swell Head! And I ran off with them into the night, laughing loud as they were. Louder, if I could've.

I stayed out that whole night and came back the next expecting the whupping of my life but the house was real quiet. Daddy was in bed and momma was sewing by candle light. She said my brother been asking after me. Wanted me to sleep with him in his bed. That's what we did. Kept each other warm. She said he missed me. Couldn't get to sleep no other way. I said I was too growed up. There wasn't no room no more. I slept in my own bed that night. I remember it felt real cold.

One day a Carnie Man arrived. Said he was from Coney Island.

I'll give you fifty dollars for that child, sir. I'll take the burden off you good folk right now and give him a good life.

Ain't innerested, said my daddy

Well, I'll up the offer to a hundred.

You got a problem with your ears, mister.

Okay. You country folks drive a hard bargain. One two five. Here in my pocket. Last and final offer.

My last and final offer is you get your fat butt off my land or you get buckshot all over it.

Rebuke to a guardian angel. That's what that is, sir. And I'll avail myself of your company no longer. God be with you. Or not, as may be.

I didn't take to school work. Wasn't scholarly inclined. Not that there was any question that I'd do anything but stay on the family business that was there under my two feet every day when I woke up, the farm my daddy bust his back to keep running. I didn't think it was dumb and I didn't think it was great. You'd have to be crazy to choose that kind of life, but I didn't choose it, it was just there. And I guess my idleness just

Swell Head

accepted it.

We thought the rate of increase might diminish in adulthood, but no. Soon we got worried he'd topple off the bed, so daddy constructed rails either side. Daddy was always constructing little things to make his life a tad more bearable. Like the periscope so he could see the sunrise and sunset, and the picture of the Laughing Cavalier we got from a yard sale.

We'd take turns doing chores, tidying, taking him his food. Having to edge round the bed now because, well, the size of him, his tiny arms nowhere near long enough to be up to the task of feeding himself. Mashed potato was his favourite. Steaks gave him trouble. Meat of any kind. I guess he was a vegetarian.

He also liked TV. *The Lucy Show*. Phil Silvers. He really liked *The Flintstones. The Partridge Family. Starsky and Hutch. Kojak. A Man Called Ironside. Miami Vice. The Streets of San Francisco. Hawaii Five-O*.

He couldn't move round the room much anymore so we put mirrors outside. He could watch cars passing way off on the interstate. He could watch them come into view over the horizon and turn to the other mirror and see them head off south.

Once a car came by, with a bunch teenagers shouting, Swell Head! Swell Head!

I said, Don't listen to them morons.

Maybe they were the morons I'd been to school with. Maybe they were a whole other bunch of morons.

Then there was the surgery. So much surgery I lost count.

What they found was that his body had atrophied. Wasn't no use no more. He was just encumbered by the dead weight of it, what the doctors said. He was absorbing it. Eating himself. But the thing was, it wasn't doing him any good. It was poisoning him. We couldn't get him to the hospital. We had to bring the hospital to him. First he had to have his arms removed, and then his legs. Two different operations. Full anaesthetic, put him out cold. No sooner he recovered from that they said,

Swell Head

Well, we're real sorry 'bout this, but there's more.

My daddy said, More what?

They said, More to do, if you want him to keep living.

He said, I do.

So in the end that tiny torso itself was amputated whole off of him – only his, what they say, vital organs remained, heart, lungs, liver, which the doctors managed to tuck up into the space within his skull cavity and sew him back up. Thank you, Dr Gordon. Thank you, medical team. Not a night I don't say a prayer for you. (And him, obviously.)

Anyways. Result was, my brother had to get used real quick to the fact that what little body he had dangling there was gone forever. He was only a head now – a big, bulbous, still-growing head.

He got awful sick after that. Thought I'd lose the feller. But he was tough. I forgot that. He was tough coming into this world and tough right through, you ask me.

Irony was, he pulled through but my momma didn't.

The strain was all too much for her. Fifteen operations over five years. But not just that. I think the caring for him wore her down, slowly but surely over the years. And the fact she had to hand him over to strangers and was powerless to help him, that finished her. Maybe she worked herself into thinking she was going to lose him and couldn't bear that so wanted to go first. Maybe she reckoned she go right up to heaven and get stuff prepared, like a good mother should.

Without her guiding light, daddy became lost and old and weak. He fell in a field of a heart attack two weeks later, almost like he planned it that way.

Soon after that people from Welfare came. Nice good-meaning folks. Concerned, but I guess that's their job.

You able to care from him here, son?

Always have.

I mean, we can move you. The county will pay. If you want to move.

Move where? I said.

Swell Head

In his best interests.

In his best interests is with me, I said.

So they went.

And that was my brother and me, all on our own...

I had my work cut out. He was outgrowing his bed again. Double bed. King-size. Chin nudging the foot of it. Cheeks hanging over either side. I moved more and more stuff out. There wasn't much room for furniture anymore. Just him and the TV.

I'd go up with his bowl of mashed potato and he'd turn his head to see me, his forehead brushing the light bulb cord. He'd nudge it from side to side like a stray curl of hair. I'd roll him upright. He'd perch on the bed, secured by pillows, making it look like a small nest under him. He was real hard to get under now, to change the bed linen and such, to wash and clean and such. It was hard work. Not that it wasn't hard work before. But the bigger he grew, the harder it got. And it was my job now – nobody else's.

I continued to read to him. New stuff, old stuff. *New York Times*. And not just the funny pages. *International Herald Tribune*.

We continued to watch TV. Oprah. Montel. Jerry.

Sometimes I smelt his hair burning and it makes me feel bad all over again.

Sometimes I heard the trucks going by.

Sometimes I heard their voices calling, Swell Head! Swell Head!

Sometimes I thought of the Carnie Man.

Sometimes I wanted nothing better than to curl up next to him in the dark and feel his warmth as he slept.

What he thought about most of the time, Lord only knew. I never did, never shall.

And that's the truth.

Guess I could have married. If the right woman came along. The right woman didn't come along, so that didn't happen, I guess. No good crying over spilt milk as they say in China.

Swell Head

'Course I had my needs over the years.

So did he.

Naturally, time to time, I did my best to ease 'em. Seemed cruel to me not to make an effort to find some way to satisfy his desires, like any man wants. Any normal man wants. Not that he was – that word, as momma used to say. She didn't like that word used in front of him for obvious reasons.

Still, there were places in Appomattox and beyond, bars mostly, where men in tight shirts hung out and dallied round certain women. Didn't take long to find 'em and didn't take Einstein to work out their occupation, like they found those guys with beer guts and froth in their whiskers so handsome they just had to populate that bar stool showing near enough all they got above the fishnets and enjoying all that fascinating talk. Moses, some o' them practically had dollar signs on their eyeballs. Not that it mattered to either party. Didn't matter to me. Sure as hell didn't matter to my brother. He sure wasn't in no state to be choosy.

Whisky was imbibed. I found it lubricated my persuasive powers and somewhat numbed the face on occasions it was slapped.

Not every girl wanted to come back. Not every girl wanted to leave the bar. Plenty wanted to do whatever it was in a motel room two blocks away like they always did. I'd explain, that'd be fine, but the problem is it ain't for me, it's for my brother. And you look like a nice person, you got a real nice face, it's only a twenty minute drive and I'll bring you right back here to your own front door. By now I'd a told them the whole story. Sometimes they didn't listen or quit and hooked themselves round some other less loquacious loser. Sometimes they half-listened, gleaning the bleary details over a procession of daiquiris. Sometimes they listened to the whole stew pot and said, Where's your car? I got an hour, tops.

It was just a story, right? She said as she stepped inside.

No.

She thought I was crazy and evidently that didn't bother her

Swell Head

till now. Been with plenty of nut jobs over the years, she was thinking. Can't afford to be picky. Let's get this done and over with, fast. I seen it in her eyes, like I seen it in the eyes of all the others. But she covered it well, hoisted her purse strap up her shoulder and smiled good teeth at me.

Nice place. Woman's touch?

Only my momma's. She's long gone.

Kiddin' me. Had you down for a married man.

I said I wasn't.

That don't mean zip. Mind if I smoke?

Down here's fine. But not upstairs. It affects his sinuses.

She looked at the cigarette in her fingers like it was an alien object and put it away. I unnerstand. She smiled again and I could see her thinking, I done lots of weird shit for people who pay for it, this is just more weird shit, that's all.

You got lots of books, mister.

He reads a lot. Not himself. I read to him, aloud.

Like a big old baby. She saw the look on my face and said, I didn't mean that. I don't know what I mean. Maybe I bettern't talk too much. I talk shit.

I think you talk fine.

Well, talking's extra and you're already on the clock. Now she took out the cigarette and lit it, playing with the gold lighter like she was practising a card trick. You got some moonshine? If that ain't possible crack cocaine will do. Jesus, I'm joking. Lighten up, pops. This place's like a mortuary.

I thought you said it had a woman's touch.

I changed my mind. I need some warming on the inside. It's bitter out there.

Jack Daniel's?

To the rim. No water. Then you can have what you paid for. You want to do it here, or in the bedroom?

Me? No. No, ma'am. I thought I made it clear. This ain't for me, miss. I'm sorry. These – services ain't...

I know that's what you *said*. Sure that's what you *said*. That's part of the game, right? The turn-on? The fantasy? The

Swell Head

kick? This fucked-up story of a brother with a head the size of a Hummer who hasn't left his room in forty years, who had his fucking vestigial baby body amputated by surgeons—

No, no. It's true. I swear. You're not here for me. You're here for him. That's the whole idea.

Okay, okay, okay. Gimme another. To the rim. No water. Let me sit down. Fuck, you've got a lot of books. All them names on them shelves, they're hurting my fucking eyeballs. Now listen. Joe in the bar? He knows me. He knows where I live. He looks after me. If I don't come home tonight he'll know about it, okay? And he saw me speaking with you, he served you drinks, he was right—

I'm not – look, I ain't some Ted Bundy. I ain't Jeffrey Dahmer, Christ. I ain't some pervert. I'm just a guy who has a brother.

Okay. Okay. Fuck…

She went quiet and drank from the glass and while she did I went to the record player and put on Billy Joel. It played 'Uptown Girl'. One of his favourites. I sat back down thinking to myself he was up there probably grinning, probably swaying to and fro like a big old bouncy beach ball, like a big old hot air balloon. I grinned too, till I thought to myself it might look weird.

What kind of dancing you good at, miss?

Dancing?

Yeah.

Twist. Disco. Jive. Guess I got my own combo, like most people. Why?

I turned up the record player. Because that's what he wants. That's what he asks for. For somebody to dance for him. Nothing physical. No intimacy at all. He just wants to watch a lady dancing.

She considered the Jack Daniel's but didn't take no more though her fingers remained entwined round it. Her eyes flickered to the ceiling but after she looked there once she didn't want to again.

Swell Head

I guess you exaggerated, right?

Exaggerated.

Yeah.

Like – embellished?

Emb—

Yeah. Knew it. Sure you did. So he's … unusual. I get it. So he wants to watch. No touch. Why didn't you say so? Won't be the fucking first time. You sure he won't touch?

He's a head. No physical contact whatsoever.

And he doesn't want to screw me.

Can't.

He doesn't have a penis, right?

None, of any kind. I swear.

Dancing…

Dancing.

She blew air, held her head the way people do before they scream, then tidied her bra and hair in that order, stood up, straightening her leather skirt and said: Okay, let's get this show on the fucking road.

She went on up the stairs, dropping her coat over the banister rail from where it slid. I followed, after turning up the Billy Joel, turning to see her long legs disappearing up to the landing.

When I got there she stood by the vanity mirror in momma's room. Her blouse was off and she was unhooking herself between the shoulder blades when she saw me and stopped.

Does he want me to take off my clothes?

That'd be nice, I said.

I tugged the curtains shut (you could see from the highway), switched on the corner light and sat in a straight-back chair.

Her skirt lay in a pool round her high-heeled feet and she swayed a little to the music. Getting in the mood of it I guess, shifting her weight from hip to hip. Hands going from her waist to her neck, sweeping her hair above her only for it to fall down again onto her shoulders.

I walked over to the door to my brother's room. Chipped

Swell Head

and blistered. Lacking in paint. I knelt down and put my eye to the key hole.

He likes it, I said. He likes it very much.

She kept on dancing. She was beautiful. Losing herself in it. I tried not to look because this wasn't for me, this was for him. But even when I didn't I could see her shadow cast on the wall and she was a dream. She was a peach.

He likes this music, I said. He likes you.

He can't see me, she said chuckling, stomach sucking and curving.

No, but he knows that you're here.

Then let him see me, she said. Open the door.

What?

Open the door, goddamn it, she said, hips still swaying to the music, wrists figure-eight-ing past her face. Let him see me. If that's what I'm here for, if that's what you brought me for, let him see me.

Next thing I remember is her scream.

And what a scream that was. Golly gee.

Reckon she never did believe it wasn't some kind of story. Never did think I was nothing but some crazy person, some pervert on the prowl. Made me wonder though, why she wanted to see what was behind the door – why did she ask that?

Anyways, she ran. Heels hammering on the stairs. All leather skirt and bra and pants of her. All chicken-flesh and blood red cheeks of her. All screeching shimmering moonlit streak in the direction of the freeway of her, coat waving behind her like a surrender flag. Guess she hitched a ride all right. Quite a few truckers tend to use that route of a night time. I sorta presume she got home okay. No reason to think different. She sure was travelling. My estimation she'd a got there by foot in the time it takes to boil an egg.

I went downstairs and made mashed potato. Whole bucket load. Guess I thought he might be after some comfort eating. After being hurt like that, I mean. Lady screaming like that

Swell Head

partial to hurt a man's feelings, in my estimation. Course, I couldn't speak for him, much as I share a bunch of his D&NA.

Some danced a little longer, some danced a little less, and only one ever stayed the night. Name of Pearl, from Georgia. When they made her they broke the mould.

I looked at his big, fond face eating away. That part of it I seen framed in the doorway of momma's room. 'Cause he'd gotten that big by then his bedroom was barely big enough to hold him. He was pressing against all four walls. Cracking the plaster, splitting the daub, dust raining down when he turned in his sleep. And his big eye like a whale's filling the doorway, like Moby Dick's. Revolving in its tired socket. Rolling left to right, up and down. Blue-red veins in the corners thick as my wrist and spread like the fingers of a branch. Big old shutter of his eyelid falling and rising, blinking at me like Methuselah at a hot rod party.

Should a told her, I guess. What to expect, I mean.

I took a sheet from momma's bed and dabbed his eye. When it got heavy I wrung it over the bathtub, fetched a book from downstairs and started reading to him.

That was a while back...

Now, when he gets dehydrated his skin cracks so I get a water pail, wet him where I can. I can't get in the room no more, so he has to turn over a little at a time. We do that. I wash out the folds in his skin real regular. Forehead. Crow's feet. Bags under his eyes. Anywhere it's partial for fungal infection to arise if not attended with the correct medication – soapy water and mild antiseptic.

I comb his big eyebrows with a rake.

When I open the door in momma's bedroom now, the space is filled with half his mouth. He's licking his dry lips. I cool them with ice cubes. Brush his teeth with Arm and Hammer, one whole tube every night and every morning.

Me? I'm okay.

I guess I might have missed out on some kind of a life. Travel. Not that I know a whole lot what travel's for. Suited

Swell Head

me fine staying right here. Looking after my brother.

He gets antsy. I get pissed at him. We argue. Sure. But generally we get along. Always have.

He gets sick. I get sick. Our age, it happens.

The doctors are good. They get him un-sick pretty fast.

Now it takes a little longer than it used to. A few more doctors than it used to.

But his heart is fine. His brain is fine.

He's healthy.

I tell the doctors what my daddy told me – that when he was a baby the people in the hospital said he wouldn't last six weeks.

They say, Well, he's done that. But we don't know how long he can go on like this. After all, look at him.

I'm looking, I said.

Man from a special home came. Business card, everything.

Said, Sir, we can look after your brother. We are professionals. We've had great experience in this area. We know what to do. We can give him drugs. Make him happy. Twenty-four hours, sir. Constant care and supervision. You name it. You're clearly not as young as you used to be, sir…

I said, You know what? Don't call me sir.

We understand. Course we do. You're family. Ain't we all got family, and nobody says it's easy. But there will be a problem. One day…

I said, You know what? Appreciate your kindness. There's the door right there.

Had a stroke last August. Now they're all over me.

Got a rail in the john, I said. Got a beeper in case of emergency. What more do you want?

Be realistic, sir. Come a time we'll have to move him. Come a time we'll have to move you. You can't live here forever. You can't look after yourself forever and there'll come a time you can't look after him, for sure.

I give them the beady glare. I'm fitter'n any of you.

Maybe.

Swell Head

I'll see you all to the grave. You see if I don't.

Well. Maybe so. You think about it, though. Because it's coming.

They left me with that, damn them. Damn them for leaving me with those thoughts. They think I don't have those thoughts all on my own? They think I don't sit at night wondering what's going to happen? Happen to him if I die first?

It's all I think about, now.

Every time I forget a tablet or get the shakes. Or get that feeling in my head when my sugar goes down or my legs turn to Jell-O. If I go or get taken away, if I take a fall, if I break a hip, if I'm in the hospital, if I'm on oxygen, if I'm not here – what happens then? If I'm not here anymore to look after him? Once I'm gone?

Who'll look after my brother then? Who'll care?

That's why I'm sitting here with the gasoline can in my lap. That's why the gasoline can is empty. It's done. I can hear the crackling and I can smell the smoke and, you know, it smells kinda sweet. I wonder what's burning for it to smell so sweet? Momma's perfume? Momma's pillows? Or just the past, the memories? And I want someone to get one of them water pails for my tears now, damn it.

I reckon I'll sit right here in daddy's rocking chair. I feel tired right now and I don't feel minded to go very far from this warmth.

And listen. He's not screaming.

He's not weeping. Son of a gun...

He's silent, now.

Listen...

Oh, yes. He's silent, my little brother... Silent as the man in the moon.

WALKING THE DYKE

Alex Langley

"Wow, to think I'm finally here in the notorious Goat's Head in Swainbury." Constance Baines smiled and took a drink from her freshly poured glass of red wine. "Cheers!"

The rotund barman grunted.

"Must be good for trade?"

The barman looked puzzled.

"Being associated with Mortimer, I mean."

"Lot of folk walk the dyke," he replied.

"Dyke?" It was Baines's turn to frown. She *was* a lesbian, and she hoped she wouldn't encounter any prejudice in this small market town. Perhaps he was referring to some strange rural ritual. However, before she could ask him to elaborate, the barman had turned his attention to a pair of newly arrived farmers.

As she moved to find a table, Constance was hailed. "He means the earthwork, very popular with hikers."

"Oh."

"It was built by some Anglo-Saxon chief, but in 'Ring of Death', Mortimer gave it a prehistoric origin."

"Of course. Silly of me not to realise."

"Sorry. I couldn't help hearing your conversation at the bar – one sided though it was." The man who had spoken was tall, gaunt and dressed in black.

Constance smiled. She was slim, pretty, wore glasses, and was at least a foot shorter than the man.

"I'm afraid – cliché that it is – that you'll find many of the locals are somewhat reticent when it comes to talking to strangers. Even more so if you mention D.M. Mortimer."

"Ah," said Constance, "but not you?"

The man in black grinned. "I'm considered a stranger myself. Join me?" he invited.

Constance sat opposite him.

Walking the Dyke

"Yes," he continued, "if you ask most of the folk around here about Mortimer and his works, you'll be lucky if you get a blank stare."

"How can they be ignorant of the fact that Mortimer immortalised this town, this very pub in his stories?"

"Oh, they're not ignorant. Well, not all of them. It's more a case of ignoring it."

"But why? D.M. Mortimer's ghost stories are classics of the genre."

"They are indeed. But even amongst enthusiasts, Mortimer isn't exactly well known."

"Well, that's something I mean to address."

"And he didn't exactly paint the locals in glowing colours."

"You mean the characters in his stories were based on real people?"

"Some of them, yes. And many of their descendents still live here."

"Really? I had no idea. Wow. Well, that will make an excellent angle for my article."

"Ah, you're writing an article, are you?"

"Yes. I'm Constance Baines; I contribute scholarly pieces to *The Canon's Scrapbook* and more general articles to *Gore Macabre* in the vain hope of educating the blood and guts crowd."

"Oh yes, I'm familiar with your work."

"Really?"

"Don't look so shocked. Some of us read more than *Farmers Weekly*. I can show you around Swainbury, if you like."

"A guided tour? Yes. That would be great. Thank you."

"Of course you know that Mortimer wrote only ten tales and the Goat's Head features in two of them, so how about another drink?"

Constance nodded. "It's quite something to be able to drink in the bar where Mortimer drank and when it comes to stories of Pan and pagan rites, well, 'The Goat's Head' is one of the

Walking the Dyke

best."

"It is indeed. Right, my round, red wine, is it?"

"Please."

So I know what a nice girl like you is doing in a place like this, but if you don't mind me saying so, you don't look like the sort of girl who would like horror literature."

Constance laughed. "Is there a look!? Just because I'm a blonde with big tits doesn't mean I'm a bimbo!"

"No, no of course not. Sorry! Don't judge a book by its cover, eh?"

Constance grinned. "Actually, I think in many cases you can. But no, you shouldn't judge on appearances."

"That's very true."

*

"We'll start in the lower part of the town. Follow me."

Setting off at a brisk pace, Constance's guide took her down narrow alleyways. "Recognise these?"

"These must be the lanes where the abbot was pursued by the abomination."

"Correct."

"That ending is so horrible. Truly a fate worse than death." Constance shuddered and it had nothing to do with the weather, which had grown colder since she'd first arrived in Swainbury.

The tour continued.

"Now you're probably thinking that this rather non-descript building has nothing to do with Mortimer's stories, and you'd be right. But this was where the old railway station from 'I'll Be Waiting For You' stood. And if you look to your left you'll see the tunnel that was haunted by 'something dark and slimy'. I would take you for a closer look, but I'm afraid nowadays you'll only find it haunted by local drug users."

After going out of Swainbury to see the remains of the earthwork, and the farm that had appeared in 'Growing Evil',

Walking the Dyke

Constance's guide took her back through the town. He, pointing out places of interest, and reciting anecdotes, and she, making notes and taking photographs.

"This orange-brick building is now a bank, but in Mortimer's day it was a library."

"I've made sure I have all my library books back on time since I read 'The Late Return'. A truly chilling story."

"And, over there..."

"It's the clock-tower from 'Strike Thirteen'."

Next he took her to see the church of St Nicholas. "A suitably Gothic monstrosity, I'm sure you'll agree."

"It's just as he described it."

"Let's take a look inside," he said opening the heavy oak door. "The oldest parts date to the fourteenth-century."

"I'm just imagining the passage in 'Service for the Damned' where Mortimer describes the black mass. Yes, I can see it all. The creature summoned up is the equal of any of James's spectres."

"I quite agree."

Constance shivered.

"You all right?"

"Hmm, yes. Someone must have walked over my grave."

"Ah. Speaking of graves... This way."

Emerging from the church, they found the weather had turned foggy.

"You couldn't have picked a better day to come to Swainbury. The cemetery is this way."

Many of the monuments were badly weathered, but as they walked through the mist-wreathed graveyard, Constance's guide was still able to point out the resting places of people that had 'inspired' characters in Mortimer's stories.

They reached an unmarked mound in the shadow of a yew tree. "Now, this is the one that'll interest you the most..."

"Of course, it's the grave from 'The Exhumed Body'. Would you mind taking a photo of me next to it?"

"Of course not."

Walking the Dyke

"But what about Mortimer's grave? Where is he buried?"

"Well, that's the big mystery. Certainly not in this cemetery, and I haven't been able to find any record of his interment."

"How strange."

"Did you know that Swainbury has another horror writer?"

"Really? Is it someone I would have heard of? Oh hang on, it's not someone who has only been published on some obscure website, is it?"

"No." He laughed. "It's Alex Waite."

"Oh my God! Alex Waite! I had no idea. God! I reviewed his last book."

"I remember it."

"God, he's awful. Badly written, poorly researched, sexist crap. Pulp horror of the worst kind – the sort that gives horror a bad name. And he lives in Swainbury?"

"She."

"Sorry?"

"Alex is short for Alexandria."

"Oh!"

"Funnily enough, she lives in the very house Mortimer lived in. It's also the house where 'A Haunting' took place. And Waite used it as the setting for her novel, *The House of Death*. Would you like to look around it?"

"I would love to, but I couldn't possibly. How could I face her?"

"You won't have to. She's away."

"You're not suggesting we break in, are you?"

"No." He laughed. "I have a key – I've been doing some work there, renovating the house. And if I can't show you his grave, the least I can do is show you where he lived."

"Oh. Well, if you're sure it'll be all right. I'd hate to miss out on the chance of looking around Mortimer's house. And 'A Haunting' is my favourite of his stories"

"Good. Follow me."

*

Walking the Dyke

"Down here. Come on." Constance was led down some steps. "Your tour wouldn't be complete if I didn't show you this."

They were in the cellar. The room was empty apart from a collection of tools. Set into the flagstones were four shackles. A chalk pentagram had been drawn on the floor enclosing them.

"This is the cellar where the Bloody Butcher cuts up his victims."

"The Bloody Butcher?" Constance frowned. "Er, I don't think I've read that one."

"You wouldn't have. I haven't finished it yet."

Constance wasn't expecting that admission, nor the blow to the head that followed it.

When she came round she found she was lying spread-eagled on the floor, chains around her arms and legs. Her clothes had been removed and her guide had changed his. He was now wearing a black dress, fishnet stockings, and a wig of long blonde hair.

"Hello, Miss Baines. I'm Alex Waite. *The Bloody Butcher* is the title of my next novel. It's about a psycho who chops up his victims, who all happen to be attractive young women. I think it will prove very popular with the readers of *Gore Macabre*, don't you?"

"Look this has gone far enough. You've made your point. Just let me go and I'll promise I'll say nothing."

Waite knelt beside the prone girl, reached out and squeezed one of her breasts. "Mmm, very nice. I'll be removing your breasts, as you've probably noticed mine aren't as big as yours. They'll suit me very well, don't you think? And as you say, there's no reason at all why a big-boobed blonde can't like horror literature, whether that's supernatural, nasty, or both. Or write it either, hmm?"

"You're mad!"

"Well, your review did make me mad, darling."

"I'm sorry. Please let me go. I'll write the best review you've ever had; you've certainly scared me."

Walking the Dyke

Writhing around, struggling to pull herself free from the shackles, tears streaming, Constance cried for help.

"As you know, the house has been recently renovated; the cellar soundproofed, so please feel free to scream as much as you like. No one will hear you."

Constance *was* screaming madly.

"I was going to cut your breasts off while you were alive, but the way you're thrashing about, they could get damaged. And we wouldn't want that, would we?" From amongst the tools, Waite selected an axe. "So I'll have to kill you first."

"Nooooooooooooooooo...!"

Waite swung the axe. The blade cleaved right through Constance's neck, her head rolled free, a scarlet fountain spurted.

"I guess you were right about me being a hack. But one thing you were wrong about is that I always do very thorough research."

THE CREAKING

Anna Taborska

Alice hurried through the forest, her basket filled with fresh herbs, and small pots of strengthening tonics and soothing balms. She had worked all night, crushing healing leaves and seeds, grinding nourishing roots and dried fungi; mixing her concoctions so that she could bring relief to the sick and ailing as soon as the sun was up.

Partially hidden by trees and thicket, her little house was a good half-hour walk from the village. It would have been easier if people came to her rather than her having to go to them, but some of those she helped were old and frail, others were very sick or busy looking after small children. Besides, the villagers didn't seem keen on walking through the forest, even during the day. This was something Alice couldn't understand. For her, the forest meant sanctuary and nurture: it hid her from the madding crowd, and provided her with food and all the plants she needed to mix her medicines and make a meagre living. And what didn't grow in the forest, grew in the marshes and fields nearby.

Alice hadn't been blessed with attractive features or an easy life. Her father had died when she was a little girl, and her mother had raised her alone. From an early age, she had learnt how to heal, and how to survive by working hard and keeping herself to herself. Alice's mother had traded remedies for eggs, milk, flour and the occasional piece of cloth to patch up clothes, and now Alice did the same.

Going to the village had been a frightening experience even when her mother was alive, but in the five years since her mother's death it just seemed to get harder. The villagers stared at her: adults whispered behind her back and children called her names. Even the people whom she helped were uneasy around her. They were grateful enough for the relief

The Creaking

her remedies brought, but Alice could sense that as soon as she'd applied the ointment they needed or handed over their medicine, they didn't like her hanging around.

The only bearable part of going to the village was the walk through the forest. Of course, Alice was in the forest practically every day collecting berries, fungi, herbs or kindling for the fire, but she loved spending time in the woods without having to 'work'. When she was strolling among the ancient trees, listening to the birds and the soft, startled noises of small creatures scurrying away in the undergrowth, she felt something akin to contentment.

Today was no different, except for the fact that Alice couldn't take her time; she needed to get to the village as soon as possible – Maggie Gray was counting on her to help her ailing daughter. The toddler had been coughing for several days now, and none of the usual mixtures of honey and herbs had worked. Alice had had to resort to mixing a blend based heavily on coltsfoot, and that had to be prepared in just the right way or it could poison the little girl rather than heal her. The sooner she could administer the medicine, the greater the chance that the child would recover. So Alice hurried along the path that wound its way to the village.

It was early morning and the sunlight was just beginning to filter down through the trees, but even at high noon the forest floor would be dark – the tall and leafy trees casting a permanent shadow. At her brisk pace Alice couldn't hear the birdsong that she usually enjoyed. Today her footsteps accompanied her, and the occasional flurry of wings as a bird fled its nest in alarm.

As Alice burst out into the clearing not far from her home, she came face to face with a young deer. Alice froze, her face breaking into a smile, and gazed at the creature in wonder. No matter how many times she came across deer in the forest, their regal grace never failed to bring her joy.

The animal held Alice's gaze, its mouth moving impassively

The Creaking

as it chewed its morning meal. Then a loud creaking sound rang out behind Alice. The deer bolted in fright, disappearing into the undergrowth, and Alice span round, but saw nothing. She stood very still, her heartbeat hard and fast. The sound came again: the wrenching, squealing, rasping sound of wood being stretched and distorted. Again and again the creaking resounded, as if a tree were being pummelled and bent by a strong wind, yet not the slightest hint of a breeze stirred in the forest. Alice wanted to run, but her legs refused to oblige. Instead, she peered into the trees, trying to see what was causing the heavy, rhythmic creak. It sounded like something was exerting a considerable amount of pressure on a large branch, but Alice saw nothing. Trying hard to conquer her fear, she placed her basket on the ground and took a step towards the sound. As she did so, the sound stopped. Alice moved forward a few paces, and the sound came again – this time right above her head. Alice screamed. She grabbed her basket and ran.

Alice kept running until her strength ran out, then stopped and looked fearfully behind her. Of course there was nothing there; what could there possibly be? As her breath slowed and her heart stilled enough for her to hear the forest around her, Alice strained her ears for the horrible sound. She heard only the wind in the trees and bushes, and the stirring of the wildlife around her, and yet the grating, jarring creaking reverberated in her head. She knew instinctively that nothing would be capable of wiping that sound from her mind. The trees and bushes around her seemed darker; the soft, familiar sounds of creatures moving through the undergrowth seemed sinister, unnerving. For the first time in her life, the forest was no longer a haven, no longer a friend; it was something to be feared. Alice realised that her fear was out of all proportion to what had happened, and yet it persisted.

That day, Alice spent as little time as she could in the village, explaining to people how to use the tinctures, balsams and

The Creaking

poultices she had prepared for them, rather than staying to administer them. She even turned down Maggie Gray's offer of a meal, although she did remain long enough to show the mother how to dose the cough mixture for her little girl. Instead, Alice packed away the food and other items that the villagers gave her in return for her services, and hurried home, going out of her way to avoid the clearing with the large creaking tree at its edge. Long before darkness fell she made sure that she gathered everything she needed for the next day, then locked herself away in her house. But try as she might, she couldn't get the creaking out of her head.

That night Alice dreamt that she was running through the forest. It was dark, and something blacker than the night was chasing her. As she ran, nettles stung her, thorns scratched her and roots tried to trip her up and send her sprawling. Alice ran blindly on and unexpectedly found herself bursting out into the clearing. She came to an abrupt halt, shocked at finding herself exposed and vulnerable to the dark malignant presence that pursued her. She moved swiftly, but silently back into the trees and listened for any sound of her pursuer. And that's when it came: the bloodcurdling screech of bending wood – the creaking that turned the sweat on Alice's back to ice. She span round, looking up into the large tree above her. Was that a black shape – a shadow crouching in the branches? Alice screamed and woke up.

For the next few days Alice continued to avoid the clearing and the tree, but her unease didn't lessen. If anything, it grew. She gathered what plants she needed for her medicines without straying any further from her house than she had to, she did her rounds in the village and hurried back home. At night she dreamt about the darkness that pursued her through the forest, and the creaking. Then one day when she got to the village, she found the villagers in a tense and morose mood. The Tyrell boy had gone missing. His abusive and permanently angry father had last seen him the night before. Old man Tyrell had been drinking in the kitchen with his friends when the boy came in to say goodnight.

"Fuck off to bed, you little shit!" Tyrell's response elicited peals of laughter from his drunken cronies.

The boy had scuttled off to bed, and that was the last anyone had seen of him. Old man Tyrell had woken up at lunchtime and gone round the house, looking for someone to vent his hangover on. He couldn't find his twelve-year-old son, so he clouted his wife, and demanded to be fed. Mrs Tyrell had gone out into the yard to call Tommy in for lunch, assuming that he'd gotten up early, made his own breakfast and gone to play with friends. But her son was nowhere to be seen.

"I can't find Tommy," she told her husband as she fearfully set his plate of food down in front of him.

"I'll kill the little shit when he gets back," he had replied.

Tyrell spent the afternoon drinking, only pausing between drinks to repeat his threat, but by the time it got dark and his wife had unsuccessfully scoured the village for the boy, his protestations had decreased somewhat in their vehemence, if not frequency. A brief torch-lit search of the village and its immediate surroundings was organised, but Tommy wasn't found.

The villagers quickly did what villagers often do in times of perceived threat: they became suspicious and mistrustful of outsiders. It was into this atmosphere that Alice arrived the next morning. She checked in on the little Gray girl and gave Maggie a fresh pot of medicine for her. The toddler's cough had lessened.

"She's getting better." Alice smiled shyly at Maggie Gray.

"Yes." Maggie pulled her daughter towards herself, away from Alice, then got a hold of herself and added without much enthusiasm, "Thank you, Alice." There was an uncomfortable silence.

"I'll be going then," offered Alice, adding nervously, "Mrs Pratt is waiting for her bunion ointment." Maggie got up silently and fetched a dozen eggs from the back of the house.

The Creaking

Mrs Pratt was in a talkative mood. Alice was hardly through the door, when the old woman told her how Tommy had disappeared the day before and how a search of the village had turned up no sign of him.

"Poor Betty Tyrell is hysterical," Mrs Pratt said with barely concealed delight, "and even old man Tyrell has been out looking for the boy."

"That's terrible," responded Alice. "I hope they find him."

Tommy had risen early the day before, grabbed a slice of bread and a piece of cheese, and crept out of the house without waking his parents. He'd decided on the previous night that he would visit his cousin in the neighbouring village. There was no point asking his parents, as his mother would defer to his father, and his father would hit him with the buckle of his belt. If he slipped out early, he could get back by teatime. His father would be too hung-over in the morning and too drunk in the afternoon to notice that he was gone, and he would be home for supper.

The boy set out across the cornfields just as dawn broke, and was at his cousin's in time for breakfast. Charlie was thrilled to see him, and his aunt and uncle made a fuss of him.

"Your parents do know you're here?" questioned his aunt.

Tommy nodded, "Uh-huh."

"And they let you come all the way here on your own?"

"Uh-huh." Tommy smiled at his uncle and aunt. He was jealous of Charlie. Charlie's dad never hit him or shouted at his mother. Charlie's mum was pretty and always smiling; not like Tommy's mother, who had frown lines and puffy tear-stained eyes, and was always sad.

Charlie's father helped the boys to make fishing rods, whilst his mother made them a hamper with bread, cheese, ham and milk, and then the two cousins set off for the river. The day was warm and sultry; the boys fished and chatted, ate and eventually dozed off in a haystack, waking up when the sun started going down and a chill crept into the air. By the time

The Creaking

they got back to Charlie's house, there was less than an hour of daylight left. As Tommy had a two-hour walk to get home, his uncle and aunt offered to let him stay the night, provided his parents wouldn't be worried. Tommy told them that his parents had said he could stay over if it got late and could come home on Sunday. He would get a hiding one way or another, so he figured he might as well delay the inevitable.

When Tommy got home, his mother ran to him and hugged him, tears of relief staining her face. "Where have you been?"

Tommy's father was sitting at the kitchen table, surrounded by his drinking cronies, who were helping him drown his sorrows and work out where to look for his boy. Before Tommy had time to answer his mother, his father got up from the table and lumbered towards him.

"I'm gonna kill you, you little shit!" Tommy didn't know whether to stay or run. He'd rarely seen his father quite so angry. "Where the devil have you been, you little shit?" Tommy cowered back as his father approached, pulling off his belt and brandishing the buckle end at his son. "Go on, tell me! Where have you been, you little shit?" The belt whistled through the air and hit the boy on the side, knocking him off his feet. His mother screamed and ran to defend her son, but Tyrell pushed her out of the way and went to take another swing at the boy. There must have been a particularly homicidal look on old man Tyrell's face, as his companions stopped laughing, and one of them decided to intervene. Jim pulled himself up drunkenly from the kitchen table, and staggered up between Tyrell and his son.

"Witch took you, did she, boy? Witch took you ... to make a potion out of your blood?"

Old man Tyrell paused, belt in hand, confused by the question.

"Witch took you and locked you up, but you got away?" prompted Jim.

"I'll kill you, you little shit!" Tyrell had regained his momentum and was about to pelt the boy again, when Tommy

The Creaking

piped up from the floor, "Yes, sir."

"Huh?" grunted Tyrell.

"Witch took me and locked me up, but I got away."

"Who locked you up?" fumed Tyrell. "Are you lying to me, boy?"

"No, sir."

"If you're lying to me, I'll kill you!"

"Witch took me and … was gonna … make me into a potion … but I got away."

"Nobody hurts my boy!" Tyrell turned to face his friends. "You hear me? Nobody hurts *my* boy!"

"We hear you, Robert." Jim raised his hand in a placating gesture, but there was no placating old man Tyrell.

"I'll kill her! I'll kill the witch!" Tyrell glared at his companions. "Are you going to sit there or are you going to help me?"

As old man Tyrell was the parish constable, they decided to help.

"Who's he talking about?" Nathaniel Jackson whispered as the drunken party spilled out of the house after Tyrell.

"Alice Goodman, I guess," mused George Hogge. "Ain't no one else around here who makes potions."

"Hang on, Robert!" Jim tried to undo what he'd done, but it was too late. He was pushed aside, and by the time old man Tyrell had finished rousing the villagers, his party was over a dozen strong. They set off to put an end to the witch who'd been killing children, draining their blood and grinding up their bones to make her unholy potions. Old Joe had been living in the village for a long time, and knew exactly how to get to the witch's house.

Alice had just cleaned up after supper, and was getting ready to mix her medicines for the following day, when she heard the voices. At first she thought she must be mistaken, but the shouting grew louder, angrier. And now she could see the flickering orange light of torches dancing amongst the trees.

The Creaking

They were getting closer, and Alice knew she should run, but it was too late, they were already here. A baying mob shrieking and snarling like beasts. "Alice Goodman, come out! Come out now or we're coming in!"

Alice stood rooted to the spot with fear. Then the door flew open and Robert Tyrell burst in, accompanied by his own personal lynch mob. Alice wanted to scream, but no sound came from her throat.

"Gotcha, you fucking witch!" growled Tyrell.

"You won't be killing any more children!" someone shouted from the back of the crowd. Alice couldn't speak, but she shook her head and held up her hands in a vain attempt to ward off the fury that was being hurled at her. Then Tyrell had her by the hair, and she was twisting in pain, being forced out into the night, fists punching her and nails scratching her, as she was half-dragged, half-carried out of her house and through the forest.

A punch to Alice's right eye screwed it tight shut as the tissue swelled up around it. Her left eye filled with her own blood from a gash on her forehead. She couldn't see, and in her fear and pain she couldn't sense that the trees around her had thinned and the undergrowth had given way to grass.

"This will do!" someone shouted. Alice recognised the voice of John Briggs. Only last week she'd cured the fungal infection on his feet with her garlic and chamomile ointment. He said he'd never forget what she'd done for him. The villagers stopped, and Alice tried to cry out to Briggs, but still no sound came from her cracked, bleeding lips. Alice threw herself forward in an attempt to break free. A violent tug to her hair ripped much of it out and brought on a fresh wave of pain.

"Stay still, witch!" It was Tyrell's voice. "Hold her, will you!"

"Give it here!" shouted Briggs.

Rough hands held her even tighter, crushing her arms. Then Alice felt something being pulled down over her head. She

The Creaking

realised what was about to happen moments before she felt the rope sting and tighten around her neck. Then she was being hoisted up off her feet, the burning pain in her neck unbearable and the breath choked out of her slowly, prolonging her agony. The last thing Alice heard was the horrific, jarring creaking as the branch bent under her weight and the darkness took her.

BERNARD BOUGHT THE FARM

James Stanger

Sloshing in the pen, their bodies encrusted in mud, pig filth and their own excrement, Bernard refuses to regret anything that he's done.

After night's dark ink has soaked the sky, the heat of the rising sun will scorch the heavens for another torture-stricken day. Before too long the force-feeding that the farmers will visit upon them – stuffing small metal tubes into their mouths, and pumping swill down their throats – will cause their bonds to break as their flesh rips like over-stuffed sacks of bloodied meat.

They are alone in the biting chill of the farmyard, alone apart from the swine that share the pen with them. The pen is tightly enclosed and isolated from other structures so that no living soul will ever be able to hear their screams, which are anyway mixed all too conveniently with the shrill squeals of the pigs. The creatures knock and nuzzle them and both men know that it is only a limited amount of time before the pigs start to bite. Swine eat anything and they need no encouragement…

*

His complexion ruddy, brow wrinkled beneath a gleaming bald pate, Bernard Crombe's anger was clearly etched upon his face. "Tell them I don't want to know; if those wops want to undercut someone they better find some other sucker, it's four-fifty a share or they can forget it." Bernard is dressed in traditional English tweed, and although his black wellington boots are slicked with mud and animal filth, he appears to be the personification of a gentleman farmer. However, looks can be deceptive – his accent is that of rural America, and there is nothing gentlemanly about him. Yet – no matter what those

Bernard Bought the Farm

upper class snobs thought – he was certain he was the equal of those who made up the highest echelons of England's rural community.

He had never tasted pork quite like the products that came from this tiny impoverished farm in East Sussex. This land was smaller than his native US, but he appreciated the methods of farming, even if there were always some improvements he felt he could make.

*

As a boy, Bernard would act as his father's lackey, forbidden to explore the farms and factories on his own. His father hailed from a foreign shore that no family member was willing to trace and had created a huge fortune by investing in a now world-famous chicken franchise. He would not spare his son even the most grisly and sickening aspects of factory farming production.

One unforgiving, blazing hot day in New Mexico, the boy had dared to roam the farm on his own. Near an outhouse, he found a malnourished hen, naked save for a few feathers, neck lolling to one side from poor health.

He let the hen rest on his lap. He felt it would make a perfect pet for him and he was sure that even with his limited knowledge he knew enough to nurture it back to health. For a few peaceful moments of loving compassion, he stroked it and caressed its saggy shivering skin. Hearing his father call for him, he clutched the hen he had named Pecky and ran to obey his father's command.

He stood next to his dad obediently with the hen cradled in his arms.

"What the hell you got there boy?"

"It's Pecky – she needs help."

"Bernie boy, I think it's time you learned a little something. Hand over that hen." The boy was unsure, but reluctantly he handed over the pathetic specimen, its cluck now no more than

Bernard Bought the Farm

a gargled splutter.

At his father's nod, Bernard and a senior member of the farm's workforce trailed a broken path towards a large open metal room. Inside, hundreds of plucked chickens hung upside down, wriggling and thrusting around in panic.

Bernard gasped at a team of people hacking and chopping chickens, not long removed from their hanging places. There were a few empty spaces awaiting other chickens, and a chain lowered mechanically so that it was at the boy's height.

"It's time to be a man for your old dad, son." His father grinned. "Fix Pecky here up on that chain and let the man take him to the table at that end of the room. You're going to cut this little bastard up with one of them big knives, and then I'm going to have him cooked up for you to eat."

It was beyond Bernard to disobey his father as to do that was to disobey God himself. So with shaking hands and a small tear for his hen friend he attached the shackles around the bird's legs.

His father smiled proudly at him, held his hand, and led him over to the big bloody table at the far end of the room, ordering the team of workers to stop what they were doing and transport the hen from its point of origin right up to where Bernard was standing.

Under instructions from his father, Bernard unfastened Pecky. He glanced into the hen's fearful blinking eye and wanted to save his pet, but then he felt the firm grip of his father's hand on his shoulders.

"I want to see you chop Pecky right up, boy."

He handed Bernard a meat cleaver, and after a moment's reflection, the boy chopped and butchered the scrawny bird in a messy carnage of blood and innards. As he repeatedly swung the cleaver, his worried look gradually turned into a gleeful smile and it was clear all memory of the beloved pet had evaporated. "Can I eat Pecky, Pa…? I guess I've worked up an appetite."

Bernard's father looked at his boy for a moment, and

Bernard Bought the Farm

chuckling, broke into a wide-toothed smile that caused his gold molar to shine. "Sure boy, but she's going to need a little paprika."

This initiation had unleashed something sinister in young Bernard, and from here onwards he planned all his own meals, and those that he would prepare for his eventual millions, with the utmost pain towards the livestock. Bernard left childhood with a formidable knowledge of the anatomical structure of poultry and along with it keen creative methods of inflicting wounds and agony on the chosen animals. He considered himself mature at fourteen. He gained weight alarmingly, and the kids at school called him 'fat retard' and 'pig fucker', but all they amounted to were words for Bernard had also gained a certain aura. This aura marked him out as a freak amongst his peers and because of it they would never physically approach him. Not that this bothered Bernard. In fact, he relished his status and cherished his intimate knowledge of nerve endings and pain receptors.

Two years later, Bernard had increased his involvement in his father's business. The older man was now little more than a distant spectre of a figure.

Gently slicing layers of skin off a living animal was one of Bernard's passions. He found pigs to be his favourite, harbouring the notion that not only was it a fact that pigs tasted so divinely salty but they resembled people, although he never thought that he was flaying an actual person.

The joy he felt derived from his deeply held belief that these beasts had the full range of emotional facets humans did and yet you could legally slay and eat them.

By twenty-one Bernard had begun to display a more sophisticated understanding of torture and on his new Ohio farm – a gift from his father – he had a reasonably sized and fully functioning factory which included high-walled and locked pens where he could conduct a series of increasingly ingenious and depraved experiments upon livestock.

The original plans for the Ohio farm were that it should

become another poultry hub to supply chicken for his father's expansion into Europe, but for the first time Bernard rebelled against his father's wishes and demanded that the factory focus on swine. After a spate of bitter rows, his father relented, unable to cope with his son's newly found steel and grit.

After a decade, Bernard was running a highly successful farm and factory supplying pork bellies to almost every Southern State in the US, and he remained extremely hands-on in his approach.

He would prepare his own meals here, and in the privacy of his own controlled environment was able to administer as much lingering pain upon his pigs as he desired. His favourite 'trick' was to hand-pick a pig from his main farm and have it brought over by a worker called Saunders, a British immigrant who was seeking residence in the US. Saunders was loyal and unquestioningly obedient to Bernard's every whim. Indeed, he would not trust anyone else to get that close to his private quarters – he could not trust anybody else.

Entering his quarters, Bernard donned a pair of yellow rubber gloves and picked up the delivered pig by its trotters, carrying it upside down as if it were on a spit roast. The feeling of power he enjoyed with the captive animal in his hands engendered an almost giddying arousal. The obvious fear in the pig's feverishly darting eyes suggested that it understood enough to experience panic, the only mercy being that its imagination could never encompass the full horror of its situation.

Taking the animal to an aluminium bench, Bernard clasped its trotters together with two long beams of metal pointing out of the bench, steel arms with a mighty grip, keeping the thrashing animal suspended about a metre from the ground.

Bernard chuckled. "Oh, the hell inside your head," he whispered, as he picked out a meat tenderiser from a rack affixed to the wall. He caressed the pig's back for a moment, closing his eyes and tilting his head towards the ceiling; his penis growing hard, he rubbed the head of the tenderiser

Bernard Bought the Farm

slowly down the shaft of his thick cock.

He toyed with the pig's curly tail, pulling it straight and then letting it go, allowing it to coil back to its original twisty spiral. Still moving the steel mallet over his private parts, he suddenly inserted his index finger into the pig's anus. His eyes closed as the pig became utterly confused and wriggled in panic.

"Oh shush! I love foreplay as much as any man, but let's get down to it!" In a flash, Bernard's eyes sprung open and he gritted his teeth as if he was in the throes of a seizure. Raising the tenderiser, he smashed it against the pig's front right leg. It squealed wildly an instant after the leg snapped.

Bernard let out a pleasurable gasp, and struck again, this time on the front left leg and again the animal erupted in a protest of screaming pain. Bernard moaned as if in orgasm. He struck the final two legs in quick succession, the snapping bone sounding like organic gunfire. The thrill Bernard felt was such that he had to sink to his knees and weakly drop the hammer. It made a dull 'dink' as it hit the ground.

Bernard quivered with a sensual delight, and he quickly removed his trousers and underpants so that he could be free from the self-made sticky mess that now clung to his thighs and crotch.

Leaping to his feet again, he made darting lines that sectioned off a piece of the pig's anatomy, for which Bernard had a special tool. It was a unique manner of carving knife, different because so fine were its teeth and so sharp was its blade that he could strip an animal of its skin and not disturb the flesh underneath, prolonging its agonised existence.

He worked quickly and carefully to avoid fatal blood loss, his joy in this method of preparation deriving from seeing the inner workings of the pig whilst it still moved. Bernard knew that this was undoubtedly a living hell for the creature, and such a notion made him almost dizzy with excitement. Keeping a steady hand and sticking to his own expertly drawn lines, he removed the pig's hide as easily as peeling an orange.

The blood oozed and dripped with satisfying thickness upon

the bench, its crimson hue enchanting him, and he could not resist licking some of it from the worktop.

When a section of skin had been stripped, it fell to the floor with a wet flop, and Bernard especially enjoyed the moment where he could saw away at the pig's udders for he knew how sensitive they were. "Like nipples," he gleefully pronounced.

He always saved this bit for last and with a swift stroke of his blade, deprived the animal of these appendages in the most agonising way imaginable. Bernard thought it most fortunate the thing was still conscious, for the finishing touch to the whole proceedings was the crowning glory in this whole ghastly pageant of gore.

Moving fast to catch the pig still alive, he moved to the metal rack and picked up a black diamond-studded collar. Tying the collar around the neck of the pig, he unfastened the animal. Bernard then placed it on its broken legs upon the floor and forced it to attempt to walk.

Bernard stared at the pig as if through x-ray glasses – he could see its muscle tissue and most of its inner organs – and as he dragged it around the floor, he boomed: "Come to market boy, c'mon! Come to market! It's time to go to market!"

The pig knew only pain and horror, its body wallowed in lagoons of abstract torment. It started to die only when bits and pieces of it began to plop out all over the floor. Like the bloodiest form of incontinence possible it shed vital organs, and then drained of blood, it fell softly to the ground, reduced to a bare skeletal structure. Now Bernard could cook it and his hungry belly would be satisfied.

It became increasingly obvious that his perversions could not be restricted solely to his own private space on the farmyard and bizarre practices began to emerge in open view of the workforce.

He handpicked still dependent piglets soon after their birth, generating assured trauma for both mother and offspring. He soon accelerated to increasingly hideous acts, with the specially chosen piglet forced to witness the mutilation of its

Bernard Bought the Farm

mother.

It soon became necessary for Bernard to quell the growing number of disgusted voices of protest from his labour force, and in Saunders he found he had a suitable enforcer of his will.

He sought Saunders' influence and advice for carrying out hirings and firings on the farm and it wasn't long before the workforce consisted of low-paid immigrants forced to keep quiet for fear of losing their jobs.

With such security to do whatever he pleased, Bernard acted with scant regard to the opinions of others as to how he treated his pigs, and Saunders was most enthusiastic in being involved in the most ghastly abuses of the animals. He even started to encourage Bernard to initiate more extreme violations.

One soil-baking day whilst brutalising a panicking sow, a gaunt farmhand holding a piglet tight, forcing it to watch their barbarism, the two men sank to new levels of cruelty and degradation.

The sadists where standing at either end of the suffering creature when Bernard suddenly cracked a grin and looked deep into Saunders' eyes. "Y'know what would be really sick? Rape this little pink bitch from behind."

There was a bestial snort of joy and smirk of acknowledgement from his right-hand man and Saunders eagerly yanked off his jeans, and tore down his underpants to reveal his erection.

Bernard admired the magnificent penis violently thrusting into the animal's arse and felt a sudden tug of affection towards a man enjoying the same depraved excesses as himself. Together they forced the sow into an unnerving rhythm of pain, with Bernard sawing away its trotters at the front, and Saunders' pelvis pounding at the back. Viscous red liquid sprayed and sloshed in the filth and mud. A crazed Bernard cried out. "Fuck her! Fuck her! Fuck that bitch sow hard!"

Saunders quickened his pace, increasingly violent as he sensed that the now trotter-less beast was beginning to give out. He breathed heavily through his nose, his grimace tight and his face contorted in demonic pleasure. The sow tried to eject the penis with excrement, but Saunders just shoved harder back into the orifice that oozed with shit, thick crimson blood and pre-ejaculate. "This is the best lube in the world!"

Bernard laughed a thunderous roar back at him.

Saunders finally orgasmed at roughly the same moment that Bernard managed to hack off the sow's snout, and as a last token of needless torture he pulled off the animal's tail.

Both then collapsed into a gory tangle, toying with various innards from the dead, still twitching sow's corpse. Adorning each other with entrails and offal, the two men suddenly realised that the farmhand was still present. His uncomprehending expression made them giggle and they embraced. From this point on their working relationship changed into one of grotesque intimacy, a sharing of experiences of bestiality.

They would bathe together, smoking Cuban cigars under the cover of twilight, Saunders sitting upon Bernard's vastly fattening thighs, his employer becoming aroused as he conjured elaborate fantasies of the fate he would visit on the doomed creature of their choosing.

"Let's use my razor-edged potato peeler," Bernard whispered to his lover. "Peel the skin in strips from its backside." Excited, he entered Saunders. "A slight variation," he gasped, as he sodomised the British man. "You take his backside. I'll use my nail-clippers this time, take the bastard's eyelids off."

When his now long-estranged father died, Bernard inherited the entire estate, save for a small Costa Rican villa, left for the mistresses to squabble over. Bernard moved swiftly in his business machinations to close down the poultry aspect of his new empire, and concentrate instead on the supply of pork products to the food industry and retail outlets. He even started his own chain of bar and grill restaurants.

Everything seemed to flourish under his new regime and

Bernard Bought the Farm

whilst holidaying in England with Saunders, Bernard found the opportunity to expand his dynasty, and excitedly called his most trusted financial executive back home, after visiting a farm on the East Sussex coast. "I found me the most fabulous livestock on the entire planet," he raved. "It's on some shit-heap of a lousy run-down farm in this fag and tranny county."

Whilst Bernard continued to put on vast amounts of weight, his lover lost it, growing painfully thin. At this stage in his life, Bernard found the day-to-day running of his business made him weary and breathless. His size was now so obscene that he needed a walking stick to move around. And it was fair question as to whether the man's blood ran with glooping lumps of fat and sticky cholesterol. The muttered rumours (never dared to be spoken aloud) within the ranks of his workforce were that it surely wouldn't be long before the old geezer was in a chair – some even formed a dead pool as to whether he would be gone within the next financial year.

He feared isolation above anything else, and secretly he became dependent on Saunders taking care of the mundane affairs of dealing with his employees. Despite all of this, he lived on with a ghastly fire fuelling him from within, and he presided over his empire like some brooding megalith, a monstrous tyrant with a heart of granite.

*

One wet day in April, they visited Dernhurst Farm, the place that Bernard sang the praises of, with the sole intention of purchasing the land and, more importantly, the livestock, for a pittance. After a furious phone conversation with a sales rep in Bologna, Bernard continued pressurising the rather wretched-looking landowner, Saunders standing beside his master and sheltering him from the deluge like an obedient lieutenant.

The landowner, Will Norton, was soaked to the bone and growing increasingly disturbed by Bernard's aggressive manner.

Bernard Bought the Farm

"It's a fair price, Mr Norton," Bernard grunted.

Norton rejected the offer. "It's a shite price!"

Bernard was growing frustrated with this stubborn yokel. Whatever offer he made, the farmer remained obstinate. He laughed as something occurred to him – this bumpkin sure was pigheaded – and for a moment he entertained cruel fantasies involving the inflexible landowner.

Norton shifted uneasily, he could sense the American's anger, but he would not succumb to this blustering businessman.

Bernard snapped out yet another poor valuation, as if ordering Norton to accept, but the latter just shook his head with a grim, if somewhat fearful signal of dismissal.

"Wipe yer brow, Saunders!" Bernard was on the verge of considering defeat, something he hadn't done in several decades. "I've faced down, burned out and crippled better men than this," he muttered. "One final offer!" he suddenly snapped.

Saunders widened his eyes slightly. The rise was modest, but broke some minor rules in their own laws of business engagement. He wondered if this was driving his partner slightly crazy. It was strange, but he could sense another motive other than money behind Norton's refusal to sell them the farm.

He whispered in Bernard's ear. "Let's go back to the hotel. We've got a team of lawyers who can make these guys' lives hell, so that they *have* to sell it us."

Norton just stood in front of them motionless, like an unmovable guardian of the farm and all that lived within its borders, and Bernard had to swallow the bitterest pill. He turned his back on the farmer with Saunders in tow, sighed and slowly walked towards the car. Abruptly he turned, "You bog-trotting fag!" he shouted, "I'll get this place even if it kills you!"

Saunders tried to drag him back to the car at a more urgent pace. Things were getting ever so slightly embarrassing and

Bernard Bought the Farm

words such as these caused unnecessary trouble for their lawyers. Was Bernie starting to crack up?

"Norton may have had his day," Bernard muttered. "Goddamn it! This place is blessed with some mighty fine swine and they ain't gonna belong to that bumpkin for long, because I know exactly how to treat pigs like them!"

He clenched his steel walking cane, and as a demonstration, he thrust the sharpened end deep into the eye of a snuffling piglet. He plucked out the organ of the now bloodied and squealing animal and pointed the end of the cane at Norton, the detached eye staring at him, dripping with blood and fluids.

Popping the item in his mouth Bernard grinned at the shocked farmer, chewed it and once again turned his back on the man. The pair walked through the lashing rain to their car, indifferent to the piglet's suffering, and the blood spurting from the animal's torn socket turned puddles crimson. Norton threw himself over the pigsty fence and cradled the animal as if it were a mortally wounded newborn child. He yelled after Bernard, who was now laughing, whilst Saunders, slightly embarrassed and even more suspicious of his lover's sanity, still managed a wry smile. He thought of Bernard as a naughty boy and regarded his act as one of mischief that reminded him of the man he fell in love with so many years ago. Sobbing, Norton clutched the young pig that wriggled and convulsed in pain.

"Stay right where you are, you fat twat!" Norton's son, Robin, dashed from the farm's outer perimeter and between the two men and the car, aiming a shotgun at them, his grim look communicating nothing but hatred. "I saw what you did, Crombe. Made me sick. But let's be honest, shall we – Dad and I both kind of expected it, and this time you ain't getting away with it."

The shotgun lent authority to his words, and after the initial surprise, Saunders detected something rehearsed. The colour had drained from Bernard's face, his hands raised in front of him, seemingly testing some sort of invisible barrier. "Hold yer horses, young fella, let's not get hasty here," he spat.

"I'll get as hasty as I like, mate. Now you hold steady or I'll blast yer balls off."

Nevertheless, Bernard seemed to consider himself invulnerable, unrepentant in his ways and unable to recognise properly the real danger he was in. "Settle down, boy! I got fifty bucks says your limey ass ain't got the balls to fire that thing anyway!"

There was a dull thud as Saunders hit the ground, Bernard's lover knocked unconscious by the handle end of Norton's pitchfork. He proceeded to kick Bernard's stick away, felling the obese man to his knees as Robin thrust the butt of the shotgun into his skull. He was out cold before he had time to understand what had happened.

*

The pair awake to the filth and stench of an enclosed pigpen at Dernhurst, far from anything and anyone. Saunders can hear snorting and squealing, and a strong smell of pig excrement fills his nasal passages as he lies face down in the cold shit and mud. This was the plan he had sensed brewing between Norton and his son, but how had it happened?

There is a searing sensation inside his brain. He remembers Norton's attack, and tastes the blood that trickles from his scalp down to his lips. He also feels a twinge of panic when he realises the consequences of an untreated open wound in an atmosphere so thick with flies. He finds a semblance of relief upon hearing the strained wheezing of Bernard's breathing; his lover is alive at least.

Bernard is naked. He feels the vicious, chilly air, and despite indulging in sexual depravity that involves a degree of discomfort for him, *this* is neither erotic nor endurable. In fact, this is hell and he wants to be out of it *now*. He has been aware of Saunders' movements for a little while now and can be sure he is alive, not that it makes matters much better. On the

Bernard Bought the Farm

contrary, being tied so tightly to the rail-thin weasel just makes it harder to escape and the bonds cut more deeply into his bulging flesh.

At first Saunders thinks that his arms and legs are numb due to exposure to the cold or even lack of movement, but when he examines his condition more carefully, he discovers to his horror that his hands and feet have been sawn off, the stumps covered in rags to stem the bleeding. He throws up suddenly, the vomit oozing down and into Bernard's mouth, prompting a volley of spitting and barely coherent insults back at him.

The numb tingling is familiar to Saunders, local anaesthetic that won't last forever. Soon the pain will arrive like a horde of barbarians, tearing and destroying all the resistance that he can muster.

He also notices that the same 'operation' has happened to the still groggy Bernard and he starts to whimper like a beaten dog, shivering and wishing for the horror to stop. Deep down, he knows that this is the start of a long ordeal and the outcome can only be bleak. Naturally, he is terrified.

That wimp Saunders must have broken, thinks Bernard. Even now he can find some defiance. And unfeeling mockery of his lover's situation is more his style.

In the light of the early evening sun, Bernard notices a broken window, and finds it gives the ability to view the extent of the atrocities visited upon them. He turns his head for a full view of his face and in a bitter comic twist sees two fishhooks embedded into his nostrils that force them right back. He wonders as to why he couldn't feel them before, but everything was so numb and feeling is only just returning.

He gulps when he realises that when the numbness wears off he will suffer unendurable pain. The reflection in the glass also reveals that long jagged rusty wires have been forced into both men's anuses. They are crudely manipulated into spiral shapes resembling pigs' tails.

Bernard's breathing becomes uneasy and he urinates out of fear. His gaze darts feverishly around, seeking a means of

Bernard Bought the Farm

escape. Unable to find any, he forces himself to become physically calm, yet mentally he is a hive of activity – there must be a way of getting out of this mess. Saunders' behaviour is the opposite, thrashing around and bawling like a starving baby, his logical brain eclipsed by a world of terror.

As he feels the first twinges of pain, Bernard soon grasps the reality of their situation – there can be only one form of escape – and he begins to yell.

Two silhouettes fall across the prone pair and Norton's voice broadcasts: "Quiet now lads – save it for later. There'll be plenty of time for all that screaming and crying. We got plenty planned for you." Saunders tries to stop his crying and manages to calm down to a wretched whimper, regarding Norton and the boy with tear-streaming eyes. Bernard can barely see them and cranes his neck up as far as it can go.

Norton speaks again. "It was almost like fate when you came to buy the farm, Crombe. We followed your work, see, and know all about what you got up to. So we thought you should personally recognise what you'll go through in the next few days. If you're lucky and we keep you alive long enough, might even be weeks." He chuckles. "We'll go easy on you tonight, lads, let you settle in and meet the locals. Mind out for their biting! When we don't feed those little blighters, they'll have a go at chewing anything. Night now and sleep well. After all that trouble, looks like Bernard bought the farm in the end."

He winks and turns away laughing with his boy, as the sun sinks in the sky and darkness descends over a farmyard that from a distance looks lonely, harmless and innocent.

TED'S COLLECTION

Claude Lalumière

The room that housed Doc Austin's collection was kept cool throughout the year, the air-conditioning maintaining a steady ten degrees centigrade at all times. Ted tried to count the cats, but he was never in the room alone, and it was hard to concentrate while chatting with Doc. Once he'd reached eighty-six or eighty-seven, but then he was interrupted. He recognised a few of the animals from when they were alive and wandering through the neighbourhood, although he didn't know their names. Doc didn't bother with plaques or anything like that.

"The domesticated ones were supposed to be incinerated, but once their people leave them at the clinic who's to know?"

Doc poured white wine into both their glasses. The vintage was from Argentina, and the bottle was golden with a hint of olive to it.

"I know, Doc."

"Of course, Ted. But you won't tell anyone, because you're my friend." That was true. Ted and Doc were friends, even though Ted was only a gangly fourteen-year-old too aware of his lack of grace and his poor sense of style and fashion, while Doc was a tall, sophisticated man approaching sixty.

Doc held his glass up to his nose and sniffed the wine. He sighed contentedly and gestured for Ted to pick up his drink. The two friends gently knocked their glasses together. Doc said, "To friendship," and Ted grinned. A flush of warmth spread through the boy as the cool liquid slid down his throat.

*

Ted earned his spending money by doing odd jobs for Doc: mowing the lawn, painting the porch, washing windows. Doc lived next door, and Ted's mother was always trying to impress the older man, dressing up and painting her face and sitting on the porch when she knew he'd be coming home from work – that kind of thing. She was the one who'd volunteered Ted's services – without consulting him. At first, Ted had been embarrassed and angered by his mom's behaviour, but Doc had explained about loneliness and said that he was flattered by the attentions of Ted's mother, even if he didn't reciprocate her feelings.

To be neighbourly and to sustain his friendship with Ted, Doc consented to sharing a home-cooked dinner with Ted and his mother every Sunday. Soon, Doc turned these events into pot-lucks, despite Justine's protests, because, as he confided in Ted, her cooking was hopelessly bland.

Ted, who didn't make friends in school, enjoyed his solitude. Nevertheless, he was happy to have Doc as a friend. He'd never really known what it was like to have that kind of companionship, and he liked it. It gave him pleasure and satisfaction, a sense of belonging he had never known could be possible.

For example, he liked it when Doc invited him to watch while he prepared a new cat for his collection. Sometimes, Doc would take in sick or wounded strays. He taught Ted how to kill them so they'd feel no pain. Some of them were too damaged for Doc's collection – Doc liked the cats to look beautiful. Ted learned how to take apart the damaged ones.

"In my biology textbook, there are pictures of people's insides. Cats aren't that different from people." Ted's gloved hands were covered in blood. He wore one of those surgeon's cloth masks to cover his mouth and nose, but he had come to love the stink of dying flesh, of the insides of bodies, and if Doc weren't watching he'd take off the mask so he could better smell those odours.

"That's right, Ted. Most mammals are very much alike. Same organs. Same number of limbs. Similar nervous systems. Similar proportions."

While Doc spoke, Ted scrutinised the dead, dissected cat.

Ted's Collection

Amidst all the blood and gore, the animal's left front paw retained the elegance the stray cat had no doubt possessed in life. Almost by reflex, Ted cut off the appendage with the surgical saw.

Ted took off his gloves and held the severed paw in the palms of his hands. In that moment, it became the most beautiful thing he had ever seen. His hands trembled slightly.

Ted suddenly remembered that Doc was in the basement with him, and he blushed, embarrassed. He stammered but finally asked, "Can I keep this?"

*

It was decided that Ted would keep his collection at Doc's house. Neither of them wanted Ted's mother to discover Ted's new passion.

Although at first Doc betrayed a hint of disappointment that his young friend's interests focused on something other than taxidermy per se, he patiently taught Ted how to preserve the items Ted harvested for his collection. Ted's collection was more modest than the veterinarian's. So far, he'd accumulated two front paws (left and right), a liver, a heart, a right ear, and a tail.

Ted discovered that he never coveted the same body part twice. Or almost never. He'd replaced the first tail that he'd collected with a better one – the right one. He learned an important lesson then.

He hadn't really wanted the first tail. That time, there was no part of the dissected cat that he'd truly desired, but he'd felt it would be a waste not to take something. Never again, he decided. He must trust his instincts, his desires. If a cat had nothing he yearned for, so be it.

*

On his way home from school, Ted noticed the ambulance that

Ted's Collection

turned off his street, heading toward downtown. A police car was parked in Doc Austin's driveway.

Ted's mother was on their porch, looking even more nervous than usual. Ted didn't like what was happening. His imagination raced too quickly, thinking up macabre and lurid scenarios, most of which ended with him in jail. He would be blamed for whatever had happened. He felt it in his bones.

He'd barely started up the wooden steps to their house before his mother lunged at him and wrapped her arms around his back.

"Mom, let go. What is it? What happened? Is Doc okay?"

Justine tried to speak, but she collapsed in a fit of tears and sobs instead. Ted rolled his eyes, raced up to his room, locked the door, and looked out the window at Doc's house, waiting for something to happen.

*

Doc died of a heart attack, his mother finally told Ted when he emerged from his bedroom after the police had gone.

That night, after he was certain his mother was asleep, Ted snuck out and slipped into Doc's house using the spare key in the flowerpot next to the back door.

Ted found his collection intact. He had amassed nineteen items, including a spine, a face, one eye, and a stomach. He still hadn't found the right skull or rib cage or tongue. Other parts were missing, too. He briefly considered moving the still incomplete collection into his room, but his mother would be sure to discover it. Also, with Doc gone, Ted realised he no longer cared to continue or maintain it.

For the first time, Ted wandered through Doc's collection without Doc in the room. He finally counted the cats. There were two hundred and thirty-nine of them.

When he finished counting, Ted discovered tears running down his cheeks. He didn't remember beginning to cry. He would miss his friend. His best friend. But everything came to

Ted's Collection

an end. Friendships. Life. Everything. He understood that.

Ted's hand was closing on the handle to his own back door when he decided to return one last time to Doc's house. He went down to the basement and found the kit of surgical tools Doc had taught him to work with. He located the bottles with the chemicals he had used. Doc would have wanted him to keep all that. He would find a way to hide his friend's legacy.

*

Ted didn't have to worry about money for his education: Doc had left a trust managed by a lawyer who was instructed to defray all of Ted's school and basic living expenses for up to ten years, as of the date Ted enrolled in college. Upon graduation, or after a decade had passed, whichever came first, whatever was left of the fund would be bequeathed to a local cat shelter.

In college, for Introduction to Anthropology, the students were asked to pair up to research and write a paper on any contemporary subculture, using the terms and theories they'd been learning in class. Ted didn't know anyone, but a girl called Nicole approached him and asked if he'd be her partner. Nicole looked like an average girl: conservative clothing, trendy leather sneakers with matching purse, medium-length auburn hair with a slight bounce, only a hint of makeup.

She already had an idea for a topic. In her dorm room she asked him, "Have you ever heard of devotees?"

Ted just shrugged, and Nicole began explaining about people who were sexually attracted to amputees. They had websites, newsgroups – there was even a small club downtown, although it didn't advertise and it didn't have a sign or anything. You had to know.

"How did you find out about it?"

Nicole's expression changed. She smiled coquettishly, which made Ted uncomfortable. "You have to promise you won't tell anyone."

Ted's Collection

Ted nodded.

"I picked you because I felt you might understand. I can tell you're not like all the others in class. There's a darkness about you. I can trust that." While she spoke, Nicole untied the shoelace of her right foot.

She hesitated. "I can trust you, right?"

Now that Nicole was nervous, Ted relaxed. "Yes. I'm good with secrets."

Nicole slipped off her sneaker and peeled off the white sock beneath.

She extended her naked foot toward him.

"You can touch, if you want." She averted her gaze.

There were only four toes on her right foot. The big toe was missing.

"When I was twelve, I cut it off with a big steak knife. I hated the way it looked. It made my foot ugly. I looted my mom's liquor cabinet and drank myself silly to dull the pain. But I've blocked it out – the pain. I can't remember it. I wish I could." Nicole bit her lip. "We had a dog, this really powerful boxer with jaws of steel, and I fed him the toe after I severed it – before I passed out. My mom tells me that when she came home the dog was licking my wound. At first she thought he'd eaten my toe, but then she saw the bloody knife."

Ted touched the spot with the missing toe. It was so smooth, despite the scar.

"I go to that club downtown, take off my shoe, and men kiss me there. Sometimes, if they—" Nicole shut up abruptly and pulled her foot back. "You probably think I'm a freak."

"I'm not shocked, you know. In fact, I'm relieved that you're not as normal as you look."

There was light in her eyes when she asked, "Tell me your dark secret."

"I don't have one," he lied.

*

Ted's Collection

The next time they met in her dorm room to work on the paper, Ted asked Nicole to bare her foot. He enjoyed looking at her naked skin, and that seemed to be the most naked part of her.

"I think you're secretly a devotee. You should come to the club with me. Anyway, you have to come to research the paper."

"I'll go with you, but I don't think I'm a devotee. It's just that I'm comfortable around you, and I like it that you're comfortable around me." Ted held her foot while he talked to her. He bent down and gently kissed the tops of the four toes.

Nicole gasped.

Ted suddenly realised what he'd done. It was the first time he'd kissed a girl, anywhere. He wasn't comfortable anymore. He felt trapped.

Almost violently, he got up to leave.

"Stay." Her voice was barely more than a whisper.

He looked down at her, hugging herself on her bed. She looked fragile, vulnerable.

He felt dizzy and sweaty, but he sat next to her anyway.

She ran her hands under his T-shirt. It calmed and excited him at the same time.

*

Nicole fell asleep, but Ted was too fidgety. His skin burned with the new sensations of sex. He looked at her asleep and felt a deep tenderness toward her. It was a new emotion, tenderness. It felt good, letting that emotion warm his heart. In the moonlight, he admired her naked body, whole save for that one missing big toe.

But it was the other big toe, the one he was now seeing for the first time, that was responsible for the strongest surge of desire he had yet experienced.

Ted knew, then, that he would have to collect it.

*

Ted's Collection

The club was called Devotion. The amputees were mostly women. Among the men, he noticed only two whose bodies were incomplete. An old man missing his right leg sat in a wheelchair nursing a drink and a scowl. A loud thirty-something guy in an even louder silk shirt held court at a table in the middle of the bar, a clown who made the two women and three men who sat with him laugh. He had a nervous tick: he kept wiping his mouth with the stump of his right wrist; the foam from his beer had made a damp spot on his sleeve.

Men and women greeted Nicole like they knew her well. The bartender greeted her by name, and Nicole responded in kind. "Hi, Germ."

Ted whispered, "Germ?"

"Short for Jeremy. I started calling him that. Now everyone does." Nicole answered a bit too loudly for Ted's comfort. He was already nervous being here. And she wasn't doing anything to make it easier for him by calling attention to them.

None of the women were whole, but most of the men were. The women dressed to emphasise their deformities, their missing feet, hands, fingers, legs. Only Nicole's was invisible.

Although everyone was clothed and nothing kinky was overtly going on, Ted, who was still not fully comfortable with either the reality or the idea of sex, was keenly aware of the thick aura of sexual tension in the place. In particular, the lustful glances both men and women threw Nicole's way made Ted awkward, as if he'd been sat in the middle of a high-stakes card game with no knowledge of the rules. As if losing would expose him as a fraud.

He felt sweat pool in his armpits, dribble down his back, dampen his temples.

Nicole sat at the bar and started taking her shoe off. A dozen people, mostly men, ogled her every movement as she did so.

Ted whispered, "I thought we were here to interview people."

"Relax. Let me get cozy." Her foot was naked now. Ted saw a few of the men lick their lips.

Ted's Collection

Ted felt his face redden. He left without another word.

Outside, he waited thirty minutes, hoping that Nicole would come find him. She didn't.

*

Ted opened the door, and there was Nicole standing outside his apartment. He hadn't seen her in two weeks.

"I handed in the paper today. I put both our names on it, even though I did all the work."

Ted had nothing to say – he no longer knew how to interact with Nicole, if he ever really had – so he kept quiet.

"Aren't you going to invite me in?"

Ted sighed; it came out sharper than he'd intended. He stepped back and nodded her inside.

With her finger, Nicole traced the edge of his bookshelf, which was filled with tomes on anatomy, biology, medicine, surgery, taxidermy, dissection. She repeated the same thing she'd said the only other time she'd been here: "You know, it's weird that you don't have any music. Or any novels. Or even porn. But it's okay. Weird's good."

Ted could barely look at her. He wanted her to leave.

"You didn't have to stop coming to class. You could have called me. Something."

Ted regretted letting her in.

"Ted! Look at me!" Nicole rushed up to him and grabbed his chin in her hand. She turned his head so their eyes met.

Ted expected to see anger, or disappointment, or … he wasn't sure what, but he was disarmed by the fragility in Nicole's gaze.

"I lied to you." The words burst out of him, with a will of their own. "I do have a secret. I guess it's a dark one, but I don't see it that way."

Nicole whispered, almost to herself, "I knew it." Ted could hear the grin in her tone.

He told her about Doc, and Doc's collection, and what Doc

Ted's Collection

had taught him, and his own abandoned collection.

"Wow." Nicole squeezed his hands.

Somehow they'd wound up sitting on his bed. Ted didn't remember getting there.

"I thought it was over. Just a phase I'd gone through."

Nicole filled the silence with "But…"

"But I realise now it was only preparation for the real thing."

This time, Nicole let the silence linger while Ted gathered his courage.

Ted bent down and grabbed her left foot, the whole one, and, with a roughness that startled both of them, took off her shoe and sock. He bit the big toe at the joint, almost crunching the bones with his teeth.

Nicole winced and swallowed hard. Her breath sped up.

"I want your toe, Nicole. This one."

She bit her lip. "Will it hurt?"

"I think so. I have some anaesthetic, but—"

She put her hand over his mouth.

"No. Don't use any. I want to feel it."

Ted's heart was beating so hard, as if it would burst through his rib cage.

She asked, "Can you do it now?"

Ted reached under the bed for his instruments.

*

Neither Ted nor Nicole ever called the other again the whole time they were in school together. Ted figured they'd both gotten what they wanted, and that was that. Sometimes, he woke in the middle of the night, remembering the tenderness he had felt toward Nicole that once – after they'd had sex. In the darkness, he craved that emotion.

*

A left arm. Ten toes – one of each. Two ears: one, big and

Ted's Collection

brown and hairy; the other, small and pink and smooth. A uterus. One of each hand. A right foreleg. Ted had sawed that one off his most recent donor, a homeless man who'd already lost a foot to frostbite. Ted had promised him money, but instead he killed him. That man had nothing to live for, anyway. All he could look forward to was a life of misery. Ted had done him a favour.

They had driven to Ted's house. Inside, Ted put him under with chloroform, tied him down, and asphyxiated him with a plastic bag. Then he'd cut off the foreleg. Later, around 3 a.m., he'd dumped the man – he never knew his name – back in the alley where he'd found him.

Ted identified his donors at first sight. He was drawn to them. Always, they were damaged souls, regardless of how flawless they appeared to those who couldn't see or didn't know how to look. Invariably, they trusted him. In Ted's desires, they found a comfort, a refuge, from the darkness that gnawed at them.

In the case of his mother, though, it had taken him years to recognise his desire. Perhaps because it had been masked by their bond as mother and son. Sometimes, he had doubts that his mother had really intended for him to take her uterus. She had been so drunk that night (the last night of her life) and depressed at having been dumped by a co-worker after less than three weeks of dating. But his instincts had always been true, and the urge was so powerful that night as she sobbed and spewed her sorrow and loneliness, sitting across from him on her ratty old couch.

His ratty old couch, now.

*

Still, in the darkness, when sleep would not come, Ted found himself remembering Nicole's naked body as she had slept after sex. For brief moments, he relished the tenderness that accompanied the memory.

Ted's Collection

Sometimes, his donors – both women and men – wanted to have sex with him. He often complied, but never again did he feel that tenderness toward anyone.

To soothe his ache, he recalled all those beautiful body parts he kept in the basement and the intensity of the attraction that had compelled him to collect them. Summoning his desire for the items in his collection aroused him. He masturbated then and, after ejaculation, slipped into sleep.

*

Ted was having a restless night when the doorbell rang at 2:15 a.m. It was getting harder and harder for him to sleep.

He barked, "What is it!" as he opened the front door, dressed in his pyjamas.

Even in her thirties, she could grin coquettishly.

With an awe that surprised him, Ted said her name: "Nicole."

*

He had talked to her about his collection for two hours before she interrupted him. Instantly, Ted was seized by both an insight and a realisation. The realisation: he had not even asked Nicole why she was here. The insight: what he missed was complicity. Only two people had ever offered him that: Doc … and Nicole.

He'd been stupid not to cultivate a relationship with her. The years he'd wasted!

"Are you even listening to me?"

Ted had missed her first few sentences. "I'm sorry. It's a shock seeing you. A good shock, though."

She blushed, and then regrouped: "Ted, I need you. I need you to do this."

"Do what?"

"Take it. Take my whole right leg. You have to do it."

Ted's Collection

"But…" Ted didn't want to disappoint her.

"But what? I was right! You're still collecting. Collect my leg. Please."

"But I only collect when I feel the urge, the desire. It has to feel right. Necessary."

"So what? This isn't for you. It's for me. I need this. And you can do it. Do this for me. I can pay you. My husband is rich. We could hire anyone to do it, but I want it – I need it – to be you."

There it was, the complicity. But – "Husband?" He blurted the word out as a disdainful question. Immediately, he regretted it.

"Yes. But it doesn't matter who he is. I told him about us, and he agreed that you should be the one to do it. We need this. It's not enough anymore, just the toes. We need more. Please."

There was a terrible feeling in the pit of Ted's stomach while he mouthed the words of his acquiescence.

*

She really did pay him. Or, rather, her husband did. One week after the amputation, a fifty-thousand-dollar cheque came by courier.

Still, Ted felt impoverished. He knew he would never see Nicole again. But that was the lesser of his two losses.

On the floor of his basement, he laid out the items in his collection. (Nicole's leg was not among them.) He had amassed more than half a whole human body. He was still missing a head, a torso, a neck, and several internal organs. But he had a brain, two lungs, both arms, a stomach, an eye … and so much else.

He rearranged the items. He stared at them. Focused on them.

He had feared this, yet he had given in to Nicole's desire, like a lovesick teenager.

Ted's Collection

Today was the anniversary of Nicole's unexpected reappearance. One year since that amputation. More than one year since he had been drawn to anyone's darkness and felt the urge to harvest a part of their body.

He no longer understood what it was that he had desired. These body parts, they were nothing more than dead organic matter. Scrutinising these dead things he had coveted with such love and had cared for with such devotion, he yearned to feel something for them. Anything.

NEW TEACHER

Craig Herbertson

In Room Three the screams had reached a scale suggestive of the last knock in a pig's abattoir. Perhaps the only comparable level of human suffering might be the fall of Jerusalem. In either case, the penultimate moments of the music lesson were blithely ignored by Peters the mathematics teacher and his younger companion, Mr Clark of history, as they strolled past the door and onwards down the sloping corridors of Bellport High School.

As they passed the firmly closed door an exceptionally bestial shout pierced the air. Peters, an experienced sadist and virtuoso of the tawse, merely paused momentarily in his stride as Mr Clark, known for his moderate views, glanced upwards with a single raised eyebrow. Neither said a thing until they reached the smokers' staffroom. It was at that moment, with an appreciable distance from the screaming and a decent interval for the mind to settle, that Mr Clark ventured a remark.

"The new teacher?"

"Music," said Peters with a hollow smile.

"Having a bit of a rough time?"

"I'm afraid it's been three days of gymnastic, vocal and pugilistic exercise for the boys ... at Mr Nugent's expense." Peters searched for his pipe. "They've just transferred him to Room Three, next to the smokers' staffroom, so that any passing masters can pop their heads around the door if the situation appears to be plummeting beyond control."

Clark found his lighter buried in his trousers. Another distant whoop of exhilaration thrilled the air. There was a sound much like a violin exploding into fragments. "Must pop in to see if he needs assistance," said Clark lighting a Capstan.

"Yes, someone will need to give him a hint or two ... in a bit. After you?"

It was difficult to make out any inhabitants of the smokers'

New Teacher

staffroom. In actuality, there was no non-smokers' staffroom but a series of minor skirmishes over the two designated rooms between Miss Hawthorn, the head of religious instruction (a grim and unremitting harridan) and her picked battalion from the German language department had seen off a more inventive, but less cohesive defence by mathematics, French and art. Now an uneasy stand-off existed. On the rare occasions where necessity required Miss Hawthorn's presence on the ground floor, she was treated to a sporadic but dense attack of foul pipe smoke, cigarette fumes and general fug by whichever of the weaker party was *in situ* – regardless of whether they desired to smoke or not. The upper storey staffroom was defended by bunches of insipid flowers, a set of graphic cancer posters, a battery of perfume sprays and a range of hidden ambushes beyond even the colourful imagination of the smokers. Each side had adopted a siege mentality and at present all bets were off as to the victor.

Through the smoke, a huddle of teachers could be seen hunched over a variety of drinks that ranged from black tea and instant coffee, to pale beverages recognisable only by a heady smell of cheap spirit. Peters and Clark, moving, like experienced skirmishers in trench warfare, manoeuvred through the battered chairs and tables to the more comfortable set of dilapidated couches.

"What's that infernal racket?" Simmons, head of art and the after-school film club, had just woken from a nightmare.

"The new music teacher," said Clark. He pushed aside a pile of ragged exam papers and a collection of filthy mugs and placed his feet precariously in the gap. "What's the film tomorrow?"

"*Deep Throat*," said Simmons absently. He pulled a flask from his overcoat. "What a bloody noise!"

"What's the new man's name?" said Mr Ball unexpectedly.

"Why on earth do you want to know?" replied Peters. "He won't be around long enough to need a name."

"You never know," said Ball: He ran the weekly sweepstake

New Teacher

on the football results. "A new face could well want to invest a couple of quid in the tote."

An almost imperceptible movement of cheek and lip indicated a wave of enthusiastic interest rippling across a series of drawn visages.

"His name's Nugent," said Clark. "I just remembered that I helped interview him in the summer break. He expressed a profound interest in church liturgy, the early history of bird watching and something about choirs. I don't recall that he demonstrated a predilection for sport…"

The enthusiastic interest collapsed like a deflating balloon.

"Did our revered Head participate in that interview or was it McVicars, our less esteemed but more intimidating deputy?"

"It was the Head," said Clark.

"That explains the appointment," said Ball languidly. "The Head's recruited a batch this term that would make Mormons look like veterans of the Hellfire club."

"What's the bloody time?" Simmons had dropped off again and only awakened when an object had struck the wall behind him with some force.

"It's only second period," said Clark. "Shouldn't you be teaching?"

"It's on the eighth floor," said Simmons with a trace of pique. "I think the lift might be broken."

The others lapsed into silence. Peters took a morning paper from his bag, placed his worn tawse on the table, and began to flick through the horses with a professional eye.

Mr Clark scowled at his coffee. His initial enthusiasm for the teaching profession had waned to the point of extinction. Looking back, he thought the enthusiasm might have lasted about a week. Now, two years down the road, Bellport High had utterly done for him. Slouching back in the seat he could see the horrific façade of the main school building reflected in the windows of the Assembly room. The towering blocks rose like a concrete insult to good taste. The flickering shadows of pupils and teachers trapped in the straitjacket of education,

New Teacher

flitted across countless windows like demonic shadow plays; boxed theatre sets that included thousands of pupils and hundreds of teachers locked in an unrelenting battle for survival and dominance.

Thank God for free periods and thank God for that mercenary bastard, Ball. He had organised a racing excursion to Musselburgh the following morning. Perhaps if he put his entire salary on a lucky horse he could jack the whole thing in. If he lost he could borrow a few quid and bury himself in beer.

Ball's friend from Manchester, an untidy man of no apparent fixed address or job, had come up to watch Musselburgh races. He stared at the tawse with a perplexed look. "What the bloody hell is that?" he said.

Peters glanced up from his paper and took the long belt in his hand and gave it a thump on the desk. Cups rattled. "It's a tawse, my good man."

"A belt, used for corporal punishment. A bit different from the cane in England," said Clark. "I don't approve of their use,"

"You *hit* them with that?"

"As often as possible," said Peters. "They stand up so…" He demonstrated with more pleasure than decency allowed. "They hold their hands up before you so, palms doubled over and then you whack them as hard as you're able."

"And that stops the little bastards misbehaving?" said the Mancunian.

"Sometimes," said Peters regaining his seat. "But in any case its one of the few pleasures I maintain at Bellport."

Clark shook his head slowly and mournfully. The sound of a trumpet ripped into the air. It was quickly stifled, fading with the slow fall of a dying elephant.

"Do you remember your probationary year as a teacher, Peters?" said Ball unexpectedly. A few faces turned the colour of semolina.

Peters said in a terse undertone, "Vividly. Twenty years ago it must have been. It was awful. New teacher—"

New Teacher

"No, no. The actual year. I need it for that horse who won the National the year you started. I'm completely stuck with this one…"

Clark stared into space. "It was only two years ago for me," he said in a whisper, "but I still remember it as a living hell."

"You get less for common assault," agreed Simmons putting a newspaper on his face.

The door opened. All hands who were not asleep reached reflexively for tobacco. It was only Miss Caruthers of geography. She lit a cigarillo with a shaking hand. "What's that bloody noise?" she said coughing irritably.

"New Teacher," came a limp chorus.

"Nugent! Jesus wept; they haven't given him that year one class have they – with Dermot, Campbell and Spawn of Satan?" Miss Caruthers moved nervously towards the window. She paused for a minute to stare across the wasteland of the playground.

"Gray's class," said Clark, "No, I think Gray's off for hitting the janitor with a bucket. In any case, even the Head couldn't be … what's the big word for stupidly overconfident?"

There was a thoughtful but barren silence. From Room Three a rising murmur of insanity began to infiltrate the ether.
Peters grimaced as he tried to relight his pipe. For a second he looked vaguely dreamy. "I think he's got that class with young Farantino and thon sweet little cherub with the scar on his cheek."

"You did that didn't you?" said Ball a little unkindly. The newspaper had just revealed several call-offs in a team he had been relying on heavily for the weekend.

"Absolutely not," replied Peters. "I only damaged his wrist. A mere flesh wound." He fingered the tawse, which he had replaced under his jacket, above the shoulder. "I think it's his class. Let me see; period three yesterday I saw them drag all the chairs into the corridor."

"What were you doing near the music rooms?"

"I had to slip out for a bit."

New Teacher

"I saw him on Monday in the afternoon being trailed by a couple of lads who had attached a donkey's tail to his jacket," said Miss Caruthers absently.

"That *was* Dermot," said Clark. "But he should have been in my class."

"It *is* Farantino's class. That smug little bastard," said Simmons. He had woken up again. "They have music in the morning then after break … is it break time?" He held his forehead histrionically, "…they come to me then, the little bastards. At least they'll have worn themselves out on this new fellow"

"Break in ten minutes," said Clark dismally. "Just a warning in case anyone has corridor duty."

Ball laughed. "A warning?"

"In the sense of warning that you *should* be on the corridors. I'm free next period," he said smugly.

"Rule one in teaching," said Simmons taking a long dram. "Never be seen on the corridor or indeed any public place when there may be pupils in the vicinity."

"Don't suppose the new fellow, Nugent – what a stupid name – has discovered that particular gem of truth in the manual," said Peters.

"Well look at this," said Miss Caruthers gleefully. "It's old Hawthorn heading across the playground looking like someone's offered to test her virginity."

"Christ," said Ball. "Don't do that. What a mental picture to take into the break. It's worse than that bloody racket."

"Get your baccy out folks."

Those teachers who had not lit up began to prepare a hasty assault on the atmosphere. A few moments later Miss Hawthorn broached the doorway. She stood for a second, visibly intimidated by the curls of grim smoke that swept across the staffroom like a spewing belt of satanic mills, then with a shrug like a lioness, she stepped one pace forward staring myopically into the room while holding the door open as wide as was possible. "What on earth is that awful noise,"

New Teacher

she said in her brittle voice.

"Noise," said Peters. "Do you hear something, Clark? You have the younger ears. A noise of some description."

Clark's face took on a stoic calm. He glanced down at his newspaper.

"There is an awful noise coming from Room Three," said Miss Hawthorne with a look of baffled incomprehension.

"I think I hear something," said Ball calculating the odds on a rather complex treble.

"Yes," said Simmons in a theatrical voice. "I rather think it might be coming from that new fellow's class – Nugget, Ungent?"

"It is unlikely to be Mr Nugent's class," said Miss Hawthorne in a strident voice, "because the Head has advised me to inform you that Mr Clark will have to cover for our colleague as he has phoned in sick this morning."

"Then who on earth is in his classroom?" said Peters. "I heard an adult's voice a moment ago. There, didn't you hear it?"

A gruff voice seemed to be grunting and bellowing at a volume loud enough to penetrate the smoke stained division between Room Three and the staffroom. Something shattered against the wall and there was a strange silence filled only by a low and disturbing chuckle.

Suddenly, Clark, who had only been idly skimming the newspaper while he thought of a way to weasel out of lesson cover, went quite white. He dropped his newspaper. It fell open at a stark photo of a lunatic escapee and a rather lurid headline which warned against approaching him under any circumstances.

Even as the staff raised their eyes towards the open staffroom door a thin trickle of dark blood was visible, snaking its way down the sloping corridor like the first grim intimation of a rupture in a dam.

It came from the general direction of Room Three.

THE IN-BETWEENERS

Tony Richards

Our main shopping street was pedestrianised a couple of years back. And since then, I have never felt particularly comfortable going there after dark. Don't ask me why, but there's something reassuring at night about the hum of a passing car, the fleeting glow of headlights.

Nowadays, the shops close their doors at five-thirty, everybody leaves the area, and there is only silence.

Broken up, this particular evening, by my footsteps. I'd been forced to park at the edge of the zone and walk the rest of the way.

I was heading for the only chemist open at this hour of the night. Not that I was ill … but the single mother's little boy in the apartment next door to mine was running a fever. And understandably, she didn't want to leave him on his own. I'd offered to go out instead.

It was freezing, a biting wind coming in from the English Channel. Birchiam had only just emerged from the grip of the heavy snows which had descended on the whole of the UK. The streets might have cleared up, but the temperature had not improved a great deal. The town stretched off around me, black as anthracite to my chilled gaze. I was alone out here.

But how true was that? One moment, there was only the repeated clatter of my shoes. And the next, I thought I heard a voice. My head swivelled around.

Birchiam is a humble little seaside community. We don't get too much in the way of crime or violence here. But when we get the latter, it is usually alcohol related. And I was just fifty yards up from the seafront, where several pubs were clustered.

"Don't know," came the voice again. "Could be."

My gaze darted to the right.

A few streetlamps were broken, off in that direction. It was difficult to make out anything, at first. But then I noticed the

The In-Betweeners

small group.

They were standing in the shelter of what barely qualified as a lane. An access route to the backs of a couple of the larger stores. The only things I'd ever seen going down there were delivery trucks. And yet these kids had claimed it as their own.

None of them had even noticed me. Until, that is, I stopped and stared. At which point, instinct seemed to overtake them. Faces turned in my direction.

There were five of them, three boys and two girls. At a guess, I put them as fifteen or sixteen years old, one of the girls perhaps a little younger. Except that – typically for our burger-fed times – the boys were larger than I'd been at that age.

Maybe it was just the cold, but they were the palest-looking teenagers I'd ever seen. It was as though sunlight had never even wandered briefly across their flesh. And my immediate thought was, *drug addicts?*

I felt myself tensing, for an assault that never came.

They just kept staring at me. Their eyes seemed huge in their grey-white faces. And had a glossy quality to them, made worse by the fact that none of these kids even seemed to blink. Their gazes bored into me. I almost flinched, it was so uncomfortable.

And then they turned away, seeming to forget me. They were in a circle, facing each other. And another word came drifting out, made dully echoey by the confined space that they were in.

"Suppose."

They were just a group of kids, out loitering for the evening, minding their own business. I supposed they had that right. And if a part of me wondered why anyone would hang around outdoors on an evening like this one…

I believed I'd done some similarly stupid things when I had been that young.

I calmed down, took a shallow breath, and continued my journey to the chemist.

*

The In-Betweeners

The little boy next door got better. And the temperature went up a few degrees. Not that it wasn't still pretty cold. There was a lot of rain. When you walked down to the seafront, which I did practically every day, the waves were high, the water a shade of grey that looked utterly lifeless and icy. Every time that the breakers crashed on the shore, a fine spray blew across and hit you in the face.

The dead tramp was found at dawn the next Tuesday by somebody walking his dog. He was known to the police, and had been seen by most people in our town at one time or another. 'Old Henry' or 'Old Harry' ... something along those lines. He was mostly seen wrapped up in plastic sheeting in one abandoned shop doorway or another, dividing his time between swigging from a can of cider, singing some vaguely obscene song, and holding out his grimy hand for money.

He hadn't drowned. He had *been* drowned, which was a big difference. The medical examination proved it. Somebody had held him down. The gulls had got to him before the walker with his dog had. It was the big story in the local news.

I went to the spot where he'd been found a couple of days later. It was about two hundred yards to the left of the old, broken-down, closed-down pier. And – despite the fact that it had been the main feature on provincial TV and in the *Birchiam Record* – there was not a sign that anything had happened. What exactly had I been expecting? Yellow tape and markers on a weather-ravaged beach?

The waves struck down upon the fine pebbles unstoppably. And a couple of gulls circled overhead, like they were still looking for scraps.

When I turned away, I saw the group of youths again.

They were on the far side of the beachfront street, and fifty yards closer to the pier than I was. Were bunched together in so tight a group they seemed to form one single body. All similarly dressed, in clothing that could have been either black or a very dark navy. Slightly shiny fabric, like they'd got it wet.

The In-Betweeners

I couldn't see from this distance, but I imagined their unblinking gazes. We stared at each other for a few seconds, and then I got uncomfortable again and looked away.

When I turned my head back, they had moved. And in the opposite direction to mine. They had crossed the road, were on the way to the pier itself. And once they had almost reached it, they climbed over the seawall and headed down under its pilings. I had done that when I'd been a little kid, I recalled. Me and my friends had pretended it was some kind of enchanted maze, down there.

But there was none of that eagerness to the way the group of youths approached the structure. They just shambled along the edge of the beach until the bulk of the old pier swallowed them up. And that was the last I saw of them, until the next occasion.

*

Birchiam was full of groups of kids like those ones, I began to notice. Maybe 'teens' was the wrong word to describe them. 'Tweens' would have been the better choice. Not children any longer, and so subject to harsher rules. But not adults either, so they had no purpose, and could not even invent one for themselves.

They hung around outside our town's little mall, or on random street corners, or in the car parks of pubs that they were not allowed to enter. Smoking. Drinking from cans. Swearing. Waiting to grow a couple of years older, so that they could stop being in between the rest of us, and find out what was really happening to their lives.

They were stranded, marooned. Becalmed. And because of that, they frightened people, much the same way they had frightened me that first night. So much energy and so little to do with it in a small town like ours. It was like discovering a small cluster of time bombs, with no way of knowing exactly when they were likely to go off.

It was February by now, still freezing. An old school friend

The In-Betweeners

who'd moved to London had come back to visit his aging parents, and had suggested that we meet up at a restaurant that night. He had no way of knowing that *La Bella* had been swallowed up by the pedestrianised zone, and got so few patrons these days it was on the verge of closing down.

The standard of the cooking had collapsed accordingly. We both ordered a lasagne that tasted as though it was coated in cheese-flavoured plastic. But we tried to ignore that, laughing and joking and catching up on each other's news. London sounded like an interesting place, but I wasn't sure that I could live there.

On the way back to my car, I heard another voice. And not a few dull, muttered syllables, this time.

"Who the fuck you staring at? What's wrong with you ... you stupid or something? How'd you like a bunch of fives?"

The group that I'd originally seen were back in that side lane. But another group, half a dozen older boys, had decided to confront them. They all had the look of being drunk, and I supposed they'd wandered up here from one of the nearby pubs. They appeared just about old enough that they could get away with being served.

The one who had been shouting lurched forwards and raised a fist.

"You gonna answer me or what?"

The younger kids stared at him glassily, their expressions impassive.

"Suppose," one of the boys said.

"Suppose what?"

"Maybe."

The older youth swung at his head. Specifically, at his mouth.

Which suddenly expanded, and swallowed up the fist and half of the forearm behind it.

The rest of the drunken mob flailed back. I could only stand there, unable to take in what my eyes were seeing.

"Aahhh! Get it off me!" the attacker yelled.

The In-Betweeners

Then he screamed with pain.

Somewhere between the restaurant and my car, I had to have fallen asleep. I kept trying to tell myself that. In which case, why was I still standing up? I had to be dreaming that as well, the same way I was dreaming the rest of this. It was the only explanation. This could not be real.

When the boy's arm slid out of that unnatural mouth, the fist was crushed and bleeding. He went away howling down the street, with his friends scurrying around him.

The face that had contorted had returned to normal. I was the only person out here with the group of teenagers by this stage. My mind was almost wholly blank, and there was very little strength left in my arms or legs.

They began to move towards me. Had to all be wearing rubber-soled shoes, because their tread made only a subtle smacking noise on the dampened concrete. I managed to draw back into some deeper shadow, frightened they would see me. Braced myself for what might happen next.

But they were only exiting the alley. Didn't even seem to realise I was there.

As soon as they'd reached the main street, they turned left and headed for the seafront once again.

They paused when they reached it, and took another left, in the direction of the pier. I stepped out from cover, just before they disappeared.

No human being could have noticed that. No one could have heard.

But several of their faces swung around, their gazes fixing on me.

And the only sensation I was aware of, after that, was running.

*

We hang onto certain rituals in our lives, the same way that our ancient ancestors used to. Getting into our car. Locking our

The In-Betweeners

door. Turning the ignition key. All acts of subservience to the God of Personal Safety. And then getting home and locking more doors. That had to be the most important ritual, ever since we'd left behind our caveman days.

I didn't sleep at all, that night. Every time I closed my eyes, I'd see that boy's whole forearm disappear inside those pallid features. What had I been looking at? Some kind of mutation?

It occurred to me the injured youth would have to go to hospital. What story would he tell the doctors? He had not only been drinking. He'd been drinking underage.

There was something less than human in our town, and I was the only reliable witness to it.

The weather was still bitingly cold next morning, with a heavy wind still blowing. When I looked out through my window, herring gulls were being spun about like scraps of paper overhead.

I made myself a light breakfast, then puked part of it up.

The idea came to me while I was washing my face with cold water. *The pier.* When I'd seen them on the move, they had been heading for the pier both times.

Spray struck me in the face again when I stopped my car and got out. It was too early in the morning for even the commuters who parked here for the train station to be in evidence, the seafront completely empty.

I went across the road beside the promenade, then clambered over the seawall. My feet hit the wet sand with a flat noise like a broken kettledrum. The light around me was as cold and dead as the sea looked, adding extra layers to the shadows underneath the pier. I could barely see anything until I went beneath it.

It had been closed down years back. No one ever goes out there. But human beings have a funny habit. If anything falls into disrepair, they don't simply leave it at that. They treat it with contempt.

Everyone had dumped their junk here. Up near the entrance, it looked like fly-tippers had been at work. Further along there

The In-Betweeners

were drinks cans, plastic bottles, piles of cigarette butts. Candy wrappers and discarded newssheets. There were even a couple of syringes and a condom.

I picked my way past society's droppings. The crashing of the breakers sounded like an earthquake, underneath this rotting wooden structure.

Then I stumbled over something which I hadn't previously noticed. I swivelled around, got my balance back, and inspected it.

The impact of my shoes had broken it up along one edge … but it looked like, at first glance, a raised ring of concentric circles in the sand. Two feet wide, maybe eight inches high. They weren't perfectly even. Then I thought I might be looking at some kind of spiral. I was not completely sure, because the light was very dim back here.

It couldn't have been fashioned by the motion of the sea. The tide never came up this far. So who had done this, some budding Dali, fashioning a surrealist sandcastle?

It looked wetter than the area around it.

I moved on and found another. Then a clump of them.

I had lived near the seashore my whole life, and thought I recognised the shapes. They were like the casts left by worms that lived beneath the beach.

But this size?

And there were other footprints all around me. But they could be anyone's.

*

I write for a living. Except I couldn't write for the rest of the day. Couldn't so much as lay the tip of one finger against an expectant key on my laptop. It would begin shaking before it got that far. What could I speculate about today … the truth? Did such a creature actually exist in any normal sense?

Go to London, my mind kept telling me. Steel yourself, and finally make the move. To a place where the Earth itself is held

The In-Betweeners

in bonds of brick and concrete, nature and its vagaries kept mostly out. I had come across some kind of mutation; I was pretty sure of that.

As so often happens when you start out early in the day, the hours passed rapidly. Some rain hammered against my window at about three in the afternoon. An hour later, I could hear my next-door neighbour telling off her little boy for spilling something. But most of the rest was a shapeless blur. I barely even realised it was growing dark until I noticed that the streetlights outside had come on. The fact was, I was very badly confused, moving around my home like an automaton.

Some walkers went by on the street below.

And a few minutes after that, I heard someone mutter, "Mmm."

I thought I recognised the tone. It had a hollow, echoing quality to it. And when I had first heard it, I'd supposed it was the high walls around the lane shaping it that way. But that wasn't the case.

I had only turned one light on, in the kitchen, where I had been making coffee. So when I went back to my living room window, I was reasonably sure that I would not be seen. I eased my head around the edge.

The youths were standing there. But not just five of them.

There were about twenty. How'd they found me? They all looked similar, very pale and glassy eyed. Their faces were rather flat, with no freckles or marks that I could see. And they were still all dressed in the same manner, which was not unusual for bands of teenagers. Dark padded jackets, black or navy blue. Jeans of the same colour. Heavy boots. There was something almost paramilitary about the way they looked.

I saw the nostrils of a couple of them suddenly expand, far wider than should have been possible. No words seemed to pass between them. But they all looked up, simultaneously, in my direction.

They started walking towards the double front doors of my apartment block.

The In-Betweeners

Which were on an entryphone system. They could not get in without being allowed.

There was movement in the corridor outside a minute later, nonetheless. I turned off that final light and stood by the wall near my apartment door, holding my breath, wishing that my pulse would stop banging so loudly.

The wood shifted slightly in its frame. I thought that one of them was trying to prise it open. Then I saw something moving on the parquet floor.

It looked like a pale worm. No, several of them. And then dozens.

They were all attached, I could see as they came oozing in. A great gelatinous mass of some writhing pale substance formed a heap on my side of the threshold. And then began changing shape again, lifting itself into the air and taking on a figure and features.

The youngest of the girls that I had seen that first night stared at me unblinkingly. Her mouth dropped open. Her lips didn't move, but a word came belching out.

"Suppose."

It wasn't a comment. It was part of their disguise. They hung around the darker, more deserted parts of our town, mumbling the same kind of inanities that most teenagers did. Up this close, I could see her clothes were no such thing. They were part of her body, but a greatly darker shade. The glittering damp look appeared to be tiny little scales.

What were these things, some deranged experiment of nature? But they'd come from their home between the land and sea, and fitted in among us, without most of us even noticing.

There was more writhing near her feet. Several others of her kind were coming through. I knew that it was useless to lash out at them. I'd seen what had happened to the drunken kid.

And so I turned tail and ran, into the bedroom. Slamming the door. Locking it. It wouldn't be long before they got underneath that as well. I went to the window, sliding it open, the icy night air hitting me.

The In-Betweeners

Tendrils were already appearing on my bedroom carpet.

This was the top storey of the block, and there was no way down. No drainpipes and no balconies. Above me was the guttering alongside the roof. I grabbed for that. It groaned and shuddered slightly, but it took my weight, allowing me to pull myself the rest of the way up.

The tiles were damp. I slithered several times before I reached the ridge, and my pulse was thumping through my whole body, my breath like the panting of a hunted animal. Had my life been reduced to just a pair of simple choices – have those things kill me, or fall to my death?

Several worm-like shapes had spiralled up and attached themselves to the gutter. More were following.

Which made me scuttle along the top of the roof on all fours, my feet still skidding.

I reached the far edge. There was a sheer drop below me. When I glanced across my shoulder again, the girl and two larger boys were making their way calmly towards me, seemingly unbothered by the slippery tiles.

There had to be some way down. I looked out further, saw a tall, bare tree.

I backtracked several yards, stood upright, and ran again. And hurled myself into the air, my arms flailing desperately.

A branch slammed into my chest, tearing through my shirt and peeling flesh away. I managed to grab hold of it just as I was falling past.

It broke.

The next branch down caught me squarely in the small of my back, flipping me over. My fingertips clung onto it, but only for a second.

I didn't even get hold of the one after that. Simply dropped across it, so that it was pinned beneath my armpits for a brief while. Pain ripped through me. I hung there like a rag doll on a washing line.

And the next time that I fell, I hit the ground.

The In-Betweeners

*

Both my legs were broken, though I only found that out much later. Consciousness left me for a while.

When I awoke, pain had become the new God of my world. It had invaded my whole frame, distorted my thoughts, and even blurred my vision. I stared through the haze above me. Vaguely, I could make out faces.

They were clustered around me, the whole group of them. Indistinct blobs of paleness and darkness. No one else had even noticed me falling. We were alone on the street.

They studied me a while. And then a mouth came open, I heard something blurting out.

"Could be."

They turned away, and melted off into the night.

I slipped into unconsciousness again.

*

Perhaps the drunken tramp they'd killed – down by the waterfront, near their home – had tried to attack them. After a couple of days, I came to understand why they had spared me.

The nurses in the hospital were efficient but rather quiet, the doctors businesslike in their examinations of me. And even while I was lying in traction, I was visited by someone who was obviously a psychoanalyst. I was being given medication, I was quite sure, that was intended to keep me calm.

A writer of bizarre, fantastic fiction, who was something of a recluse, had not changed his clothes or shaved in a couple of days, and who had thrown himself off the rooftop of his apartment block, only a nearby tree preventing him from taking his own life.

Who'd accept a word I told them?

Who'd believe me?

You?

www.ingramcontent.com/pod-product-compliance
Ingram Content Group UK Ltd.
Pitfield, Milton Keynes, MK11 3LW, UK
UKHW041410180426
11947UKWH00007B/45